T0061613

SAGUARO SANCTION

Praise for the National Park Mystery Series

"An exciting, rewarding puzzle."
—*PUBLISHERS WEEKLY*

"As always, the highlight of Graham's National Park Mystery Series
is his extensive knowledge of the parks system, its lands,
and its people."
—*KIRKUS REVIEWS*

"Intriguing . . . Graham has a true talent for describing the Rockies'
flora and fauna, allowing his readers to feel almost as if they were
trekking the park themselves."
—*MYSTERY SCENE MAGAZINE*

"Graham has crafted a multilevel mystery that plumbs the emotions
of greed and jealousy."
—*DURANGO HERALD*

"Graham has created a beautifully balanced book, incorporating
intense action scenes, depth of characterization, realistic landscapes,
and historical perspective."
—*REVIEWING THE EVIDENCE*

"Only a truly gifted novelist is able to keep a reader turning pages
while imparting extensive knowledge about the people, the landscape,
and the park system. Scott Graham proves yet again that he is one of
the finest."
—CHRISTINE CARBO, author of
A Sharp Solitude: A Glacier Mystery

"A winning blend of archaeology and intrigue, Graham's series
turns our national parks into places of equal parts
beauty, mystery, and danger."
—EMILY LITTLEJOHN, author of
Shatter the Night: A Detective Gemma Monroe Mystery

SAGUARO SANCTION

A National Park Mystery
By Scott Graham

TORREY HOUSE PRESS

Salt Lake City • Torrey

This is a work of fiction set in a real place. All characters in this novel are fictitious. Any resemblance to actual events or persons, living or dead, is entirely coincidental.

First Torrey House Press Edition, March 2023
Copyright © 2023 by Scott Graham

Published by Torrey House Press
Salt Lake City, Utah
www.torreyhouse.org

International Standard Book Number: 978-1-948814-75-1
E-book ISBN: 978-1-948814-76-8
Library of Congress Control Number: 2021952965

Cover art by David Jonason
Cover design by Kathleen Metcalf
Interior design by Rachel Leigh Buck-Cockayne
Distributed to the trade by Consortium Book Sales and Distribution

Torrey House Press offices in Salt Lake City sit on the homelands of Ute, Goshute, Shoshone, and Paiute nations. Offices in Torrey are on homelands of Southern Paiute, Ute, and Navajo nations.

ABOUT THE COVER

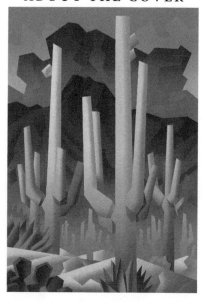

"Saguaro National Park is one of my favorite spots in Arizona for camping and inspiration. I always have a feeling of deep peace when walking among the stately, silent saguaros. To me, this is the real Garden of Eden."

Acclaimed Southwest landscape artist David Jonason painted *Saguaro Storm*, a portion of which appears on the cover of *Saguaro Sanction*. Combining a keenly observant eye and inspiration drawn from a number of twentieth-century art movements, including cubism, futurism, precisionism, and art deco, Jonason achieves a uniquely personal vision through his vividly dreamlike oil paintings of the American Southwest. Jonason connects on canvas the traditional arts and crafts of the Southwest's Native tribes with the intricate patterns in nature known as fractals. "For me as a painter," he says, "it's a reductive and simplifying process of finding the natural geometries in nature, just as Navajo weavers and Pueblo potters portray the natural world through geometric series of zigzags, curves, and other patterns."

Saguaro Storm (36×24 inches, oil on canvas, 2018) is used by permission of The Jonason Studio, davidjonason.com.

For my son Logan,
with thanks for sharing his extensive
knowledge of border issues with me

PROLOGUE

They deserved to die, all three of them.

She had ridden the cresting wave of her excitement all through the night. After months of preparation, tonight, finally, she would meet her goal.

She'd begun the trek not long after midnight, leaving the outskirts of the city and striding into the desert ahead of Javier and Mendes, who grumbled at her command that they not use lights.

Cactus branches reached out from the darkness. She shoved past them, ignoring the thorns piercing her shirtsleeves and embedding themselves in her flesh, while behind her Javier and Mendes yelped and muttered bitter curses in Spanish.

Her schedule had been ambitious from the start. Big ideas required big ambition, after all. Besides, the schedule was determined not by her, but by the calendars. She'd merely tasked herself with meeting their requirements. Now, over the next twenty-four hours, the schedule required her to bring her plan to fruition.

The light evening rain shower had ended by the time she set off into the desert with her two hired hands. As she led them through the night, the clouds gave way to a star-filled sky and the desert exuded its pungent after-precipitation scent, filling her lungs with purpose.

The three young men met her at the rocks as planned. But when they admitted they had not completed their task, claiming exhaustion and the weight of their cargo, her excitement gave way to outrage. Others had completed the journey with similar loads over the past weeks and months. Who did these three think they were, abandoning her final, precious delivery in the desert somewhere to the south?

Fury swelled inside her, a loosed beast demanding retribution. She pressed her fingers to the looped length of razor wire in the front pocket of her pants, the coils warm from the heat of her thigh.

She drew the looped wire from her pocket, slipped her fingers through the steel rings at each end, and stretched the wire taut. The young man who had done the talking did not see her movements in the dark. But when she slipped the wire over his head and cinched it tight around his neck, he felt the full force of her wrath in the slash of the wire through his skin—just as she felt it, too, in the warm spray of his blood across her face.

PART ONE

"This high figure with a duck on its head, brightness rounding into every pecked divot. It looked like it was carrying the sun."

—Craig Childs, *Tracing Time*

1

Rosie Ortega inhaled deeply and noisily through her nostrils. "I've never smelled anything so good," the fourteen-year-old declared.

"You sound like a horse," said Carmelita, Rosie's sixteen-year-old sister.

"Neeeiiigh!" Rosie whinnied. She shook her head, her curly, black hair bouncing off her round cheeks. "If I was going to be a horse, I'd be a wild horse. Especially around here. The desert smells sooooo delicious."

Carmelita swept a loose lock of her long, dark hair over her shoulder. "It'd be hard to find something to eat, though, with all the thorns."

Rosie stopped in the middle of the rocky path she and Carmelita were traversing with their mother, Janelle Ortega, and stepfather, Chuck Bender, along the spine of a ridge in the Sonoran Desert of southern Arizona. Chuck and Janelle were dressed for the hike in broad-brimmed sunhats, long-sleeved cotton shirts, and loose pants. The girls sported running tights, stretchy nylon tops, and ball caps. Chuck wore heavy leather hiking boots, while Janelle and the girls wore their favored light-weight trail-running shoes with marshmallowy soles.

Chuck halted behind Janelle and the girls. The boulder-studded ridge snaked ahead of them beneath the blue late-October sky. A quarter mile back, a group of hikers strode along the ridgetop trail in a tight bunch. The hikers included Saguaro National Park Superintendent Ron Blankenship, a park ranger accompanying Ron, and the five-member research team Ron had assembled at Chuck's request for today's observational study.

Desert greenery blanketed the slopes dropping steeply away from both sides of the ridge. Hundreds of saguaro cactuses towered like multiarmed power poles above the low mantle of desert foliage, which included prickly pear cactuses with pads the size of dinner plates; barrel cactuses as big around at their midriffs as fire hydrants; and spindly ocotillo, their long, thin gray branches thrust toward the sky. Halfway down the west face of the ridge, a line of brown volcanic cliffs thirty to forty feet high cut through the vegetation, running parallel with the ridgetop.

Chuck sniffed the air. It had rained the evening before, when a low-pressure system had passed through Arizona. With the clouds departed and the morning sun heating the east side of the ridge, the powerful scent of the moist desert filled the air. The scent, sweet and tangy with an undertone of pine, issued from the many creosote bushes dotting the hillside among the cactuses. The pores of the tiny, resin-coated creosote leaves, wide open to absorb last night's precipitation, emitted the unique smell, as distinctive as any in nature.

Despite the nervousness thrumming in Chuck's belly about what today would bring, the pleasing odor invigorated him, putting him in mind of the outdoors-oriented life he'd shared with his family since becoming husband to Janelle and stepdad to Carmelita and Rosie six years ago, after far too many years as a lonely bachelor.

Over the course of his two-and-a-half-decade career as an independent archaeologist, it was the scent of the drying Sonoran Desert, even more than the stunning desert scenery itself, that had led Chuck to bid regularly for contracts here in southern Arizona. He drove south from Colorado two or three times each winter to work the bids he won, escaping the snow and cold of the mountains to complete the fieldwork portion of his Arizona contracts. The work trips enabled him to enjoy the warmth and beauty of the low-elevation desert straddling the US-Mexico border. As an added bonus, after infrequent rainstorms like the one yesterday evening, he was treated to the wondrous Sonoran scent as well.

"If you ask me, Rosie," he said, "there's no better smell on earth."

He'd left their Rocky Mountain–ringed hometown of Durango in southwest Colorado a few days ago, during the first cold snap of autumn, to begin work on his latest archaeological contract in Arizona, scheduling his two-week stay in Saguaro National Park to overlap with the girls' weeklong fall break from Durango High School. Yesterday, Janelle and the girls had driven the five hundred miles south from Durango to his campsite, one of half a dozen bare gravel pads in the park's maintenance yard available to scientists and construction contractors working temporarily in the park. The yard was generally quiet and deserted, used primarily for long-term storage. The half dozen sun-bleached campsites, complete with electrical hookups and sewer drains, were shoehorned between beige aluminum storage garages lining one side of the yard and the base of the ridge along which Chuck now hiked with Janelle, Carmelita, and Rosie.

Despite the increasing heat of the day, a chill ran up Chuck's spine. He and Janelle had rousted the girls and set out up the ridge before sunrise, as the stars faded from the sky with the coming of dawn, for a specific reason beyond simply enjoying the desert at its after-rain finest. Six years ago, Janelle had placed her full and unreserved trust in Chuck, leaving the only life she'd known in inner-city Albuquerque, New Mexico, to marry him and move with the girls to his small hometown of Durango. This morning, for perhaps the first time since they'd married, he was placing his full and unreserved trust in her.

"I'm glad we got up so early," Rosie said, gazing at the cactus-studded slope aglow in the morning light, "even if everything's so prickly."

Saguaro National Park was home to thick stands of saguaro cactuses growing where moist air gathered periodically against rounded hillsides and rocky ridges. The park was comprised of two separate districts, on the east and west sides of Tucson. The fast-growing city sat in a shallow bowl between the two park sectors, with the rugged Santa Catalina Mountains rising at the city's northern edge.

Chuck turned his back to the rising sun and looked out from the top of the ridge, which ran through the park's west-side Tucson Mountain District. At the foot of the ridge, the park gave way to the flat scrublands of the Tohono O'odham Reservation. The lands of the Tohono O'odham people stretched west for fifty miles from the park boundary, and south for sixty miles to the US border with Mexico. At 2.8 million acres, roughly the size of the state of Connecticut, the reservation was the second largest in the US, after only the Navajo Reservation that encompassed parts of Arizona, New Mexico, and Utah to the north.

Rosie raised and lowered her shoulders in an exaggerated shrug. "I guess maybe I wouldn't want to be a horse around here after all."

Last year, in her eighth-grade Colorado Environment class, she had studied the herd of wild horses that lived in remote Disappointment Valley west of Durango near the Utah border.

"You'd be surprised," Chuck told her. "The desert supports an amazing amount of wildlife, including wild horses. Well, wild burros, anyway."

"Burros?" Rosie asked.

"Donkeys," Carmelita said. "Right?" she asked Chuck.

"Yes," he answered. "Burros are small donkeys with extra-long hair. They were brought to America by the Spanish conquistadors along with horses."

"*Sí, burro*," Janelle said, emphasizing the double *r*'s in the word with the rolling trill of a native Spanish speaker. "That's Spanish for donkey."

"Well, then," said Rosie, "hee-haw!"

"In some parts of the Sonoran Desert," Chuck said, "feral

burros are so plentiful they're destroying the plant life and driving out native animals like desert bighorn sheep."

"Is somebody going to round them up, like they did the horses in Disappointment Valley?" Rosie asked.

She had learned in class, and reported at home over dinner, the story of the federal government's controversial roundup of the burgeoning herd of nonnative equines in western Colorado a number of years ago. The feds had chased the feral creatures across the sagebrush-covered floor of Disappointment Valley with helicopters, resulting in injured horses and fiery protests by animal-rights activists.

"The desert is too rugged for that. They're using contraceptives instead."

"I know what those are. So does Carmelita." Rosie's mouth turned up in a sly grin and she adopted a singsong tone. "Don't you, Carm?"

Carmelita's eyes narrowed but she did not respond.

Chuck filled in the silence. "Prophylaxis is an excellent tool when used for the right reasons."

"Oooo," Rosie said, giggling. "The *right* reasons. I know all about those, too."

"We're talking about burros," said Chuck.

Rosie chortled. "No, we're not."

"Enough of that," Janelle cautioned. "Let's stick with where we're at. We're on a beautiful hike in the desert, a world away from the cold and mountains we left just yesterday."

Chuck pointed at a rocky outcrop half a mile ahead. "The trail tops out up there and drops into an arroyo. There's some nice shade under the palo verde trees in the bottom of the drainage."

He did not add that, assuming all went as planned, a pair of young men would be waiting for them in the shade beneath the trees.

Rosie set off up the trail, followed by the others.

"Is that where the pictographs are?" she asked Chuck, speaking over her shoulder to him past Carmelita and Janelle.

"Yep," he replied. "Except they're not pictographs, they're petroglyphs. Pictographs are ancient pictures painted *on* stone. Petroglyphs are pictures carved *into* stone."

"Pet-*ro*-glyphs," Rosie said, breaking the word into individual syllables. "You try it, Carm."

"Petroglyphs," Carmelita repeated. "And pictographs. They're two different things, whereas hieroglyphs are both."

"Hie-*ro*-glyphs," Rosie repeated. "How come you know so many words?"

"From studying vocab for my SAT, for college."

"You're already doing that?"

"I took my Pre-SAT back in April."

Carmelita had scored in the highest percentile range on the preliminary version of the college entrance exam given to all Durango High School sophomores. Since the start of her junior year this fall, she'd added several hours each week of college-entrance-exam study to her already packed schedule.

"I'm going to miss you when you leave," said Rosie.

"Whoa. Hold on, there," Janelle said as they hiked. "Carm's not going anywhere for a looong time."

"But when I do," said Carmelita, "I'm going a looong ways away."

"Depending on how much it costs."

"Which is why I'm studying so hard, so I can get a scholarship."

"Well, then," said Chuck, "why don't you define hieroglyphs for us?"

"Hieroglyphs are symbols painted on walls or carved into stone that contain a message. They have meaning. They're an early form of writing commonly associated with the ancient Egyptians."

"Perfect," Chuck told her.

"Yeah, Carm, perfect," Rosie echoed.

"Do you remember," Chuck asked her, "why I'm doing the work I'm doing here in Saguaro National Park?"

"I know it has something to do with petroglyphs and hieroglyphs and all that stuff."

"*Correcto*," he said, imitating as best he could the trill Janelle had given the double *r*'s in *burro*. "Like Carm said, the ancient Egyptians developed a written language based entirely on symbols, or hieroglyphs. Other early peoples also communicated with hieroglyphs, like the Ojibwe in the Great Lakes region and the Mayans in Central America. I've been contracted to study whether any of the petroglyphs carved into rocks in the Sonoran Desert by the Hohokam—the ancestors from a thousand years ago of the Tohono O'odham people who live in this area today—might, in fact, have hieroglyphic qualities."

"I bet they have all kinds of secret meanings," Rosie said.

"You're not the only one who thinks so." Chuck glanced over his shoulder at the research team hiking along the ridge. "Harper Longworth, the head of the Anthropology Department at the University of Arizona, is convinced at least some of the petroglyphs in the park are symbolic. Ron Blankenship, the park superintendent, is on the fence. He brought me here to have a look and let him know what I think. My findings will help him decide how to proceed. If the petroglyphs are proven to be just pictures, they'll continue to be protected, and that will be that. But if they're proven to be part of an ancient hieroglyphic language developed by the Hohokam, that's a whole other thing entirely. A finding of that sort would lead to much more extensive study of the petroglyphs in the park, and on the Tohono O'odham Reservation, too."

"So you're, like, a judge?"

"Ron wants me to give him my honest opinion as an outside observer."

"Chuck is known for being a straight shooter," Janelle said

to Rosie. "Nobody ever accused him of bending to the will of anybody else, that's for sure. He won't even bend to my will—and believe me, I've tried."

Chuck grinned. "I do the dishes, don't I?"

"Sometimes."

"Mostly," Rosie groused, "you make me and Carm do them."

"That's my prerogative," said Chuck.

"Your what?"

"Carm, would you like to take that?"

"Prerogative," Carmelita said. "A right or privilege of an individual or group."

"Geez, Carm!" Rosie exclaimed.

"It basically means I'm the boss," said Chuck.

"Not of me," Janelle said.

"Not of me, either," Rosie added from the front of the line.

She stopped abruptly in the middle of the trail and screamed.

2

Rosie's screech died in her throat. She hurried forward and crouched in the trail.

"Hey there, big guy," she said, reaching down.

She straightened and thrust her hand toward Carmelita, Janelle, and Chuck. On her palm rested a dark, hairy spider the size of a donut. The spider—a western desert tarantula—began to move, crawling around her outthrust hand on its long, jointed legs until it hung upside down from the back of her hand.

"That tickles," Rosie said, giggling.

She turned her palm facedown, returning the tarantula to an upright position on the back of her hand. The spider immediately began to crawl around the side of her hand once more.

"That thing's huge," Carmelita said.

"And hairy," said Rosie.

"They don't bite, do they?" Carmelita asked Chuck.

He watched the spider circle Rosie's hand. "Almost never."

"I've picked up lots of them around Durango," Rosie reported, "and I've never once gotten bitten."

"Lots of them?" Janelle said. She closed her eyes and shook her head. "You've never told me anything about that."

"You never asked."

The tarantula's round thorax was brown and black and covered with fine hairs. A pair of pincer-like appendages called pedipalps curved outward between its front legs.

"You were right when you called him a big *guy*," Chuck said. "You've got yourself a male there, same as the ones you picked up in Durango. October is tarantula mating season here in the desert. That's why your spider-man is out and about."

The spider continued to loop Rosie's hand as she turned her palm up, then down, then up again. "You can tell he's on a mission." She squatted and extended her hand close to a rock sticking up in the middle of the trail. The tarantula crawled onto the rock, descended the stone's steep face with its grippy claws, and ambled across the trail in the same direction it had been headed before Rosie picked it up.

"He's searching for females in their burrows," Chuck said.

"Not *burros*?" Rosie asked, rolling the *r*'s.

"Nope," Chuck said with a smile. "Burrows—little caves female tarantulas dig in the ground and live in for years. The male shows up and taps the ground outside. If the female is receptive, she'll strum the web she's built in her burrow, inviting him in."

"No contraceptives required," Rosie said, staring at the spider.

The tarantula reached the side of the trail, its pace slow and steady, its direction unvarying.

Carmelita leaned forward, studying the spider along with Rosie. "You're right," she said to her sister. "He's on a mission. He's totally ignoring us. It's like we're not even here."

"Which tells you a lot about males," Janelle said. "No matter what the species is."

"When male tarantulas set out across the desert in search of a mate," said Chuck, "they never change their direction. Either they find a female or they don't."

"You mean he's on, like, a death march?" Rosie asked.

"Or a life march, you could say. Males don't set out across the desert until they're close to the end of their lives." He pointed at the tarantula. "That guy will either find a mate or he'll die trying."

Rosie waved at the tarantula as it disappeared into the brush. "Goodbye, dude. I hope you get lucky."

"Rosie!" Janelle admonished.

"Well, I do. He's working pretty hard."

"And," Carmelita added, "he's waited a long time."

Janelle jetted a burst of air between her lips. "Seriously? Both of you?"

Chuck looked back along the trail at the approaching group of hikers, now just a couple hundred yards behind them. "We should get moving," he said to Janelle.

She stiffened. "Right."

The trail descended from the high point on the ridge into an unnamed arroyo that petered out on the flat desert scrubland of the Tohono O'odham Reservation. The drainage began in a crease where the end of the ridge fell precipitously to meet a low, rounded hill in the middle of the national park district. Together, the ridge and hill served as a saguaro-studded uplift separating the paved urban landscape of Tucson to the east from the largely undeveloped lands of the Tohono O'odham Reservation to the west. At the foot of the ridge, palo verde trees sprouted on both sides of the gravel channel running down the middle of the arroyo. Long, needled branches extended to the edge of the wash from the trees' vibrant green trunks.

Rosie marched down the path, her feet pounding the rocky ground. Several inches taller and significantly leaner than her little sister, Carmelita bounded after Rosie in her cushioned trail-running shoes, as light on her feet as a gazelle. Janelle trailed after the girls. She was lithe like Carmelita and short like Rosie, her hair coal black like both her daughters.

Chuck followed the three of them down the switchbacking trail. The many hours he spent working outdoors on archaeological digs kept him in good physical shape. Even so, at nearly fifty years old, his aging knees ached with each descending step. His stomach churned as he walked, the brief excitement of the tarantula already replaced by his returning anxiety about what lay ahead.

He stepped into the open with Janelle and the girls from behind a head-high prickly pear cactus that shielded the end of the trail from the channel at the base of the ridge. On the near side of the drainage, a navy blue flag hung on a flexible fiberglass pole. Beneath the flag, a light blue plastic barrel the size of a beer keg with a spigot at its base sat on a waist-high metal frame. Eight dark brown basalt rocks the size of refrigerators lined the far side of the wash. Outstretched palo verde branches shaded the large volcanic stones. Despite the brief rain yesterday, the gravel in the bottom of the arroyo was dry, the ground beneath the small rocks having soaked up all the previous evening's moisture.

"What's this?" Rosie asked, stopping beside the plastic container.

"Water." Chuck scanned the wash beyond the barrel but spotted no signs of movement. "It's for unauthorized migrants—border crossers traveling through the desert."

"You mean, *sneaking* through the desert?"

Janelle stood next to Chuck, her hands curled into fists at her sides. She searched the channel and surrounding vegetation along with him, her eyes darting.

"They move at night and hole up in the shade during the day," Chuck explained to Rosie. He pointed at the channel curving around the north end of the ridge. "They follow open drainages like this one as much as they can."

He laid his hand on the plastic tank, waiting. A gentle morning breeze flowed up the wash. No one stepped into the open from the thick vegetation lining the sides of the channel.

"Is that how Grand-*papá* and Grand-*mamá* got here?" Rosie asked, using the Spanglish terms she and Carmelita had adopted as youngsters for Janelle's parents, who lived in Albuquerque.

"Your *abuelos* came to the US on work visas when they were teenagers," Janelle said. "They applied to become citizens after that."

Rosie rested her palm on the plastic barrel next to Chuck's.

"How come there's water for people way out here in the middle of nowhere?"

Chuck slapped the half-full barrel with the palm of his hand. The deep-throated *pop* resulting from his slap echoed down the arroyo. Still, no one emerged from the brush. "A humanitarian group called Humane H$_2$0 places these out in the desert so the migrants won't die of thirst. But others sabotage them by emptying them or shooting holes in them or adding gasoline to the water to sicken or kill the people who drink it."

Rosie blanched. "Why would they do *that*?"

"They don't want anyone else coming to America after their own ancestors came here."

Janelle clucked her tongue. "There's more to it than that," she said to Rosie. "Lots more. But suffice it to say, most people believe immigrants should come to the US through legal channels like your *abuelos* did."

"Except," said Chuck, "gaining citizenship is a lot harder today than it used to be. It's almost impossible. Meanwhile, the countries south of here have so many problems that people are willing to risk their lives crossing the border and walking through the desert to get away from them."

"Like I said," Janelle told Rosie, "it's complicated."

"Very," Chuck agreed.

He scrutinized the sides of the channel. Nothing.

He turned to Janelle with his brow furrowed. Now what?

The sound of hiking boots striking rocks on the trail reached the bottom of the arroyo, signaling the approach of the others.

Chuck pointed at the dark boulders lined along the opposite bank of the wash.

"Those are what we came out here for this morning," he told the girls, expressing half the truth. "I hiked here and checked them out on my own a couple of days ago. The petroglyphs are on the far sides of the rocks, facing away from the drainage."

"Cool," Rosie said.

She dropped her hand from the barrel and walked halfway across the channel toward the line of boulders. She came up short.

"Someone's there!" she exclaimed, staring past the rocks into the speckled shade beneath the palo verde trees.

Chuck hurried with Janelle and Carmelita to Rosie's side. A man lay on his back on the bare ground beneath the trees. One of the man's arms rested in the sand at his side. His other arm lay across his stomach. Above his draped arm, the man's chest was still. Even from this distance, it was clear he was dead.

Chuck's breath caught in his throat. "Stay here," he directed Rosie and Carmelita. He scurried with Janelle out of the wash and between the boulders.

Janelle collapsed to her knees beside the body. She rocked back and forth, her hands clasped to her chest, staring down. "Francisco," she moaned. "Oh, *Dios mio.*" She looked up at Chuck, tears streaming down her cheeks. "It's Francisco," she said, sobbing. "Oh, God, it's Francisco."

Chuck had met Janelle's cousin a couple of times on trips to visit Janelle's extended family in Juárez, across the border from El Paso in the Mexican border state of Chihuahua. Francisco was in his late teens, thin and bony. His dark eyes, sunken in their sockets, stared unblinkingly at the tree branches overhead. Beneath his jawline, a dripping red slash encircled his neck. Flies alighted, buzzing, on the bloody ring. In the calm air beneath the trees, the metallic smell of blood overrode the piney scent of the drying desert.

The skin of Francisco's face was smooth and unblemished, his upper lip shadowed by a wispy mustache. He wore scuffed work boots, torn jeans, and a western-style plaid shirt with snap front pockets. His thick black hair was tangled and unwashed. The tips of his fingers were ripped open, white bone showing through flaps of bloody skin. A worn ball cap lay on the ground next to him, and an empty canvas rucksack rested on the ground beneath his back, its straps looped over his shoulders.

Chuck bent and put his arm around Janelle, drawing her to him. "He's dead," he said gently. "I'm sorry. There's nothing we can do for him."

"Someone killed him. He was murdered," Janelle said. She choked back her sobs. "And it's all my fault." She jerked her shoulders from Chuck's encircling arm and looked wildly around her. "Carlos. Where's Carlos?"

Chuck searched, too. Francisco's twin brother was nowhere to be seen.

"There's someone else!" Rosie hollered.

Chuck whipped around. Rosie pointed downstream from the middle of the channel.

"Carlos!" Janelle cried, scrambling to her feet. She charged from beneath the trees and sprinted down the arroyo, her shoes crunching in the gravel. She dropped to her knees beside a second person, who lay on the ground next to the wash at the end of the line of boulders.

"He's breathing!" she cried out. "He's alive!"

3

Janelle stared at the person lying on the ground before her. The person was not Carlos. Rather, he was a boy of perhaps fourteen, several years younger than her twin cousins.

The boy lay on his back, arms at his sides and eyes closed. Blood seeped from the back of his skull, staining the sand beneath his head, but his chest rose and fell in regular rhythm.

Janelle put two fingers to the boy's neck. His pulse was strong and steady.

The boy was short and pudgy, with blunt-cut black hair. He almost certainly was from Guatemala, Honduras, or El Salvador, the three northernmost countries in Central America, known collectively as the Northern Triangle, from which so many minors were venturing to the US. He wore blue jeans and a torn green T-shirt. His feet were clad in sneakers. One of the soles of the shoes was partially separated from its tattered canvas upper, revealing a dirty white sock with a hole in its side.

Janelle gripped the boy's shoulder. He did not react. She gave him a gentle shake. He lay still and unmoving on the ground.

The boy must have been attacked by whoever had killed Francisco. She sat back and scanned the brush around her. Still no sign of Carlos. She glanced up the arroyo at Francisco's body lying beneath the trees. Tears fell from her eyes and rolled down her face. She bowed her head, her chin pressed to her chest. "Francisco," she sobbed. She clasped her hands, her fingers tightly intertwined. "Francisco, I'm so, so sorry."

Chuck, Carmelita, and Rosie arrived from higher in the drainage and stood over her.

She rested her hand on the boy's shoulder. "He's unconscious," she told them. She brushed the tears from her cheeks and took off her daypack and set it beside her. "There's no telling how badly he's hurt. We need to get him out of here. He needs a trauma center."

She gazed across the arroyo at the dense greenery lining the far side of the channel. How long had it been since the attack? Were they in danger?

"I'm sure whoever did this is gone," Chuck said, also eyeing the thick vegetation at the edge of the channel. "But I'll have a quick look around to be sure."

"Be careful."

"You know it."

He made his way up the arroyo past the end of the trail, his head swiveling.

Janelle withdrew from her daypack the substantial first aid kit she'd carried with her while hiking in the backcountry since completing her paramedic training a year ago.

"Call 911," she directed Carmelita, aware even as she removed latex gloves and gauze bandages from the kit that any care she provided the unconscious boy would do little to determine his fate, which instead lay in the hands of medical professionals at a hospital.

"There's no service down here," Carmelita noted, holding up her phone. "I'll head back up the trail. I had three bars a little ways up."

"No," Janelle said with a brisk shake of her head. "Sorry. We'll have to stay together until the others get here. We don't know what we're dealing with yet."

Rosie looked up the drainage. "Here they come."

The seven people who'd been hiking along the ridge emerged one by one from behind the prickly pear cactus at the end of the trail. The first five, four women and a man, wore various versions of desert-hiking garb—long-sleeved shirts, lightweight pants, and ball caps or broad-brimmed sunhats. Two men wearing park service uniforms—black boots, gray slacks, green shirts, and ball caps bearing the arrowhead-shaped National Park Service emblem—stepped into the open behind the others. One of the uniformed men was a law enforcement ranger, identifiable by the bulky handgun holstered at his waist and the thick bullet-proof vest pressing out from beneath his shirt.

The two uniformed rangers and the people in hiking clothes—the research team, gathered this morning to assess the petroglyph rocks along with Chuck—stopped and stared at the unconscious boy sprawled in front of Janelle and the girls.

Chuck returned from higher in the wash and spoke with the unarmed ranger, who was lanky and clean-shaven, in his mid-fifties, a few years older than Chuck. They were too distant for Janelle to hear their conversation. The ranger hunched his shoulders, listening intently, his eyes flicking to the injured boy. Chuck tipped his head toward the far side of the channel. The ranger stared along with the others at Francisco's body lying in the shade beyond the petroglyph rocks. Everyone strode down the wash to the injured boy and Janelle and the girls.

"This one's alive?" the unarmed ranger asked Janelle, his face pale.

"He's unconscious," she said. "His respiration and pulse are steady—for now."

The ranger groaned.

"He needs help, Ron," Chuck said to him.

Janelle looked up at the uniformed man. Saguaro National Park Superintendent Ron Blankenship had awarded Chuck the contract to study the petroglyphs in the park and had assembled the research team at Chuck's request as well.

Ron squared his shoulders. "Right."

Carmelita raised her phone to the superintendent. "There's no cell service down here."

"Lance," Ron said, turning to the armed ranger. "Would you head back up the trail until you get a signal?"

"Sure," Lance replied.

The second uniformed ranger was in his late twenties. He had a weightlifter's physique, wide at the shoulders and slender at the waist, his pronounced thigh muscles bulging beneath his pant legs. A brass badge glittered on his broad chest and his park service cap was pulled low over his smoky gray eyes. Buzz-cut blond hair showed beneath his cap.

He spun away from the group.

"But…" Carmelita said softly.

Janelle spoke up on her behalf. "My daughter's phone had a strong signal a little ways up the ridge," she said to Ron. "It's new, with an improved antenna."

Lance turned back. "Fine with me if she comes along," he said to Ron.

"What about me?" Rosie asked.

"I need you here," Janelle told her. She looked up at Carmelita. "Go. Your phone may be his best hope."

Carmelita and Lance jogged up the channel and disappeared behind the prickly pear cactus, returning to the trail up the ridge.

Janelle put on the pair of latex gloves from her medical kit and probed the back of the boy's head with her fingers, finding a gaping wound. She placed the gauze pads over the wound beneath the boy's skull, taking care to move his head as little as possible. She beckoned Rosie to her side. "Kneel down and put your hands over his ears. If he tries to move, hold his head still."

Rosie dropped to her knees and pressed her palms to the sides of the boy's head. Chuck, Ron, and the research team tightened their circle around her and Janelle, who addressed the superintendent.

"I don't think there's anything more we can, or should, do for him at this point," she said. "There's no benefit in moving him."

Ron tipped his head forward. "After the call goes through, the medevac chopper will be here PDQ." He sighed. "We've got them on speed dial at this point, I'm afraid." He shoved his cap higher on his forehead and massaged his brow with his fingertips. Turning to Chuck, he said, "I need to take a look at the deceased. Care to join me?"

The two men headed up the wash along the line of petroglyph rocks. A woman in her forties knelt beside the injured boy, opposite Janelle. Locks of brunette hair fell from the woman's sunhat. Her walnut eyes were so luminous they nearly leapt from her olive-toned face. "Can I do anything?" she asked. She reached behind her and gave her daypack a tap. "Would water help? I've got plenty. Or I could get some for him from the water tank."

"Not now," said Janelle. "But maybe if he regains consciousness. Is your water in a liter bottle?"

"It is," the woman said, pulling the bottle from her pack.

"Good. Keep it handy, would you? If he vomits and we need to turn him on his side, we can use it as a cervical roll to stabilize his neck."

Janelle looked up at the empty blue sky, willing the medevac helicopter to appear above the wash despite the departure of Carmelita and Lance only a couple of minutes ago.

She squeezed her eyes shut, holding back a fresh onslaught of tears. The blame for the injured boy—and Francisco's death and Carlos's disappearance—rested in significant part with her.

"Ron's right," said the woman. "They'll be here pretty damn quick. This has become a regular spot for pickups."

Janelle blinked away her tears. *Focus.* No one on the research team knew who Francisco was or how he'd come to be here, and now was not the time to reveal that information. "Because of the water tank?"

The woman nodded. "You'd think it would be just the opposite. That's what Border Patrol thought at first. They were totally against placing water stations out here in the desert. They figured the migrants would use the water to keep heading north. But instead of giving border crossers the extra boost they needed to keep going, the water had the opposite effect. The migrants who were in the worst shape—women and children, mostly—couldn't bring themselves to leave the tanks. Instead, they either called for help or waited and gave themselves up to whoever came around. These days, Border Patrol supports the water stations because they reduce the death count. I don't care who you are, it sucks to come across dead bodies in the desert. I convinced Ron to let Humane H_2O place the tank here in the park a few months ago. Everybody thought it would be too close to Tucson to do any good, but it's resulted in a steady stream of distress pickups." The woman's eyes strayed up the wash to Francisco's body. "I thought we'd be checking out the petroglyphs today," she concluded with a shrug, "but what are you gonna do?"

"I'm not sure why you're acting surprised, Martina," a swarthy man with black hair said to the woman. His voice was deep and rumbly, like Rosie's.

"Meaning what?" Martina asked him.

"Meaning it was you who got the water station put in here in the first place. It was you who turned this spot into a gathering place for migrants." He looked down at the unconscious boy. "Just not, normally, like this." He addressed Janelle. "I'm Joel Henry, natural resources officer for the Tohono O'odham Tribe. I work with Humane H_2O on behalf of my people." He waved up the drainage at the blue barrel resting on the metal stand at the foot of the trail. "I was pulling double duty today, checking out the petroglyphs with Vivian here—" he glanced at a stout female member of the research team standing next to him "—and checking on the water level in the tank. It's not close to any roads, so refilling it is quite an operation, with a whole team of volunteers hiking in here with backpack tanks every couple of weeks."

"The Tohono O'odham government actually pays Joel for the work he does with Humane H$_2$0," Martina said to Janelle.

Joel dipped his chin. "Before the water stations, my people were spending a fortune dealing with migrants who either got into trouble while crossing the Tohono O'odham Nation, or who died on our lands. Everybody was overwhelmed—our police, our medical examiner, our search and rescue team. We can't stop the migrants from coming, but at least we can try to keep so many of them from dying, or almost dying." He grew solemn, looking up the wash at Ron and Chuck standing over Francisco's body. "Even with the water, though, death came to this place today. I just wish we'd gotten here in time to stop it."

Martina looked at Janelle. "We're talking murder, is that right?"

Janelle nodded. "Strangulation." She looked away before Martina could see the distress in her eyes.

Martina addressed Joel. "If we'd have gotten here any earlier, we might've wound up dead ourselves."

"All of us together would've scared them away," Joel countered.

"You're probably right." Martina turned to Janelle. "I came here from Voyageurs National Park in Minnesota a couple years ago. I knew I was in for something completely different when I came, what with the desert and all." She glanced at Joel. "But I didn't give much thought to all the people who would be out here in the desert."

"There are lots of desperate people crossing the border," Joel said.

"Desperation I can handle. It's all the dying I can't get used to." Martina eyed the sizable medical kit at Janelle's side. "You sure came prepared."

"I'm a paramedic." Janelle looked at the boy's rising and falling chest. "His respiration is staying steady. That's good, at least."

Rosie shifted her knees in the gravel, her hands covering the boy's ears. "*Mamá* works for Durango Fire and Rescue," she told Martina, a note of pride in her raspy voice. "That's the fire department in our town—except *Mamá* rides in the ambulances. She even drives them sometimes."

"What about you?" Martina asked. "What do you do?"

"I'm on the dance team. And the improv team. That's comedy and acting put together. But I'm missing our big show, the Durango Fandango, because we came here instead." She looked up the drainage at the dead body. "I saw him first." She glanced at the injured boy. "I saw them both first."

"You don't seem too upset by it," Martina observed.

"Everybody dies," Rosie said. She didn't yet know that Francisco was—or had been—her second cousin. "That's what Dad says. He studies dead people."

"That'd be Chuck," Janelle explained to Martina. "Bender."

"Ahhh," said Martina. "I'm beginning to put the pieces together."

"He told me I could help when I got here," Rosie said. "That's why I'm missing the Fandango. He's teaching me to be an archaeologist, just like him. He's the expert of all experts."

"So I've heard."

"Are you an archaeologist, too?"

"Not by training. I'm the naturalist for the park's Tucson Mountain District, here on the west side of the city. I've overseen a couple of Hohokam digs the last couple of years, but mostly I run outreach programs for schoolkids and conservation organizations and big donors to the park. We go out on day hikes, meet for lectures, that sort of thing." She raised her hand to Janelle in introduction. "Martina Ricci."

"No uniform?" Janelle asked her.

Martina's hiking outfit was well used, her cotton shirt and pants stained with dirt and worn at the knees and elbows, the toes of her hiking boots speckled with grime. The brim of her straw hat was battered and broken, and a long, curved feather, brown with gray stripes, extended from her hatband.

Martina rolled her eyes. "Uniforms are ridiculous in the desert. The heat rashes? Oh…my…*God*. I refuse to wear them in the backcountry. Ron's used to it by now. He blames Minnesota. He says I've still got ice in my bones." She gave the tip of the feather in her hatband a flick with her finger. "This is an osprey feather. It reminds me of where I came from. There are a million fish hawks in Voyageurs, but not a one of them in Saguaro."

"What's your role on the research team?"

"The petroglyphs are one of the main reasons I came here. When I was posted at Voyageurs, I got involved in studying an old canoe trade route used by the predecessors of the Ojibwe people that ran through the middle of the park. I researched the similarities between the petroglyphs carved on granite outcrops along the Voyageurs route and those found in Saguaro. When the naturalist slot opened up here, I applied for it."

"Minnesota to Arizona—that must have taken some getting used to."

"I'm still getting used to it. I was at Voyageurs for five years—or, as they like to say in Minnesota, five winters. I grew up in Chicago, so I didn't mind the cold. But all the indoors time started to get to me. When the Saguaro job came along, I figured, why not? I've been through two summers out here so far. I thought when I moved to Arizona that I'd be outdoors seven days a week, 365 days a year, basking in the sun. But it turns out that's not how the desert works. It's the flip side of Minnesota. To live here, you have to be willing to spend a lot of time indoors in the summer with an air conditioner blowing in your face."

Janelle glanced at the petroglyph rocks lining the edge of the wash. "The Hohokam people didn't have any air-conditioning."

"No, but the Tohono O'odham do, and they make good use of it, just like everyone else."

Vivian, the Tohono O'odham woman standing next to Joel, nodded. "You got that right."

"I often wonder what life must have been like for your ancestors," Martina said to her. "It couldn't have been easy."

Janelle looked at the unconscious boy, then up the line of rocks at Francisco. "For a lot of people, life isn't easy today, either, air-conditioning or not," she said.

She credited her younger brother, Clarence, for the good life she, Carmelita, and Rosie had enjoyed since she'd met and married Chuck six years ago. After Clarence had graduated from the University of New Mexico School of Anthropology, he had hired on with Chuck as a temporary employee for Chuck's one-man firm, Bender Archaeological, Inc., based out of Chuck's aging Victorian home in Durango. Clarence had come to respect his new boss and had introduced Janelle to him.

These days, Clarence lived in an apartment in Durango and made his living as an archaeologist-for-hire for Chuck and other local firms when there was work to be had, and as a bartender in downtown Durango between archaeological digs. While Janelle, Chuck, and the girls were in Arizona this week, Clarence was looking after their family cat, Pasta Alfredo, in Durango.

Janelle often wondered about the type of life she'd have had if her parents had never come to the US. Would she have risked the journey north, like Francisco and Carlos and the injured boy on the ground in front of her? That haunting question, along with its never-to-be-known answer, had played a significant role in her suggesting she could meet Francisco and Carlos at the water station in the park and help them with their claims for asylum in the US. But now, Francisco was dead—murdered—and Carlos was missing and perhaps dead as well.

She stripped off her gloves, her eyes downcast. Reaching out, she squeezed Rosie's wrist.

"Ouch, *Mamá!*" Rosie protested, wiggling her arm while keeping her hands over the boy's ears.

"*Lo siento, m'hija,*" Janelle apologized, letting go. "It's just, this poor boy."

Up the wash, Carmelita appeared from behind the prickly pear cactus, followed by Lance, as they returned to the bottom of the arroyo. Lance crossed the channel to Chuck and Ron, who stood over Francisco's body, while Carmelita descended the drainage to the injured boy and those gathered around him.

"We got through right away," she reported, stopping next to Rosie. "Lance knew exactly how to get things moving."

Rosie looked up at her older sister with a devilish grin. "You mean, he shot the moves on you?"

Carmelita's cheeks reddened. "Give it a rest, Rosie."

Rosie's smile disappeared. "I know, I know," she acknowledged. "Somebody died." She looked down at the unconscious boy. "And he might die, too." She twisted to look at Lance, who was speaking with Ron. "He sure is a hunk, though."

"You're not the first to notice that," Martina said.

"It's for my improv team," said Rosie. "We're supposed to listen to people really close, then make up jokes about them."

"But," Janelle said, "your jokes are supposed to be nice, not mean. That's the rule."

"What's mean about a hunky dude shooting the moves on Carm?"

"*Rosie,*" Carmelita warned.

The boy seized suddenly, his entire body shaking. Rosie tightened her hands at the sides of his head while Janelle held his arms, keeping him from striking the ground or himself with his fists during the seizure. The boy relaxed after several seconds, the seizure coming to an end, and lay still, his eyes closed.

Janelle sat back from the boy. Movement caught her eye. A short, heavyset man in a black T-shirt and low-slung jeans appeared at the foot of the trail. Large silver stud earrings filled his earlobes and his smooth black hair swooped to his shoulders.

Janelle's jaw dropped. It was her brother, Clarence.

4

Chuck stared at Clarence, attempting to wrap his mind around his brother-in-law's unexpected arrival in the arroyo. Liza, Clarence's girlfriend, appeared from behind the prickly pear cactus as well.

Liza, in her late twenties like Clarence, was short and broad-shouldered, her arms tattooed and heavily muscled. She wore a sisal sunhat, T-shirt, shorts, and sturdy hiking boots. Her black hair fell far down her back in a long braid.

A member of the Ute Mountain Ute Tribe, whose homelands encompassed a swath of mountains and high desert west of Durango, Liza made her living as a whitewater rafting guide on trips down the Colorado River in Utah and Arizona. Liza and Clarence had met in the spring on a rafting trip through Cataract Canyon in Canyonlands National Park and had dated between Liza's river trips in the months since. As the rafting season slowed with the onset of fall, the two had spent an increasing amount of time together in Durango.

But now, inexplicably, here they were in the Arizona desert instead.

Chuck crossed the channel to them.

"Surprise," Clarence said, lifting his shoulders in a self-conscious shrug. He was bareheaded, his dark hair tucked behind his ears, his big earrings shimmering in the sun.

"What are the two of you doing here?" Chuck demanded.

"We..." Clarence cast an uneasy glance down the arroyo at Janelle and the girls. "We picked up Enrique and Yolanda in Albuquerque and brought them here," he admitted to Chuck.

"You *what*?"

Clarence squirmed, twisting his boots in the gravel. "They insisted. They threatened to drive here on their own if we didn't take them. What else were we supposed to do?"

"Not we, *you*," Liza said. "You're the one who decided."

"They begged," Clarence said to Chuck. "We…I…didn't have any choice." He lowered his voice. "*Familia*. That's all *Mamá y Papá* are talking about right now."

"Uncle Clarence!" Rosie called from where she knelt over the injured boy, her hands at the sides of his head. "I'd come say 'hi,' but I can't!"

"I can see that," Clarence called back to her.

"There's a medevac chopper on the way," Chuck explained.

Ron approached from beneath the trees. "This is a crime scene," he said sternly, stopping in front of Clarence and Liza.

"We didn't mean to intrude," Clarence said. "We hiked here to surprise *mis sobrinas*—my nieces."

"I'm going to have to ask you to leave."

"Of course," said Liza.

"This is Liza Cuthair," Chuck said, introducing her to Ron. "She's a rafting guide on the Colorado River." He tipped his head at Clarence. "And this is my brother-in-law, Clarence Ortega. He works with me on my contracts when I need him."

"Anything we can do to help?" Liza asked the superintendent.

"You can get out of here," Ron snapped. "There are too many people here as it is. The injured victim will be airlifted out. After that, we'll secure the scene and call in one of our ISB special agents, along with the medical examiner and the sheriff's department."

"ISB?" Clarence asked.

"The Investigative Services Branch of the National Park Service. It's a pretty busy operation these days, with the parks so full of visitors."

Clarence looked past the superintendent at Francisco's body. "What's going on?"

Ron stepped sideways, blocking Clarence's view. "I'm not at liberty to say."

"Could we at least check in with my sister before we leave?"

"As long as you keep it brief." Ron paused. "Just so you know, I'll be getting your contact information from Chuck. You both should expect calls."

Liza inclined her head. "Understood."

Ron turned on his heel and returned to the body.

Chuck led Clarence and Liza down the wash to the injured boy and the others. "That's Francisco back under the trees," he said softly. "His body."

Clarence stopped and grabbed Chuck's arm. "Francisco?"

Chuck drew him on down the drainage. "I'm sorry to have to tell you."

"He's...he's *dead*?"

Chuck nodded grimly. "He was strangled. I haven't told Ron who he is yet. Everything's been happening too fast."

"*¡Jesu Cristo!*" Clarence exclaimed beneath his breath. He pointed ahead at the injured boy. "Is that Carlos?"

"No. We don't know who he is. We don't know where Carlos is, either."

"*Dios mio*," Clarence moaned.

"I'm sorry, Clarence," Liza said as they walked. "And you, Chuck. Tell Janelle and the girls I'm sorry, too, when you have the chance, would you?"

They reached the injured boy and those encircling him.

Clarence put his arm around Carmelita. "You doing okay?"

"He's alive," she said of the boy. "That's the good thing."

Rosie looked up from where she knelt at the boy's head. "But the other one's dead."

Liza rested a hand on Rosie's shoulder.

Vivian gazed across the circle at her. "Liza? Is that you?"

Liza's eyes grew wide. "Vivian? Vivian Little Boy?"

"One and the same."

Before he'd come to Arizona, Chuck had gotten to know Vivian on a series of video conference calls he'd scheduled with the research team for planning purposes. She was sturdily built, with ruddy cheeks and a firm jawline. The brim of her cap curled tightly around her temples, accentuating her high cheekbones. Her dark hair cascaded down her back.

"What are you doing here?" Liza asked her.

"The boundary of our nation is just west of here." Vivian swung her arm, taking in the broad expanse extending from the base of the ridge. "All that out there is Tohono O'odham land." She aimed her square jaw at Liza. "The bigger question is, what are *you* doing here? I have a hard time imagining you out in the desert. You're a long way from any whitewater."

Liza tapped Clarence on the arm. "I came with this guy."

"He's our uncle Clarence," Rosie explained.

Vivian extended her hand to him. "I'm the cultural preservation officer for the Tohono O'odham people," she said. "Liza and I guided together for a couple of seasons on the Salt before I got on with the tribe."

A thumping sound came from beyond the ridge. The sound quickly grew louder, pulsing through the air.

A tall, blond, middle-aged member of the research team turned her ear to the sky. "That's the U of A Medical Center helicopter," she said. "I'd recognize it anywhere. Its landing path goes right over my office. Hear how deep it sounds? Its engine is twice the size of most medevac choppers, which enables it to fly way south into Mexico to pick up Americans who need help there."

Harper Longworth was chair of the Anthropology Department at the University of Arizona in Tucson. In her forties, she was six feet tall and weighed little more than a hundred pounds. She was skinnier in person than she'd appeared to Chuck on the video calls—though, admittedly, he'd only seen her onscreen from the shoulders up—so skinny in real life, in fact, that it seemed the slight breeze flowing up the arroyo might knock her over. Tendrils of Harper's wispy, straw-colored hair stuck to her pale, perspiring neck, and the logo of the University of Arizona, a blocky, bright red letter *A* outlined in dark blue and white, was silkscreened above the breast pocket of her khaki shirt.

As the helicopter drew nearer, the beat of its rotors shook the ground under Chuck's feet. The injured boy moaned and dug his fingers into the sand, wrestling to sit up. Rosie grasped the sides of his head while Janelle and Martina secured his torso and legs, holding him in place.

The boy's eyelids fluttered open and he looked frantically from side to side, his dark eyes filled with dread.

"*¡Carlos!*" he yelled. "*¡Corre, Carlos, corre!*"

5

The injured boy went limp beneath Janelle's hands, his eyes falling closed and his arms sagging at his sides.

Janelle stared down at the boy, her heart racing. *Carlos*, he had said. And *corre*. He had hollered her cousin's name, yelling, "Run, Carlos, run!"

"Would you please keep an eye on him?" she asked Martina, scrambling to her feet.

At the park naturalist's nod, she strode up the wash, angled between two of the petroglyph-bearing rocks, and approached Francisco's body.

Standing next to Francisco, Ron and Lance tilted their heads back, looking at the sky, as the chuff of the helicopter grew louder.

Janelle stopped at her cousin's feet. Whatever had been used to kill him had done maximum damage—the slash across his throat was deep and straight and extended from ear to ear.

Ron turned to her. "I need you to back off. I don't want the murder scene contaminated—any more than it already is, anyway."

The superintendent's words reached her as if from a great distance. She clamped her hand over her mouth as she looked down at Francisco, barely aware of the presence of Ron and Lance next to her cousin's body, or of the approaching medevac helicopter in the sky above.

Tears burned the backs of her eyelids. She'd seen Francisco and Carlos just weeks ago in Juárez, when she'd driven with her parents to El Paso and they'd crossed the border bridge to visit her father's brother and sister-in-law, Miguel and Consuela, the parents of Carlos and Francisco. Her twin cousins had attended the big family gathering Miguel and Consuela had hosted that evening at their home on the outskirts of the border city, singing and dancing to *música tejana* in the dusty courtyard late into the night.

Though Francisco and Carlos were identical twins, their personalities were as different from one another as could be. Francisco was loud and brash. He stroked his thin mustache lovingly with his thumb and forefinger when he talked, and his boisterous laughter was contagious. Carlos was reserved and clean shaven, avoiding eye contact and conversation.

At the end of the evening in Juárez, Francisco had led a snake dance around the courtyard, his arms raised high above his head, swaying his skinny hips and singing along with Flaco Jiménez's mournful *Los Barandales del Puente*. At the urging of his relatives, Carlos had joined his brother and the other dancers, shuffling his feet at the end of the line with his head bowed.

Despite the stark differences in their personalities, Francisco and Carlos were alike in their shared desire to come to the US. The night of the dinner, Francisco had told Janelle of his and Carlos's constrained lives in Juárez. They rarely left home for fear of being kidnapped and forced into servitude for the drug cartels that controlled the Mexican borderlands. They had concluded, in agreement with their parents, that they had no choice but to leave their home city. Their choices were to head south and seek their fortunes in Mexico City, far from the lawless border region, or cross the border and seek asylum in the US.

"*Primero intentaremos solicitar el asilo*," Francisco told Janelle that night. "First, we will try for asylum. If that does not work, we will go to the south. But we cannot stay in Juárez."

Carlos nodded somberly at Francisco's side.

Francisco asked what Janelle thought of their plan to cross the US-Mexico border in the remote desert and turn themselves in to immigration authorities in Tucson, sixty miles north of the border, lessening their chances of immediate deportation by officials stationed at the El Paso border bridge. She agreed with their reasoning and offered to help, suggesting they cross in October, when she and the girls would be in southern Arizona with Chuck.

Her offer of aid had come easily in Juárez, surrounded as she'd been by family. But she'd grown increasingly anxious on the drive home from Mexico. Legal though any support she provided her cousins might be, helping them still came with risks, and those risks applied not only to her, but to the girls and Chuck as well.

It was her good fortune that she'd been born in the US. To what lengths was she morally required to go in helping members of her family on the Mexican side of the border?

She dropped off her parents at their home in Albuquerque and returned to Durango, where she sat Chuck down at the kitchen table and told him of the offer she'd made to her cousins.

"I appreciate what you're trying to do," Chuck said when she finished. "But you can't help them, you just can't."

She reached across the table and took his hands in hers. "I know you're right. I came to the same conclusion on the way home. I'll let them know, with my apologies."

"Apologies for what?" Carmelita asked, appearing in the kitchen doorway.

"Um," said Janelle. "We were…uh…"

Chuck looked at Carmelita from his seat at the table. "Your *mamá's* cousins in Juárez asked for her help crossing the border."

In all the years Janelle had been together with Chuck, she'd never known him to speak anything but the truth to the girls, so his frankness now came as no surprise. She followed his lead. "The twins, Francisco and Carlos, your second cousins, want to apply for asylum in the US. They didn't really ask for my help. I offered it."

"But now you're going to back out on them?" Carmelita said.

Janelle bit down hard on her lower lip.

"Why?" Carmelita asked.

"There are risks involved, to Chuck and his work, and to you and Rosie."

"What sort of risks?"

"I offered to meet them in the desert and take them to the immigration authorities in Tucson. Your grand-*papá* and grand-*mamá* would serve as their sponsors in Albuquerque until their cases are heard."

"That doesn't sound very risky. It doesn't sound illegal, either."

"Your cousins would be in a bit of a legal gray area by coming that far north before presenting themselves to immigration."

"Your meeting them wouldn't have anything to do with that, though, would it?"

"No, it wouldn't."

"What's the problem, then?" Carmelita looked from Janelle to Chuck. "*Familia*," she said. "That's what you're always talking about. It's why we drive to Albuquerque to see Grand-*papá* and Grand-*mamá*, like, every other month. Francisco and Carlos are *familia*, too. How can we not help them?"

Silence settled in the room. Janelle looked across the table at Chuck.

"*Familia*," he said to her, a thin smile climbing onto his face. He turned to Carmelita, his smile growing bigger. "Guess you'd better start studying up on what it takes to be a human smuggler."

She grinned back at him. "Smugglers are called *coyotes*," she said, using the Spanish pronunciation. "There's good money in it, from what I hear."

She padded back down the hallway in her socks. Chuck turned to Janelle, his smile disappearing. "If you—we—help them, it wouldn't technically be criminal, right?"

"Correct, it wouldn't be."

"So what do you think?"

"I want to know what you think."

He looked at the empty doorway where Carmelita had stood a moment ago. "I hate to say it, but I think she made pretty good sense." He directed a grudging smile at Janelle. "*Familia.*"

Now, beneath the palo verde trees, Ron leaned forward, catching Janelle's eye. "Did you hear me?"

She jumped, startled. "Yes, of course."

"I'll give you the same warning I gave your brother. We'll be talking to you and your husband as the investigation gets underway, since you were the ones who found the body. We'll want to know anything you can think of that might help with the investigation."

Janelle stared at the ground. Anything that might help—like, for starters, who the murder victim was. "We'll be ready for you," she said.

She wiped away her tears and stepped back from Francisco's body, her eyes on the gaping slash around her cousin's neck.

Not criminal? How horribly wrong she'd been.

The medevac chopper soared over the ridge and settled on the flat gravel channel. A pair of flight nurses in full-body suits hopped out of the side door and conferred with Ron as the helicopter rotors slowed. Janelle approached and reported the boy's condition to them. They thanked her, returned to the helicopter for a stretcher, and loaded the injured boy onto it. The nurses lifted him into the chopper, which climbed back into the air with a roar of its powerful engine, the blast of wind from its rotors sending bits of gravel scuttling across the wash.

The helicopter disappeared beyond the ridge, heading back toward Tucson. Janelle returned down the channel to the others, still gathered at the spot where the boy had lain.

"That was fast," said Rosie, looking after the departed chopper.

"They know what they're doing," Liza agreed. "By the way,

you did a good job helping your mom before the helicopter came."

"Yeah," Rosie acknowledged. "I did."

Liza and Rosie had become fast friends during Liza's extended stays with Clarence in Durango the past few weeks. Liza and Carmelita, on the other hand, hadn't hit it off so well. Not yet, anyway. Janelle suspected that had to do with their similar temperaments—both were independent-minded and intensely competitive—plus the fact that Liza's relationship with Clarence had resulted in his spending less time with Carmelita than in the past.

Carmelita and Clarence had jogged together a couple of times a week for the last two years, and Clarence had shed a few pounds in the process. He hadn't exercised with Carmelita since he'd taken up with Liza, however, and the hiatus showed. Here in the drainage, his stomach protruded over the waistline of his pants, casting a round shadow on the ground in front of him.

Carmelita looked past Liza at Clarence. "Did I hear you right? You brought Grand-*papá* and Grand-*mamá* here?"

"We swung through Albuquerque and picked them up," he said with a nod. "They're back at the hotel."

Janelle turned to her brother. "You didn't tell us you were doing that."

"They wouldn't let me, *hermana*. They knew what you'd say."

"How'd you find us out here?"

"Carm posted a couple of pics on her feed this morning during your hike."

Janelle rounded on Carmelita. "What were you thinking?"

"We've talked about it a million times," Carmelita responded. "I have to put up posts to build followers, and I have to build followers to get sponsored."

For the past year, as @ClimberCarm, Carmelita had been posting pictures online every other day or so of her rock climbs and trail runs. She also posted pictures of her many podium finishes at competitive rock-climbing events around the Four Corners region during the spring, summer, and fall sport-climbing season. Her active presence on social media was aimed at gaining enough followers to be offered free rock-climbing gear and running shoes from manufacturers in return for displaying their products in her posts.

"Hey, there, ClimberCarm," Vivian said to Carmelita, waving to her. "I follow you, too."

Janelle stared at Vivian. "You follow Carmelita?"

"I follow ClimberCarm," Vivian said. "Liza put me on to her." She faced Carmelita. "I love your mountain pics, especially when there's snow. It's a nice break from all the sun and heat around here." She turned to Janelle. "When it comes to outdoor stuff, I try to follow as many people of color as I can. There aren't that many out there, especially women. Not yet, anyway." She directed her thumb at Carmelita. "It's good to see girls like her carving out some space for themselves online. It's about time, if you ask me."

Liza nodded. "If anybody deserves sponsorships, it's you," she told Carmelita, rubbing her arm. "You'll get there, just you wait and see."

Carmelita tensed at Liza's touch, but she did not pull her arm away.

Ron strode down the wash with the young law enforcement ranger, Lance, at his side, and ordered everyone to leave the scene of the murder. Lance stood next to the superintendent, his black boots planted in the loose rocks of the wash, his trunk-like legs spread wide. He rested his hand on the butt of the big silver handgun holstered at his waist.

Before Janelle started back up the trail, she turned for one more look at Francisco's body lying beneath the trees. From where she stood across the channel, her cousin appeared asleep, as if he was simply taking a nap before finishing the last of his trek through the desert to Tucson. But the cloud of flies buzzing at the gaping wound in his neck told her otherwise.

She fought back more tears. She should have stuck with her realization after leaving the family gathering in Juárez that helping her cousins seek asylum in the US was a bad idea. But she hadn't.

She was responsible for Francisco's death and Carlos's disappearance. Now, it was up to her to do whatever it took to find Carlos and learn who had killed Francisco. Her *familia Ortega* deserved no less.

6

Janelle hiked along the spine of the ridge, returning to the maintenance yard with the others. Everyone stepped aside when a pair of uniformed Border Patrol officers passed them halfway along the ridge, headed for the arroyo. Like Lance, the officers wore holstered pistols and body armor that made their chests stick out like pro football players.

A dozen search and rescue team members hiked by next. They wore lugged hiking boots, plastic helmets, and heavy cotton pants and shirts, and carried huge backpacks festooned with coiled ropes, steel pickets, and shiny alloy belay devices. At the end of the line, two rescuers rolled a wheeled wire stretcher between them. The stretcher was designed to roll accident victims out of the backcountry on the single mountain-bike wheel welded beneath the stretcher's center point. One rescuer gripped a pair of handles at the front of the rolling stretcher, while another guided the litter with a matching pair of handles at its rear.

Back at the maintenance yard, Janelle gathered with Chuck, the girls, Clarence, Liza, and the five research team members in the square of shade beneath the camp trailer awning.

"When you said 'the Salt,' were you talking about the Salt *River* back there, Viv?" a colorfully dressed member of the research team asked Vivian. The woman was trim and fit and in her late twenties. Her long-sleeved cotton shirt was hot pink, her hiking pants mauve. Her face was heavily made up—red-rouged cheeks, sky-blue eyelids, eyes outlined in deep purple, and lips thickly coated with gloss that matched the bright pink color of her shirt. Her dark hair, bunched beneath her sunhat, was as curly as Rosie's.

"Yep, Era," Vivian confirmed.

"Impressive," Era said. She addressed the group. "The Salt River runs big on snowmelt each spring from the mountains of the White River Apache Reservation all the way to Phoenix. People come from everywhere to run it. I've always sworn I'll do it someday."

"We were pretty much the only female guides on the river, weren't we?" Vivian said to Liza. "The only Natives, too." She looked out across the flat, dusty maintenance yard. "When it's running full blast, the Salt couldn't be more different than this," she noted to the group. "It's the steepest raftable river in North America. But it only runs for a few weeks each year, and then, just like that—" she snapped her fingers "—the snow's all melted and the river's gone."

"I'm so busy in the spring," Era said. "That's my excuse for not running it yet. Spring's the most important time of the year for us botanists." She offered her hand across the circle of people to Liza. "Erasmus Maldonado, lead botanist for the city of Tucson—the *only* botanist for the city of Tucson, if you want to know the truth."

Rosie eyed the colorfully outfitted botanist. "You sure have an unusual name."

"I get that a lot," Era replied. "My parents were scientists, the same as me. They were into Charles Darwin, like, big time. His brother's name was Erasmus."

"Why didn't they name you Charles?"

"It wasn't girly enough, I guess."

"Is that why you wear such bright clothing when you go hiking?"

Erasmus smiled. "I hadn't thought of it that way."

"You look like a flower."

"Well, I *am* a botanist."

"Erasmus doesn't sound very girly to me."

"Everyone calls me Era for short."

"My real name is Rosa, which means rose in Spanish. But everybody calls me Rosie even though it's just as long."

"Those are both beautiful names." Era cocked an eyebrow at Rosie. "We make a good pair, don't we? You're named for a flower and I look like one."

Janelle half-listened to the ongoing conversation, her thoughts on Francisco's body, and on Carlos, missing. Had Carlos been murdered, like his twin brother, his body yet to be found? Or was he perhaps lying out in the desert somewhere, injured, like the boy?

She sighed and looked toward Tucson, where the helicopter had headed with the boy. Somewhere the boy's mother was worrying about her son, not knowing what had become of him. "The kid never had a chance, did he?" she said, still looking out from beneath the camper awning.

The tall, willowy professor, Harper, followed her gaze toward the city. "He still has a chance—a good one, if you ask me. He's alive, at least." She looked around the circle, taking in her fellow researchers. "In a way, the boy is like the petroglyphs we were supposed to observe today."

"How so?" asked Vivian, the Tohono O'odham cultural preservation officer.

"Academicians, myself included, long believed the petroglyphs of the ancient Hohokam people in the Sonoran Desert were merely stylistic—nothing more than artistic doodlings." The professor's cadence was slow and measured, her words clearly enunciated. "We had no sense the carvings might express messages of some sort, much less that they might contain messages associated with the ancient Hohokam trade route stretching south all the way to the lands of the Mayan people in the Yucatán."

The professor inclined her head to Martina and continued.

"Your research of the petroglyph-marked trade route through Voyageurs in Minnesota opened a lot of people's eyes, my own included. I now believe the Hohokam carvings in this region may convey messages of some sort. Your work since you've come here has helped expand my perception of the kinds of messages that might be involved." Harper glanced at Janelle. "The boy almost certainly traveled here from Central America, the southern terminus of the Hohokam trade route in the 1100s. Back then, trade items with the Mayan people consisted of seashells and toucan feathers. The route remains in use today, but the items of commerce are markedly different, including heroin, marijuana, and trafficked human beings. Any messages conveyed in Hohokam petroglyphs and in carvings at the southern end of the route may echo through the centuries to today—perhaps offering descriptions of the route, or pointing out potential dangers along the way."

Vivian wagged her head at the professor. "I don't know about all that, Harper. The kid just wanted a shot at living the so-called American dream. The idea that some old messages carved into rocks had something to do with his journey? I know you're chair of the Anthropology Department at U of A and all, but I'm not buying it, not even from you."

"Nothing I've said before has convinced you, Vivian," Harper said. "I wouldn't expect anything I'm saying now to change your mind, either."

"What if Harper's right?" Martina asked Vivian.

"So what if she is?" Vivian replied. "I don't have time for all this mumbo-jumbo about secret messages my ancestors might or might not have carved into rocks a thousand years ago. My job is to protect the culture of *today's* Tohono O'odham people through our O'odham language preservation courses and our art and dance classes."

"But you came here to look at the petroglyphs with the rest of us this morning."

"I'm just doing what I'm told. Chairman Begalia loves the messages-on-rocks idea. He figures if it proves true—and maybe even if it doesn't—it might attract petroglyph peepers and bring some tourism money to the Tohono O'odham Nation, which would help us deal with the problems we face right now, today, as opposed to a thousand years ago. The boy is an example of one of those problems. We're being overrun, literally, by migrants crossing our lands and—" she sighed "—dying on our lands." She looked at Martina and her lips rose in an unexpected grin, taking Janelle by surprise. "As for you, you don't have any business telling me my people's business. We've got enough trouble surviving as it is after you white folks showed up here in the desert and took all the good, watered land at the foot of the mountains."

Martina returned Vivian's smile. It appeared the two enjoyed sparring with one another.

"First off," Martina said, "I just got here a couple years ago. Second, I'm not white. Not Anglo-Saxon white, anyway. I'm one-hundred-percent Italian-American, through and through. My grandparents were hassled plenty when they showed up in Chicago, even though they did it the legal way, with papers and green cards and citizenship classes."

"I don't believe," Vivian said, "that any of the hassle your grandparents faced involved the word *genocide*, like it did with my people, did it?"

Martina's smile faded. "You're right about that."

Harper clapped her hands together. "Guess we should get out of here." She waved at the researchers' cars lined in front of the aluminum-walled storage garages on the far side of the maintenance yard. "I want to get back to my office and see if I can track down what's become of the boy."

As soon as the researchers were out of earshot, crossing the sunbaked yard to their cars, Janelle grasped Chuck's elbow and turned him to her. "The boy yelled Carlos's name," she said. "And *corre*. You heard him. He was yelling for Carlos to run."

"Whoever Carlos is," said Rosie, her eyes on the researchers as they bid farewell to one another and climbed into their vehicles.

Janelle watched the departing researchers, too. "Do you think they suspect anything?" she asked Chuck.

Rosie crinkled her nose at Janelle. "Suspect what, *Mamá*?"

From across the yard, Martina raised a hand in farewell. Janelle released Chuck's elbow and waved back, her arm stiff. Martina climbed into a white pickup truck with the park-service arrowhead emblem on its doors and drove away.

Two other park-service trucks—presumably belonging to Ron and Lance—remained in the parking area in front of the garages, along with a white SUV with the circular Border Patrol emblem on its front doors and the rescue team's assemblage of dusty SUVs, mini-pickup trucks, and sedans.

Janelle turned to Chuck as soon as Martina disappeared on the road leading over a rise to the Tucson Mountain District Visitor Center. "It's time. We have to tell her."

"Agreed."

She faced Rosie, who stood beside Carmelita with her back to the camper. "You know Chuck is here to study the petroglyphs in the park, right?"

Rosie put a hand on her hip. "That's, like, totally obvi."

Janelle pressed her lips together. "What may not be totally *obvi* to you is that we're here for another reason, too. You heard the name the boy called out."

"Carlos."

"That's the name of one of your cousins from Juárez."

"Ohhh."

"Your *primo*," Clarence added.

"Your second cousin," Janelle clarified. "Carlos is the son of Grand-*papá*'s brother. You've never met him. Carlos had a twin brother named Francisco." She paused. "Until today."

"Had?" Rosie asked.

"The dead body," Carmelita explained. "The murder victim—that was Francisco."

Rosie took a backward step, coming up against the trailer, her eyes growing big and round. "My cousin was the dead guy?"

"Who you had never met," Janelle said.

"What about the boy who was hurt?"

"We don't know who he is."

"Why did he call out our other cousin's name?"

"We don't know that, either. Not yet, anyway." Janelle straightened. "We've told you before how fortunate you are to have been born in the US instead of Mexico."

Rosie nodded.

"For a long time, *las familias* of your grand-*papá* and grand-*mamá* had good lives in Mexico," Janelle said. "When your *abuelos* came to the US, they weren't necessarily escaping from Juárez, they just wanted to see what life was like in the States. After they came, though, things got worse and worse across the border."

"Because of drugs," Carmelita said.

"And everything that comes with them—corruption, kidnapping, bribery, murder," Janelle confirmed to her and Rosie. "That's why we haven't taken the two of you along with us when we've gone with Grand-*papá* and Grand-*mamá* to visit family in Juárez, just to be safe. For a long time, Mexicans fled across the border into the US to escape what Mexico had become. Lately, migrants from Mexico have been replaced by a flood of people from Central America instead." She looked at Rosie. "But plenty of Mexican people still cross the border looking for better lives— young people, especially."

"*Incluyendo mis primos*," Rosie said gravely.

"Yes. Including your cousins."

Clarence put his hand on Rosie's shoulder, but she shook it off and glared at Janelle. "You *knew* they were coming, didn't you? We were supposed to meet them today."

"That's why we left so early this morning on our hike," Janelle admitted. "The plan was to link up with them at the water station and let the research team see them there."

Rosie rounded on Carmelita. "You knew, too, didn't you?"

"Only because I overheard," Carmelita told her. "But," she said, turning to Janelle, "I still don't get why we needed to meet them."

"They aren't—weren't—eighteen yet," said Janelle. "They could cross the border and apply for asylum, and then, as minors, they could be placed with family members until their cases were heard. For Carlos and Francisco, that would be your grand-*papá* and grand-*mamá*."

"Why didn't they just present themselves at the border in Juárez?"

"It's only a few weeks until their eighteenth birthday. The authorities at the border have been known to detain seventeen-year-olds until they turn eighteen, at which point, as adults, they can be deported back to Mexico, or held in jail in the US until their cases are decided—which takes months, sometimes even years. So Francisco and Carlos decided to come overland instead. We were going to take them to the immigration office in Tucson, then to your grand-*papá* and grand-*mamá* in Albuquerque." She narrowed her eyes at Clarence. "But your uncle brought your grandparents here instead."

Clarence raised his hands to her defensively, his palms out. "They were so excited. They couldn't wait."

"But what happened instead was…" Rosie urged Janelle.

"We found Francisco's body." Her throat constricted as she envisioned her cousin's slashed neck.

"*I* found him. I saw him first."

"Yes, you did," Janelle said, pressing on. "Then the boy yelled Carlos's name, which tells us Carlos was there with Francisco, or somewhere nearby. The two of them phoned us before they crossed the border three days ago, but we haven't heard from them since. We think their cell phones don't work on this side of the border." She turned to Chuck. "We have to get back out there. We have to find him."

Chuck pointed at the entrance to the maintenance yard. "Take a look."

Janelle turned to see a Pima County Sheriff's Department SUV arriving, followed by a white panel van with the words "Pima County Office of the Medical Examiner" on its side. The SUV and van parked next to the other vehicles.

"The investigation will take at least the rest of the day today," Chuck said. "Probably tomorrow, too, after the ISB agent gets here."

"We can't just leave Carlos out there," Janelle said. "I'm sure he knows Francisco is dead. He'll be cut off from the water for as long as the investigation takes."

"I agree," Carmelita said. "Carlos is all alone. He may be hurt or dying of thirst. We have to find him." She crooked her finger, drawing the others around her.

7

Carmelita sped up the trail ahead of Chuck, climbing the ridge from the camper with him for the second time that morning. Despite hiking as fast as he could, he still fell steadily behind her. She waited for him at the top of the ridge. He reached her and bent forward, hands on his knees, gasping for air.

A helicopter flew toward them from the city. A distant speck at first, the chopper roared nearer, a giant insect clawing the sky. The sun glinted off its black-and-white metal skin, the gold decal of the Tucson Police Department glimmering on its side. The police helicopter roared over the ridge, close above their heads, its rotors shaking the rocky ground. Chuck straightened, still breathing hard, as the chopper swung north and descended into the arroyo.

Back at the campsite, beneath the shade of the trailer awning, Carmelita had suggested that, despite Ron's admonishment to everyone to stay away from the murder scene, Chuck could return to the petroglyph rocks under the guise of continuing his contracted work.

"You can tell him you'll stay out of the way of the investigation while you study the petroglyphs," she said to Chuck. "You can say you're just trying to stick to your schedule, that you don't have a lot of time." She tapped her chin with her finger. "And I should come with you." She hurried on before he or Janelle could lodge an objection. "If you find Carlos, you'll need someone who can talk to him."

Over the six years Chuck and Janelle had been together, Chuck's ability to speak Spanish had improved from nonexistent to rudimentary. Meanwhile, over those same years, Janelle had spoken Spanish and English to Carmelita and Rosie in equal measure, resulting in their fluency in both languages.

Carmelita turned to Janelle. "It'll be okay for me to be out there. It'll be like Bring Your Teenager to Work Day or something."

"I want to go look for Carlos, too," Rosie said.

"What if," Janelle proposed, "you come with Clarence and Liza and me to check in on Grand-*papá* and Grand-*mamá* instead?"

"Grand-*papá* and Grand-*mamá*? Sweet!"

Across the maintenance yard, a pair of uniformed deputies from the sheriff's department SUV conferred with a middle-aged woman from the medical examiner office's van. The deputies and medical examiner shouldered backpacks from their vehicles and strode past the camper and up the trail. Chuck gave them a ten-minute head start before he and Carmelita set out.

Now, atop the ridge, he watched as the police helicopter swooped out of the arroyo, having completed its flyby of the murder scene, and soared over the maintenance yard. From his high vantage point, the yard was a square of gravel sided by the metal garages. The black ribbon of pavement leaving the yard split outside the exit, one road headed toward the visitor center, the other climbing over a low hill to the western suburbs of Tucson, where tan stucco homes with red tile roofs lined street after street.

Beyond the suburbs, a handful of high-rises comprised the city's central business zone. Adjacent to the downtown district, beige sandstone classroom buildings and the red-brick medical center of the University of Arizona abutted a palm-lined boulevard. Beyond the university campus, housing developments, golf courses, and strip malls stretched for miles to the foot of the rugged Santa Catalina Mountains and rounded Rincon Ridge.

Evergreens cloaked the summit of Mount Lemmon, the tallest peak of the Santa Catalinas, rising to nine thousand feet in elevation north of the city. High on the peak, a ski slope received just enough snow to open a few weeks each winter.

Rincon Ridge, half as tall as Mount Lemmon, bordered Tucson to the east. The boundaries of Saguaro National Park's Rincon Mountain District encompassed the uplift. Saguaro cactuses grew thick on the lower slopes of the ridge, pointing skyward like quills on a startled porcupine. Piñon and juniper trees swathed the ridge's mid-slopes, and a grove of ponderosa pines capped its summit, dark green against the blue mid-morning sky.

"What was your backup plan for meeting Carlos and Francisco if they weren't at the water station?" Carmelita asked over the roar of the helicopter, which flew past the maintenance yard and followed the ribbon of pavement leading back to the city. She stood in the middle of the trail with her hands on her hips, barely winded from the climb.

Chuck wiped sweat from his forehead. "We didn't really have one. We'd planned to be in touch with them by phone along the way. The last time they checked in—when they were about to cross the border three days ago—they said their group had food and water bottles and a map of the water stations along the way."

"Their group?"

"They paid a coyote to help them get across the border. Usually, smugglers lead migrants all the way north to spots where they're picked up on highways beyond the Border Patrol checkpoints. But Carlos and Francisco planned to travel through the desert on their own after they crossed. They figured the odds of not getting caught were better if they weren't with a bunch of people. I imagine their 'group' was all the others they were with at the border who were being guided by the coyote."

"But they weren't alone when they got to the water station. They were with the boy."

"Unless the boy was already there."

"True. How many miles is it from the border to the park?"

"Sixty. Their plan was to walk twenty miles a day and meet us this morning."

"So, Carlos and Francisco made it sixty miles on foot through the desert in three days. That means they're in good shape—and *that* means Carlos would've had the physical ability to escape when Francisco and the boy were attacked." She scanned the spine of the ridge and the slopes falling away on either side. "I bet he's alive and hiding somewhere close by. He might even be watching us right now, for all we know."

A gust of wind coursed up and over the ridge, buffeting Chuck. The wind was hot and dry, as if yesterday evening's rainstorm had never happened. The piney scent of moisture that had perfumed the desert just hours ago was gone, the precipitation either trapped in the now-sealed pores of the surrounding cactuses and shrubs or evaporated into the parched air.

"If you're right, how do we let him know we're here?" Chuck asked.

"We keep heading for the water station and look for him to signal us at some point along the way."

"How will he know it's us?"

"He'll expect us to be looking for him."

"The problem is," Chuck said, "the more I think about it, the more convinced I am Ron will send us away if we just show up again unannounced." He grunted. "I'd prefer to get closer without being seen, but it's next to impossible to move through the desert if you don't follow an open route like the trail."

Carmelita peered down the west face of the ridge, which fell to the flat scrubland of the Tohono O'odham Reservation. Halfway down the slope, the dark band of basalt cliffs extended the length of the ridge. A narrow shelf of horizontal rock topped the vertical band of cliffs, protruding from the slope.

"Or the top of a cliff," she said, pointing down from the ridgetop trail at the shelf running along the crest of the cliff band. The ledge was visible through breaks in the vegetation covering the slope. "Every cliff I've ever climbed has a ledge at its top. It looks like the one down there runs all along the cliffs. Plus, it's almost entirely hidden from the trail." She ticked her finger north along the slope. "See where the cliff band wraps around the far end of the ridge? That'll put us right above the water station. We can keep an eye out for Carlos from there."

Chuck followed the stone shelf with his eyes. He nodded. "We'll be able to see when everyone leaves, at which point we can drop on down into the arroyo and search for Carlos all we want." He turned to Carmelita. "Excellent idea."

Her face flushed. "*Gracias.*"

He stared at the thorny cactuses blanketing the slope between the ridgetop and the band of cliffs. "But how do we get down there?"

"Verrrry carefully."

Carmelita wound her way down the slope in the lead, pirouetting around the thick trunk of a saguaro and sidling past the thorny arm of a cholla cactus. Below the cholla, she ducked beneath the long boughs of an ocotillo cactus, avoiding the sturdy thorns, thick as nails, lining the ocotillo's wood-like branches.

Chuck descended the pebbly slope behind her until, after only a few steps, he slipped and fell. He slid downhill, out of control. Needlelike thorns littering the ground drove through the seat of his pants and into his skin before he dug his heels into the slope and came to a stop. Wincing, he plucked the thorns from his stinging backside and continued his descent to the shelf atop the band of cliffs, grateful to join Carmelita there without further mishap.

"Just as I hoped," she said, gazing at the stone platform jutting from the side of the ridge.

The shelf ranged in width from two to four feet. Cactuses sprouted on the slope immediately above the ledge, largely screening it from the trail above.

"We'll have to duck under some of the branches," she warned Chuck, "but it should work."

The exposed basalt cliffs were remnants of the region's fiery past, as was a massive plug of stone rising two thousand feet into the air far to the west.

"That's Baboquivari Peak," Chuck said, pointing at the distant monolith. "It's volcanic, the same as these cliffs we're standing on. Carlos and Francisco would have walked past it on their way here." He waved his hand. "This whole area was a cauldron of lava-spewing volcanos three hundred million years ago. Baboquivari is what's known as a lava neck—a hunk of magma that cooled inside a volcano after it went dormant. The soft outer layer of the volcano—the tuff—eroded away, leaving the hard inner core—the neck—behind. The Tohono O'odham people consider Baboquivari the center of their spiritual world. According to their beliefs, their ancestors emerged from a cave at the base of the peak onto the earth's surface after a great flood."

Carmelita stared out at the desiccated lands extending from the bottom of the ridge to the jutting plug of lava. "Not much chance of a great flood happening around here nowadays."

"Which is why it's so hard for migrants like your cousins to travel through here on foot," Chuck said. "If you can believe it, though, a few million years ago this entire region was a tropical rainforest, complete with swamps and jungle sloths, after the volcanic period ended and before today's dry period began."

Carmelita set out along the rock shelf ahead of Chuck. He followed, placing his steps on the rough stone surface with care, his arms extended for balance. He crouched every few feet to pass beneath the outstretched branches of the cactuses and shrubs growing above the cliffs. Each time he rose back to a standing position, he scanned the desert, searching for any sign of movement that might be Carlos.

Carmelita led the way several hundred yards along the rock shelf, coming to a V-shaped cut in the cliff wall. She stopped and stared into the cut. "Is that what I think it is?" she asked, pointing downward.

She dropped to her knees and peered over the edge of the cliff, her eyes fixed on something below.

Chuck crouched at her side and looked down with her.

"My God," he whispered.

8

Rosie launched into the arms of her grandparents.

Seated on the couch in their Tucson hotel room, Yolanda and Hector Ortega hugged their granddaughter between them and looked questioningly up at Janelle, tears glimmering in their eyes.

While driving with Rosie, Clarence, and Liza to her parents' mid-priced hotel next to the interstate at the edge of the downtown district, Janelle had broken the news of Francisco's death and Carlos's disappearance to them by phone.

"Have you learned anything more?" Hector asked, clutching Rosie to him.

"I'm afraid not," she said. She pulled the door closed behind her. Clarence and Liza sat on the edge of the bed, while Janelle leaned against the dresser, facing her parents. "You know you shouldn't have come," she told them. "That's what we'd agreed."

"We had no choice, *m'hija*," said Yolanda in her accented English, including Liza in the conversation.

Yolanda was in her late fifties. The caramel skin of her face was smooth and unwrinkled. A smattering of gray streaked her otherwise black hair, which was cropped just below her ears. She wore a flowered blouse, navy slacks, and sensible loafers.

Hector was short like Yolanda and round like Clarence, his pronounced belly the result of decades of Yolanda's delicious home cooking. His face was burnished by the sun after decades of outdoor construction work in New Mexico's high desert. He wore a plaid western shirt and dark blue jeans cinched tight beneath his stomach.

Janelle's parents had worked numerous low-wage jobs after immigrating to Albuquerque as teenagers. They had paid cash for an inexpensive lot in the city's rough South Valley neighborhood, and had built by hand on the lot, on evenings and weekends, the small stucco home they lived in to this day.

Yolanda and Hector had remained close to their relatives in Juárez, regularly crossing the border for weddings, funerals, and *quinceañeras*, the birthday celebrations beloved by Mexicans for girls turning fifteen.

Still wedded to the traditions of their birth country twenty years after coming to the US, Yolanda and Hector had raided their meager savings to throw Janelle a fancy *quinceañera* in Albuquerque on her fifteenth birthday. Janelle had threatened to boycott the party, rebelling against the traditional role of *quinceañeras* in Mexican society to introduce girls of marriageable age to potential husbands. But when Yolanda and Hector told her they would hold the celebration with or without her, she turned to sabotage instead, arriving at the party in a black crepe dress, torn black leggings, and scuffed military boots, her eyes ruled with black eyeliner and her lips coated with brown lipstick.

To their credit—Janelle saw now, as the mother of two headstrong teenage daughters herself—Yolanda and Hector welcomed their goth-costumed daughter to the celebration with hugs and smiles. The party attendees took their cue from her parents, embracing her and wishing her well.

Despite, or perhaps because of, Yolanda and Hector's loving response to Janelle at the *quinceañera*, a schism opened between her and her parents in the months that followed, leading Janelle to take up with a group of hardcore kids at her high school in a misguided display of teenage defiance. Her rebellion reached its zenith when she became pregnant at seventeen by her then-boyfriend, a small-time South Valley drug dealer in his early twenties. Not until her second pregnancy, with Rosie, did she break up with her no-account boyfriend and return to the waiting arms of her parents. After Rosie's birth, Janelle devoted herself to the girls' future as well as her own, earning her high school diploma and working as a receptionist in a doctor's office while her parents provided childcare.

When Carmelita had turned fifteen, Janelle had given no thought to throwing a *quinceañera* for her. Only once as Carmelita's birthday approached had Yolanda inquired whether a Mexican-style fifteenth birthday celebration was in the offing for her granddaughter, to which Janelle had replied with a terse "no." At that point, Janelle and the girls were four years into their new lives in Durango with Chuck.

"Carm's having a plain-old birthday party at the indoor rock-climbing gym with her friends," Janelle explained to her mother. "You and *Papá* are welcome to come for that if you'd like."

"Oh, *m'hija,*" Yolanda lamented. "A *quince* would be such a good thing to do in honor of Carm's *familia Mexicana.*"

Janelle did not budge, and Carmelita's rock-gym party went off without a hitch, with Yolanda and Hector in attendance— happily so, as best Janelle could tell.

In the hotel room, Rosie stepped back from her grandparents' embrace. "We're sorry we didn't find Carlos," she told them. "But I bet he's still alive. A boy who was hurt really bad yelled his name."

Clarence leaned toward Yolanda and Hector from the bed. "We *think* he said Carlos's name."

"Nope," Rosie insisted, shaking her head at her uncle. "He said it. I was there. I heard it." She turned back to her grandparents. "That's why Carm is out there looking for him with Dad."

Yolanda gasped. "Carmelita is doing *what*?"

"She's fine," Janelle assured her mother. "There are all sorts of people out there right now. Rangers, sheriff's deputies, search and rescue. It's a mob scene."

"A...a mob?" Hector stuttered. "I don't understand."

"Neither do we," Janelle admitted. "That's why Chuck went back—to see what he can find out."

"But he took little Carmelita with him?"

"She's not so little anymore, *Papá*. She insisted on going."

"She wouldn't take no for an answer," said Rosie. "She made a boyfriend there already. He's a park ranger named Lance. His muscles are, like, huge."

Janelle aimed a withering look at Rosie, then said to her parents, "He's not her boyfriend. They just went up the ridge together to call 911."

"Only the two of them," Rosie said. "All alooone."

Janelle exhaled through her teeth. "They went to call 911," she repeated to her parents. She turned to Clarence and Liza. "The question is, what do we do while we wait?"

"We need to find out what the boy knows," Liza said. "If he can tell us."

"But how do we find him?"

Liza pulled her phone from her pocket. "With this."

Liza requested Harper's contact information from Chuck and texted the professor, who reported the injured boy had been admitted to the University of Arizona Medical Center.

Janelle attempted to convince Rosie to stay at the hotel with Yolanda and Hector, but Rosie harrumphed, crossing her arms over her chest. "Carm got to go with Dad," she said, "so I get to go with you. And that's *final*."

Janelle's parents agreed to remain in the hotel room and promised to hold off on contacting Miguel and Consuela in Juárez, awaiting official confirmation of Francisco's death and allowing more time for Carlos to turn up as well.

The wide streets of Tucson were crowded with midday traffic as Janelle drove past the downtown high-rises on the way to the hospital. Clarence and Rosie sat crammed together in the backseat, while Liza thumbed her phone in the front passenger seat next to Janelle.

"What else are you finding out?" Janelle asked her, braking to a stop at a traffic light.

"Harper says Antonio has regained consciousness, at least somewhat. He's in a regular room instead of intensive care. The room number is 443."

"His name is Antonio?"

Liza nodded, eyes on her phone. "That's what she says. Antonio Suarez—according to whatever ID they found on him, anyway."

"*Antonio*," Rosie cooed. "I like it."

Liza twisted to look at her. "You sound like your uncle. He's just the sort of person who would fall for someone he doesn't even know."

Janelle glanced at Clarence in the rearview mirror. His dark eyes sparkled at Liza.

"I fell for you before I met you, that's for sure," he told her. "All it took was one look across the river at you." He elbowed Rosie. "That's because I recognize a good-looking woman when I see one."

"You're lucky you didn't say 'women,'" Liza said.

"I know better than that."

"So do I," Rosie said. "*Solo* Antonio. *Ningun otros.* Only Antonio. Nobody else."

Janelle sighed as she pulled away from the light. "Let's just hope he really is doing better, like Harper said."

They stepped out of the elevator onto the fourth floor of the hospital. A nurse with carrot-orange hair rose from his seat at the nurse's station in front of them.

"We're here to see Antonio," Rosie announced to him.

The nurse rolled his eyes. "Of course, you are," he said. "That kid has got to be the most popular illegal we've ever had here."

"*Inmigrante*," Clarence corrected him. Then, in English: "Migrant."

"Says you."

Clarence glowered at the pale-skinned nurse. "*Sí*, says me."

The nurse jerked his thumb to the right. "That way," he said, tightlipped.

They trooped down the hallway.

"What did he mean by 'popular'?" Rosie asked.

"Sounds like we're not the first ones to track Antonio down," Janelle said. "Tucson has a strong migrant support network. That's one of the reasons Carlos and Francisco crossed where they did, along with the respect the Tohono O'odham people show migrants by placing water stations on their land."

Their steps echoed on the hard linoleum floor of the hallway. Cooled air, smelling faintly antiseptic, blew down the fluorescent-lit corridor, which was lined on both sides by doors to patient rooms.

They turned a corner and came to an abrupt halt. Several rooms down, a clutch of men and women stood in the hallway. The majority of the people were Anglo and middle-aged or older, their outfits ranging from faded T-shirts and torn shorts to creased slacks and collared blouses.

"Like I said," Janelle noted, "there are people in Tucson who really look after migrants."

The group was gathered outside a closed door to a patient room. Janelle checked the room number: 443. She tucked her hair behind her ear. Given the crowd gathered in front of the door, how were they to get into Antonio's room and question him in private?

She studied the group more closely. It included three of the five members of the petroglyph research team: Joel Henry, the Tohono O'odham natural resources officer who worked with Humane H$_2$0 on behalf of the tribe; Martina Ricci, the Saguaro National Park naturalist; and Harper Longworth, the chair of the University of Arizona Anthropology Department.

Janelle wasn't surprised to see Harper. The professor's campus office was next door to the hospital. It made sense that Joel was here in support of Antonio as well, given his work with Humane H_2O.

But what was Martina doing at the boy's room?

9

"Harper stepped toward them as they resumed their approach. Janelle considered Rosie's declared crush on the injured boy. She spoke to Rosie out of the side of her mouth, her voice low. "Would you mind asking the professor if you can go in and see Antonio?"

Rosie nodded emphatically. "Sure thing."

They stopped before Harper. "It's good of you to come," the professor said.

"Wouldn't miss it!" Rosie exclaimed.

"Thank you for giving us his room number," Janelle added quickly.

"His head wound is superficial, which is good news," said Harper. "He suffered a significant concussion, but there's no sign of serious brain injury."

"I think he's cute. Can I go in and see him?" Rosie asked, wasting no time.

"He's pretty wiped out," said Harper. "They're limiting his visitation quite severely."

Janelle rested a hand on Rosie's shoulder. "Rosie's his age. It might do him some good."

"Plus," Rosie said, "I helped save him."

"Hmm. He's clearly frightened—as he should be, I suppose," Harper said. "You may be right." She turned to the door. "Let's see if we can get the two of you in there, shall we?"

She knocked lightly, turned the handle, and led Rosie and Janelle inside. A single hospital bed took up much of the small patient room, which was quiet and dimly lit, the television off and the window curtains drawn. A plump human frame was outlined beneath a blanket on the narrow bed.

A Latina nurse in magenta scrubs stood at the foot of the bed. She was young, barely out of her teens, and held a tablet computer. She raised her hand to them, stopping them just inside the doorway. "He's had too many visitors already. He needs to rest."

"These two found him," Harper told the nurse. "They saved his life. They just want to check on him. They won't be long."

The nurse's hand wavered.

"I'll wait outside," Harper said. She left the room, closing the door behind her with a gentle click.

"How is he?" Janelle asked the nurse, her eyes on Antonio.

The nurse glanced at her computer. "He's doing surprisingly well, considering what he went through." She looked at Janelle. "You saved him?"

"We did what we could—which wasn't much, really. Mostly, we kept an eye on him until the flight team got there."

"I kept his head from moving so he wouldn't hurt himself, like *Mamá* told me to," Rosie said. "She's a paramedic."

"Good," the nurse said, smiling at Rosie. She turned to Janelle. "I considered paramedic training myself, but I decided on nursing instead. Ambulance work sounds so intense."

"It is," Janelle said. She pointed at Antonio, lying beneath the bedcovers. "But this comes with its own kind of intensity."

The nurse dipped her head. "They're pushing me to transfer to intensive care, but I keep telling them I'm not ready."

"You'll know when it's time—if ever."

Antonio's feet shifted under the blanket.

"May we?" Janelle asked.

"I'll work on my charting," the nurse said, lifting her tablet. "Just a couple minutes, though. I'm supposed to be keeping everybody out."

"We'll be super-fast, we promise," Rosie said.

She approached the bed. Janelle stood with her at Antonio's side. The injured boy wore a patient gown, the bedcovers tucked beneath his arms. His hair was combed and his face cleaned of dust and sweat. Other than a sliver of white bandage showing at the back of his head, he appeared uninjured. His eyes were open but unfocused—most likely dulled by medication. Even so, a small smile curled the corners of his mouth as he looked up at them from his pillow.

"*Te recuerdo*," he said.

"We remember you, too," Rosie replied, also in Spanish.

"I flew in a helicopter," Antonio said, continuing in Spanish, wonder in his voice. "I remember that, too."

"You're lucky," Rosie said.

"You pressed on the sides of my head." Antonio's smile grew wider. "What is your name?"

Rosie studied her feet, suddenly bashful. "Rosa."

"A beautiful name for a beautiful girl."

She hid a smile with her hand.

The nurse sat on the edge of a padded chair in the corner of the room, her head bowed over her computer, tapping at the screen.

Janelle cleared her throat, catching Antonio's eye. "You said a name when we were in the desert with you. You said 'Carlos.'"

The blood drained from Antonio's face and his smile disappeared. "Yes."

"Who hurt you? Who did this to you?"

The nurse glanced up from her seat.

Antonio traced circles on the blanket at his sides with his fingertips. His words came in a rush, his eyes wide open. "We carried them as far as we could, but we had to leave them behind. They were too heavy. We left them near the big rock mountain, where there is a road. It would be easy to go there and get them. Francisco told them so. But they said we had to go back and show them the place. Francisco said no, we would not go back. That was when they...they..." His voice died away.

"Please," Janelle implored him. "What happened to Carlos?"

Antonio's body quivered beneath the blanket. "We were so tired and we had come so far. They were very angry. Francisco screamed, and then, very quickly, he stopped screaming and fell down. I yelled for Carlos to run. I ran, too, but I was not fast enough." He looked up at Janelle from the bed. "Is it true what they have said, that Francisco is dead?"

Janelle drew a breath and nodded.

Tears filled Antonio's eyes. "They must have thought I was dead, too. Or else they were in a hurry to catch Carlos. He was the fastest of us, but I think they were very close behind him." Antonio's eyelids drooped.

Janelle laid a hand on his shoulder. "You can rest now. You're safe here."

His eyes fell closed, forcing out tears that ran down the sides of his face.

She turned to the nurse. "*Gracias.*"

"*De nada,*" the nurse replied, her Spanish coming easily. She rose from the chair and returned to the foot of the bed.

"*Mejor si ellos no saben,*" Janelle said, tilting her head in the direction of the door. "Better if they don't know."

"*Por supuesto.* Of course."

Janelle touched Rosie's arm and they turned to leave.

"*Buena suerte,*" the nurse said. "Good luck."

Clarence and Liza stood in the corridor outside the room with Harper, Martina, and Joel from the research team. Janelle and Rosie stopped before them.

"How's he doing?" Martina asked.

"He's tired," Rosie said. "But he said I was beautiful."

"He's right about that."

"I told him my real name, Rosa."

"Era told you your name is beautiful, too, didn't she?"

"You mean the flower lady?"

Martina nodded. "Erasmus."

"Erasmus," Rosie repeated. "I'm starting to like it."

"I think she'd take that as a compliment." Martina looked at Janelle. "How did he seem to you in there?"

"He was very weak. But the nurse said he's doing as well as can be expected."

"Did you get any sense from her about when the rest of us might be allowed in to see him?"

"I think it'll be a while. He was barely conscious. She said she's been told to keep people out."

"But," Rosie said, "we got to see him because we saved him."

"We all did," said Janelle, taking in the three researchers with her gaze. "We got there just in time."

"Or too late," said Martina, "depending on who we're talking about."

Janelle swallowed. According to Antonio, Francisco had screamed and fallen to the ground when his neck had been slashed.

"The way I look at it," Martina continued, "Saguaro is my responsibility. It's awful that someone was murdered in the park—in *my* park. I know Ron and Lance are out there trying to figure out what happened, and I know it'll officially be up to the ISB agent to run the investigation. But if there's anything I can do to help, I want to do it. That's why I'm here at the hospital right now, in fact."

Joel and Harper nodded, and Joel spoke.

"We all know how common migrant deaths are from the elements," he said. "But this was murder, and it took place right on the edge of the Tohono O'odham Nation."

"Over the years," Harper said, "I've watched Tucson grow from a little blip on the map to a city of half a million people. I understand that murders are going to happen here nowadays. But I agree with Martina. This one feels personal because it happened at the petroglyph rocks." She turned to the park naturalist, her eyes narrowing. "Speaking of which, I heard you say this morning that it was your idea to put the water station out there by the rocks. I hadn't realized that was the case."

Martina's face grew dark, her eyes flashing. "I'd think you'd be happy I convinced Ron to allow the station to be placed out there. You're the one who's so into helping the migrants."

Harper straightened to full height, nearly a foot taller than Martina. "Location, location, location—that's what I'm referring to. You, of all people, know how important the petroglyphs are. Yet your water station has drawn crowds of people to the site."

Martina's arms went rigid at her sides. "I did what was right, and you know it. The last segment of the route to Tucson was completely without water. There were deaths occurring on that stretch every few months." She turned to Joel. "You know perfectly well what I'm talking about. I asked your opinion first, before I ever went to Ron."

Joel nodded. "Harper, you have to admit she's right. There hasn't been a single dehydration death on the last section of the route since the water station was added."

"I'm not disagreeing about the need for a station," Harper said. "I'm referring to its placement right there with the petroglyphs. We all know how often rock art is being vandalized these days, all across the country."

Martina puffed her chest. "The migrants could care less about trashing the petroglyphs," she said. "They're too exhausted to be thinking about defacing anything. They're just trying to survive. Besides, the location is perfect in every other respect. It's just after crossing the flats, there's good shade, and it's right before the final push to Tucson. Plus, it's at the end of the trail to the petroglyph rocks, which makes it handy for refilling."

"That's easy for you to say," Joel said. "It takes ten of us, all carrying water-tank backpacks, to fill the barrel. It's been getting emptied so fast lately that we've been having to hike out there to refill it every couple of weeks."

"Which shows you how good the location is," said Martina. "The water is getting used, which means it's saving lives. *That's* what's important. That's the whole point." She turned to Harper. "If you've got a problem with the location of the station, then I'm afraid that's all on you."

"As a matter of fact, I *do* have a problem with it," said Harper. "So much so, that I've put in a formal request with the park service to have it removed."

"What do you mean, the 'park service'? Did you go over Ron's head?"

"I sent my request to DC. I know some people there."

"Oh, of course you do," Martina snapped. "You academic types, so willing to use your back channels and friends in high places to get what you want."

"I'm only doing what's necessary. I grew up in Tucson. I'm devoting my life to this community—and to protecting its past. There's a reason the petroglyph rocks are unnamed and don't appear on any maps. There's a reason the trail to them from the maintenance sheds isn't on any maps, either, and is used only by those with special-use permits to study the petroglyphs. If I'd have had any say in the matter, no water station ever would have been allowed anywhere near those rocks. The petroglyphs are a priceless link to the past." She looked at Joel. "You know that. All true Arizonans know that, Native or not." She looked back at Martina. "It's only a newcomer like you who would think placing the water station out there next to the rocks was a good idea."

"All I did was make the proposal," Martina responded. "Joel's the one who ran it up the line. Plus, it was Ron who gave the official approval for the water station in the park, not me."

"Ron is the superintendent of Saguaro National Park,"

Harper said. "As much as he's a steward of the park, he's a political animal first. The park abuts the Tohono O'odham Reservation. The Tohono O'odham people have decided the best thing they can do is facilitate the safe movement of migrants across their land along a primary route by lining that route with water stations. For Ron to say no to a final station on the route would have been political suicide for him."

"I—" Martina began.

But Harper cut her off. "Did you really believe you were the first to think about placing a water station at the bottom of the ridge? Of course, you weren't. Those of us who care about the welfare of migrants have talked about it for years. But we care about the petroglyphs, too. In fact, we've been looking for ways to direct the migrant route away from the rocks entirely. But when you proposed the station to Joel, he had no choice but to present it to Chairman Begalia. And when Begalia brought it up with Ron, there was nothing Ron could do but allow it." Harper huffed. "What good did your water station do out there today, anyway? It's supposed to save lives, but it sure didn't do that this morning, did it?" She pointed at the door to Antonio's room. "That young man in there is lucky to be alive. The other one is dead—murdered—because of you."

"Granted, today was unfortunate," Martina said. "But who knows how many lives have been saved since the water station was installed? Overall, given how much it's being used, I'd give the station an A-plus." She turned to Joel. "Wouldn't you?"

Joel raised his hands. "Don't you drag me into this. As the resources officer for the Tohono O'odham Nation, I'm for the petroglyphs *and* the migrants. It's not as simple as one or the other."

"It is if we change the route," said Harper.

"I'm willing to listen," he replied. "And I'm sure Chairman Begalia will, too."

The chilled air flowed down the hospital hallway.

"Sounds like," Rosie said, "you all finally found something you can agree on."

Harper, Martina, and Joel exchanged uneasy looks.

"Maybe so," Joel said finally. "I'll talk to Vivian and see what she thinks. She knows every inch of the backcountry out there. If there's any way to direct the migrants away from the rocks, she'll know what it is."

"Whew," Janelle said, emerging from the hospital with Rosie, Clarence, and Liza. "They really got into it in there, didn't they?"

"They were getting along just fine until you came out of the room," Clarence said.

"The talk of the water station is what set them off. Kind of surprising to hear how against it Harper is. She even put in an official request to have it removed. It'll be interesting to hear what Chuck thinks."

She called him as they walked through the heatwaves rising from the parking lot, the air in the city smelling of asphalt and diesel exhaust. His voicemail picked up. She ended the call and tried Carmelita. That call went straight to voicemail, too. She stopped in the middle of the lot, her phone clasped between her hands.

"They're not answering. Neither of them."

10

Chuck retrieved the fifty-foot length of thin but strong rescue rope he kept in the bottom of his daypack and sat down at the top of the cut in the cliff. He slung the cord around his back and gripped it with his right hand, ready to tighten his fingers around the rope, acting as a brake on it in the unlikely event Carmelita fell during her down-climb of the distinctive, V-shaped break in the cliff known to rock climbers as a dihedral.

Carmelita secured the rope around her waist with a bowline knot. "On belay," she told him, snugging the cord above her hips.

"Belay is on," he confirmed, lifting his hand to display his hold on the rope.

She descended the dihedral with ease, her hands and feet pressed to the opposing stone walls of the cleft. Chuck allowed the cord to slide through his fingers as she worked her way downward. With his left hand, he held the rope out from the rock to keep the cord away from any cracks in the cliff that might ensnare it.

"Off belay," Carmelita reported when she stood on the dirt shelf at the foot of the break in the cliff, thirty feet below.

Chuck released the rope. "Belay is off."

With the cord still knotted around her waist, Carmelita turned to look at what she'd spotted from above: a petroglyph in the shape of a spiral chipped into the wall of the crevice. The spiral appeared as a light-colored line circling outward against the darker surface of the rock. The spiral, a foot across, was carved low on the wall, its center point even with her knees.

"Well?" Chuck asked.

She turned away from the spiral and faced the opposite wall

of the cleft. "You were right!" she exclaimed. She reached forward and her hand disappeared to her wrist, cut off from his sight by the outer edge of the rock flake. "It's exactly what you predicted."

Chuck's heart pounded in his chest. "You're sure?"

The bill of her cap rocked up and down. "You can totally see the chip marks." She looked back and down at the spiral. "It looks like they line up perfectly."

"If only today was June twentieth."

"Or December twenty-first."

"Unless it's equinoctial, in which case we should have been here last month, on the twenty-second."

"Or on March twentieth." Carmelita gazed up at him, her eyes aglow. "This is *so* incredible."

"I can't believe it," Chuck agreed. He looked longingly at the spiral chipped into the rock at the base of the cliff. "I have to see it up close," he said. "Put me on belay, would you?"

He slung the shoulder straps of his daypack around the trunk of a mesquite tree at the top of the cliff, fashioning a makeshift anchor above the dihedral, then ran the rescue cord through the straps of the pack and knotted the end of the rope around his waist. Below, Carmelita untied her end of the rope, sat down on the dirt platform at the bottom of the cleft, and rewrapped the loosed cord around her back. She gripped the line with her fingers, ready to catch Chuck if he fell, just as he'd been prepared to catch her.

"Belay is on," she reported, taking up slack in the rope with her left hand.

"On belay," Chuck replied.

He descended without difficulty, gripping the same holds Carmelita had used on her way down.

He squatted on the landing at the foot of the crevice and stared at the spiral. The petroglyph had been chipped into the rock face with care—the spacing between the line circling outward from the spiral's center was precisely equidistant loop after loop. Where the line ended after a dozen loops, the rock artist had chipped a tiny circle and an outward spray of lines, creating a shimmering sun at the spiral's end.

Chuck rose and turned away from the petroglyph. Directly in front of him at head height, a wedge-shaped opening had been hacked at an upward angle through the facing edge of the dihedral. The angled opening revealed a slice of sky high above the cliff. He ran his fingers along the rough edges of the opening—hewn, it appeared, by an ancient stone mason at the precise angle necessary to enable sunlight to lance through the cut on two specific days each year and shine on the carved spiral in the shape of a thin triangle, with the point of the triangle striking the center of the spiral.

"It's a dagger!" he exclaimed to Carmelita. "An actual sun dagger!"

She smiled.

He looked from the wedge-shaped opening to the petroglyph, judging the gradient of the invisible line running between the two. "The angle looks right to me, too," he said. "Hard to say if it's equinoctial or solstitial, though. That would take some serious measuring to figure out. Either that or, like we were saying, it would take being here on the correct days of the year." He pointed at the thin slice of sky visible through the opening. "When the sun comes over the ridge on the solstices or equinoxes, its rays will pass through the slot and project onto the spiral in the shape of a dagger. It'll do that on either the summer and winter solstices, which would make it a solstitial sun dagger, or on the spring and fall equinoxes, making it an equinoctial dagger." He lowered his hand. "The old ones were incredible astronomers. Not that anyone knew it, though, until the first discovery of a sun dagger in modern times, on Fajada Butte in—" He paused, waiting for Carmelita to fill in the words.

"Chaco Canyon," she said. "In New Mexico."

"You got it. The Chacoan people built villages in the canyon over several centuries using perfectly squared sandstone blocks dry-stacked together. Then, after all their hard work, they left the canyon in the 1200s, never to return. Fast forward to 1977, when a volunteer who was surveying petroglyphs in the canyon noticed a slice of sunlight passing through slabs of rock on a sandstone bluff called Fajada Butte. The wedge of light struck a spiral petroglyph chipped into a facing wall on the butte. The light was shaped like the blade of a knife, which is where the sun dagger name comes from. It turned out that the point of the dagger struck the center of the spiral each year on June twentieth and December twenty-first, the summer and winter solstices."

He glanced back and forth between the wedge-shaped cut in the wall and the spiral petroglyph. Crouching, he looked up through the wedge, attempting to determine where the sun would need to cross the sky for its rays to pass through the opening and strike the center of the spiral.

"I wish I could tell for sure if it works," he said, rising. "That is, if the sun actually shines on the spiral on specific dates, and if so, whether it would be on solstice days or equinox days."

Carmelita pressed the tip of her forefinger to her chin. A small white spot remained on her skin when she took her finger away. "I wonder…" she said. She took out her phone, tapped its screen, and turned it to Chuck. A lined representation of the surrounding peaks glowed on the face of the phone, Baboquivari Peak the most prominent among them.

"It's my peak locator app," she explained. "It uses satellites to show what mountains are around you. I use it on my trail runs."

"What does it have to do with the sun dagger?"

"See the line?"

She extended the phone closer. A thin blue line angled from the top to the bottom of the screen.

He nodded.

"It marks the path of the sun through the sky today," she

explained. "That's the default setting. But the app allows you to set any date you want." She tapped at the screen. "There, see?" She again turned the phone to Chuck.

He leaned forward. The date "June 21" showed in one corner, and the blue line cut across the middle of the screen.

Carmelita positioned the phone between the spiral and wedge. "Check it out."

The trajectory of the blue line matched the invisible line running from the center of the spiral through the wedge and on up into the midday sky.

"What do you think?" she asked. "Does that prove it?"

"I'd say it proves that it *might* be a functioning sun dagger and that it *might* be solstitial—but it'll take a lot more data to be sure, including somebody being here in December or June." He looked out at the desert. "The discovery of the sun dagger on Fajada Butte led to a massive effort to see what other spirals might be struck by the sun on the right days of the year, resulting in the identification of dozens more sun daggers, some solstitial, some equinoctial. Amazingly enough, though, sun daggers have only been found here in the southwestern US, and nowhere else on the planet."

"It makes sense that the ancient Hohokam people made solar observations around here," Carmelita said, "where the sun shines pretty much every day of the year."

"The Hohokam people were all about the sun," Chuck agreed. "In fact, many of their sun daggers were centerpieces of shrines, with other sun-venerating petroglyphs chipped into nearby rocks around them. Researchers have found all sorts of offerings left near sun daggers, too." He paused. "Which reminds me…"

He stepped to the edge of the landing, where the mouth of the dihedral gave way to the sloping bottom half of the ridge. A handful of palo verde trees, rising thirty to forty feet above the ground, grew along the base of the ridge. Beyond the palo verde trees, the flat scrubland of the Tohono O'odham Reservation stretched to the west, a sea of mesquite trees and creosote shrubs. There was no movement at the base of the slope or on the flats beyond that might have been Carlos moving through the desert, nor was there any sign of anything that might be considered an ancient offering associated with the sun dagger.

He turned away from the cleft opening. "There's one other place to look."

He slipped past Carmelita into the shaded recess extending into the base of the cliff, peered into the shadows, and froze.

A cylindrical stack of what at first appeared to be interwoven sticks sat at the back of the crevice.

"Whoa," he whispered, realizing what he was seeing.

Carmelita stared into the dim recess along with him. "What in the world are those?"

"Bones. A whole bunch of them."

"Why are they here?"

Chuck squinted at the stack of beige bones at the back of the slot. "They may have been left by animals. Since the time of saber-toothed tigers, carnivorous cats have dragged their kills into protected places like this to do their eating."

"But they're in a perfectly round circle. Plus, it looks like they're braided together somehow."

"Cats are meticulous creatures. The stack could be the work of a very fastidious mountain lion. But to your point, yes, I'd say it's much more likely that the bones are part of a shrine left by the Hohokam people as an offering to the sun. The fact that the bones look like they're interwoven supports that idea. So does the location next to the sun dagger. As far as I know, this dagger has never been reported publicly, which means you and I are almost certainly the first people to lay eyes on it in modern times—and the first to see this pile of bones, too."

He dropped to his hands and knees and leaned into the shadowed interior of the recess to get a better look at the bones.

The improved view revealed a larger bone resting atop the cylinder of smaller bones. He sat back, startled, smacking his head on the rock wall beside him.

"Virtually everything the Hohokam people did in the Sonoran Desert, where day-to-day survival was so difficult, revolved around growing and procuring food," he explained to Carmelita, rubbing his skull and attempting to make sense of the larger bone atop the stack of smaller bones. "Their primary source of calories was fast-growing beans planted in drainages that flooded after summer thunderstorms. But they hunted wild game, too. A single deer or bighorn sheep would have provided a lot of protein. It makes sense, then, that they'd have left bones from their kills at a sun dagger site as an offering to their gods."

He cleared his throat.

"What is it?" Carmelita urged him.

"The third possibility," he said, staring at the large bone, "relates to the southern Hohokam trade route, which extended from the Sonoran Desert to the Yucatán Peninsula. The Hohokam people traded with the Mayan people who lived on the peninsula and farther south in Central America." He looked Carmelita in the eye. "I bet you know what the Mayans are best remembered for."

"Their ruins," she said. "Their big temples and cities all grown over with vines in the jungle."

He nodded. "One of the key focal points of life in the Mayans' famous city-states was the elaborate ritualism they practiced in their temples. Many of their rituals were centered on human sacrifice, which they practiced in various ways—decapitation, bloodletting, torture, you name it. By far the most common form, though, was when they led the sacrifice victim along a stone-paved path and up a stairway into a temple, where a priest cut into the victim's chest and pulled out the heart, preferably while it was still beating."

"Yuck."

"The sacrifices were seen as offerings of nourishment to the gods in the form of human blood."

"Considering that their big fancy city-states are now ruins, all their killing didn't do them much good, did it?"

"It didn't do them any good at all. Governance of the city-states collapsed in the mid-1000s, at the height of the Mayans' practice of human sacrifice, leaving splintered and warring groups behind. The Hohokam people didn't begin trading with the Mayan people until the 1100s, a hundred years after the implosion of the city-states. Even then, though, the remaining Mayans continued to practice human sacrifice—which the Hohokam traders almost certainly witnessed."

Chuck returned his gaze to the pile of bones, including the largest one resting on top.

"What are you getting at?" Carmelita asked.

"There's never been any indication that Hohokam traders might have brought the practice of human sacrifice north from the Yucatán and practiced it here in the Sonoran Desert, until—" He pointed at the large bone.

Carmelita's eyes widened.

Chuck's phone buzzed in his pocket. He knew from earlier texts that Janelle and the others had been headed to see the injured boy at the hospital.

He pulled out his phone. The incoming call was from Janelle. His phone stopped buzzing as the call ended.

In the quiet of the cleft, Carmelita's phone buzzed immediately after his. She checked its screen.

"Is that *Mamá* calling you?" he asked her.

"Yep."

"Me, too." He held up his hand to her, requesting that she not answer. "We'll call her right back. In fact, I'll text her." He thumbed Janelle a quick message: *Will call shortly.* "Now, to finish up real quick," he said to Carmelita. He pointed at the back of the crevice. "See the biggest bone, right on top?"

She nodded.

"I think it's a human femur."

Carmelita clapped her hand over her mouth. "You mean, somebody's leg bone?"

He nodded. "See the end, where it—?"

"Don't move!" commanded a voice from the top of the cliff.

Directly above, a hand extended past the edge of the dihedral, holding a gun.

PART TWO

"Once you think of the spiral not as stationary but rotating, rock art begins to move. These wound-up circles become gears turning in an elaborate and elemental machine."

—Craig Childs, *Tracing Time*

11

Janelle held up her phone. "Chuck texted that he'd call back 'shortly,' but he hasn't yet."

She stood with her back to the dresser in her parents' hotel room, having returned with the others from the hospital.

"Give him time," said Clarence as he and Liza settled once again on the edge of the bed. "Cell service is spotty out there."

"What did you learn at the hospital?" Yolanda asked Janelle from her seat next to Hector on the couch.

"Your *nieta* got us in to see the boy, Antonio," Janelle said, glancing at Rosie. "He told us Carlos ran off during the attack." She spared her parents Antonio's description of Francisco screaming and falling to the ground. Still, the vision of Francisco's garroted neck rocked her yet again, making her stomach clench.

Rosie sat on the sofa next to Yolanda and Hector. "Antonio said they left something in the desert that was too heavy for them to carry."

"What could that have been?" Hector wondered.

"Not water," said Janelle. "There were stations all along their route."

"*Drogas*," Clarence declared. "That's the only thing it could be. That's what people kill each other over on the border."

Rosie's eyebrows shot upward. "You think Carlos is a druggie, Uncle Clarence?"

"No, *sobrina mía*. What I'm saying is, I think he and Francisco might have been forced to be mules for one of the cartels." He dipped his square chin at Janelle. "I thought about it on the way back from the hospital, *hermana*. What would the three of them have been carrying across the desert that was heavy and worth killing for?" He answered himself: "Bales of marijuana." He turned to Rosie. "Even with all the legal weed in the US these days, there's still lots of money to be made bringing it across the border illegally."

Rosie put the tips of her forefinger and thumb to her lips and inhaled between them, as if sucking on a joint. "There are lots of potheads at school," she said. "They come to class after lunch totally baked, with their eyes all, like, glassed over."

"They're too young to buy from legal pot shops," said Clarence, "so they buy it illegally instead. America's potheads are keeping the Mexican drug cartels in business."

Liza rested a hand on Clarence's arm. "Do you think Carlos and Francisco's coyote sold them out to the drug runners?"

"I wouldn't be surprised. The only thing coyotes care about is money. They team up with the cartels to force migrants to act as mules and haul marijuana through the desert, threatening to kill the mules' families if they don't do as they're told. The cartels get their cocaine and meth and pills across the border by hiding it in cars and trucks. But marijuana is too bulky, and drug dogs at the border can sniff it out no matter how well it's packaged."

Janelle pooched her lips. "The boy, Antonio, said they got tired and left 'them' near the 'big rock mountain.' He said there was a road nearby."

"'Them' would be the marijuana bales. Show me Carlos's route again, would you?"

She opened the map on her phone and turned its screen to Clarence. "Chuck helped Francisco and Carlos figure out the best way to come, based on the water stations. Humane H_2O posts the locations online."

On the phone map, the route Carlos and Francisco had planned for themselves glowed as a red line in the shape of an upside-down L.

She traced the line with her fingertip. "They were to work their way north through the Tohono O'odham Reservation, then east to meet us in the park." She relayed what she'd learned online after agreeing to help Carlos and Francisco with their journey, information that had been backed up by what Joel Henry from the Tohono O'odham Tribe had said at the scene of Francisco's murder. "Officially, the tribe is against placing water stations on its lands. That keeps them in good standing with the US government. Under the table, though, the Tohono O'odham government works with Humane H_2O to keep a series of water stations on the reservation replenished. Migrants who die or need to be rescued on the reservation cost the tribe a lot of money. The tribal government allows the water stations in the hope that the water will make for fewer deaths and fewer rescue operations."

"Antonio said Carlos ran away," Clarence noted. "That means he's out in the desert somewhere, all alone, probably a long ways from the water station by now. And that means Chuck and Carmelita are not going to find him."

"Which means it's up to us to find him instead," said Rosie.

"I assume," said Clarence, "that Chuck and Carm are out of cell range in the arroyo right now. It could be a while before they call back." He glanced out the window at the hotel parking lot. "We have two cars. We can divide and conquer, and cover twice as much ground."

"Are you suggesting we drive around in circles out in the desert until we somehow stumble across him?" Janelle asked.

"Not circles. Roads." Clarence held out his hand. "Your phone, please."

She tossed it to him. He studied the map and looked up. "We have to think like Carlos. I'm guessing he headed back along the same route he took to get here. He knows the way, which would make it easy for him to move fast. Plus, he knows where the other water stations are."

"You think we should follow his route backward?"

"*Sí*. As closely as possible, anyway, in our cars. I think it's our best shot."

She twisted the corner of her mouth. "I think so, too."

Janelle cast a longing look at her phone in the center console of her mini-SUV as she drove west out of Tucson, trailing her parents' sedan on Highway 86 toward the sprawling Tohono O'odham Reservation. She straightened in her seat and looked away from the phone, focusing instead on the busy road ahead.

Chuck would call as soon as he had service. She just had to be patient.

Still, it was almost two o'clock, well over an hour since he'd texted. How long would she have to wait?

Ahead, Clarence was at the wheel of her parents' car, accompanied by Liza, Yolanda, and Hector, while Janelle and Rosie were teamed together in Janelle's vehicle. Clarence drove past the junction with the county road leading north to the Tucson Mountain District of Saguaro National Park—and to Chuck and Carmelita. It took every bit of Janelle's willpower to follow her brother past the turnoff.

She rolled her shoulders, her eyes on the traffic-packed highway. Chuck and Carmelita were fine. Maybe they'd found Carlos by now and just hadn't made it back to cell phone range to check in yet.

The road descended from the low hills bounding Tucson on the west and headed in a straight line across a broad expanse blanketed with creosote bushes and mesquite trees. They passed a sign welcoming them to the lands of the Tohono O'odham people.

Rosie looked out at the nondescript scrubland of the reservation from the front passenger seat. "Where are all the saguaros?"

"The way I understand it is, they grow on ridges and hillsides that capture moisture from the air, the same as other cactuses," Janelle replied. She waved a hand at the surrounding vegetation, consisting of the creosote and mesquite and a smattering of furry cholla cactuses. "Out here on the flats, it's mostly just scrub brush. The lack of thorny cactuses makes it easier for migrants to walk through this area. Plus it's flat. That helps, too."

Rosie put her palm to the side window. "It's hot, though. I can feel it through the glass."

"That's nothing compared to summer."

"Do you think we'll find Carlos?"

"He made it all the way from the border to the park, which means he's strong. And he escaped the attack at the water station, which means he's resourceful, too."

"What if the others—the ones who killed Francisco—find him first?"

Janelle's stomach seized again at Rosie's mention of Francisco. "Carlos will know to stay out of sight. Plus, assuming Clarence is right and Carlos is heading back the way he came, he knows where he's going. That should help."

"There's a lot of space for him to hide in, that's for sure."

Janelle closed her eyes, opened them. The scrubland extended into the distance from both sides of the highway. Rosie was right. How would they ever find Carlos out here? She glanced again at her phone. "At least we've got the map of his route."

Rosie plucked the phone from the console and brought up the map on its screen. She pointed at a moving blue dot marking their progress across the desert. "I see us." West of the moving dot, the route Carlos and Francisco had planned to take through the reservation glowed bright red. "We'll hit their line in a few more miles."

"*Sí*. We're getting close to where we'll turn off. Highway 86 is the only paved road running east-west between the border and the park. They were planning to parallel the dirt road that cuts the other way, north-south, through the reservation. It has water stations all along it. When we get to the road, we'll follow it south, toward the border. Clarence and Liza and your *abuelos* will follow it north."

A rugged mountain range rose to the south, the only break in the monotonous desert plain. Dark green pine trees blanketed the summit of the range's northernmost peak, which loomed above the highway. Half a dozen white metal domes glittered among the trees at the top of the mountain.

"What are those?" Rosie asked, pointing at the domes.

"Observatories. They're for looking at the stars at night through the clear Arizona air. The mountain is called Kitt Peak."

"See all the trees on it? I don't think it's the big rock mountain Antonio talked about."

A semitruck and trailer heading the opposite direction on the highway rocked the SUV with a blast of air as it passed.

"There's a mountain south of Kitt Peak called Baboquivari Peak. It sticks up more than two thousand feet, and it's nothing but bare rock. According to Chuck, it has petroglyphs all around its base. Baboquivari is right next to the dirt road Carlos and Francisco were to follow through the reservation. It's why I wanted to head south on the dirt road instead of north. I'm wondering if it's where they might have left their loads of drugs."

"But that would be where whoever killed Francisco would be going, too."

Janelle worked her jaw back and forth. "They won't be out here in the middle of the day."

"Unless they're chasing Carlos."

"Unless that," she admitted.

They passed the turnoff to the paved road winding up Kitt Peak to the observatories and continued across the desert plain until the moving blue dot on the phone map met the bright red line marking Francisco and Carlos's route from the border. A few car lengths ahead, Clarence slowed, waved at Janelle and Rosie from his open driver's side window, and turned north from the highway onto an unmarked dirt road headed into the scrub. Janelle turned left and drove south on the same road where it crossed the highway.

Dust rose behind the mini-SUV as she accelerated down the dirt road. Creosote bushes and mesquite trees grew close on both sides of the track. The bushes rose waist high, while the trees formed a canopy above, topping out at twenty feet. Together, the trees and bushes blocked any views deep into the scrub.

Though the bulldozed track leading south from the highway was narrow, it had been graded recently and was free of jarring washboards. Janelle maintained a steady thirty-miles-per-hour speed for several miles, passing Kitt Peak on the left. South of the tree-covered peak, a stone prominence appeared on the horizon, its summit poking above the mesquite canopy.

"That's gotta be it," said Rosie, eyeing the rocky pinnacle.

They rounded a gradual curve in the road.

"There's a water station!" Rosie cried out, pointing ahead.

Janelle slowed. Like the station in Saguaro National Park, a blue flag on a tall pole waved in the breeze above an opaque blue barrel resting on a metal frame. The water-filled tank sat in a graded opening at the side of the road. She braked to a stop beside the barrel and she and Rosie climbed out.

Shielding her eyes with her hand, Janelle peered past the barrel into the desert. Nothing. If any migrants were in the vicinity, they were keeping that fact to themselves.

"Car-los!" she called. "Carlos! Are you there?"

The sigh of the afternoon breeze sifted through the mesquite branches.

Rosie circled her mouth with her hands. "Carlos!" she hollered. "Car-*los!*" Only the sound of the wind in the trees greeted her shouts as well. She turned to Janelle. "*Nada, Mamá.*"

"We're a long way from the park. It'd be almost impossible for him to have come this far since last night."

"I don't see any marijuana, either."

"Neither do I. But Baboquivari Peak looks pretty close. Shall we give it a try?"

Beyond the water station, the road climbed a barren alluvial fan extending west from the low ridge that connected Kitt Peak with Baboquivari Peak. The deposit, a mile-wide formation shaped like a handheld fan, consisted of eroded gravel spilling downward from the ridge and spreading out onto the flat valley floor. At the top of the deposit, Baboquivari Peak came into full view to the south, from base to summit. The giant plug of chocolate-brown basalt soared high into the sky, a rugged combination of sunbaked cliffs, jutting ledges, and shadowed crevices.

"Wow," Rosie murmured, staring at the peak.

"Wow is right," said Janelle.

The dirt road descended the south side of the alluvial fan and reentered the mesquite-creosote scrub. Rounding a bend, they came upon a white pickup truck headed toward them. Janelle pulled to the side of the road to allow the truck to pass. The pickup neared. She stiffened, recognizing the driver.

Seated behind the wheel was Vivian Little Boy, the cultural preservation officer for the Tohono O'odham Tribe.

Vivian eased to a stop with her open driver's side window facing Janelle's.

Janelle rolled down her window. "Fancy meeting you here," she said over the sound of their idling engines.

Vivian grinned, her white teeth gleaming. She was alone in her truck. "I'm the one who should be saying that to you. This is my land, not yours." She rested an arm on the truck's window frame. "Did your husband send you out this way, too?"

"You're here at Chuck's request?"

"Yep. To take some shots for him."

"Shots?"

"Pics, photos, of the Baboquivari petroglyphs. He asked if I'd be willing to come out here and work my way along the base of the peak and capture as much of the rock art for him as I could. I know all about him and his background, so I said sure, no problem." Vivian lifted a long-lensed camera from the passenger seat of her truck, displaying it to Janelle and Rosie. "I took a ton of pictures for him, which was easy to do. There are lots of petroglyphs along the bottom of the mountain. The Hohokam really respected that hunk of lava, the same as my people do now."

"Didn't you say this morning that you don't believe the Hohokam petroglyphs convey any messages?"

"Yes, I did say that. But I certainly wouldn't mind if your husband proved me wrong."

"What kind of proof is he looking for?"

"He said he wants his own digitized collection of pictures so he can study and manipulate them on his computer."

Janelle's eyes strayed to the craggy peak rising to the south. "I guess you've got it all covered for us, then."

"You can follow me back to the highway if you want."

"Thanks, but we're fine. I'd like to have a closer look at the mountain. It's a pretty impressive hunk of stone."

"ClimberCarm would like it, that's for sure." Vivian looked past Janelle at Rosie. "You'll like it too. The nearer you get, the more impressive it gets. From the base, it feels like it's going to fall right over on top of you."

"Yikes!" Rosie cried, holding her hands over her head and smiling.

"How's the road to it?" Janelle asked.

"It's in good shape," said Vivian. "The rain didn't reach this far south yesterday. Just make sure you don't miss the turnoff. There's a pile of rocks—a cairn—marking the spot, but you could miss it if you're not careful."

Rosie stopped smiling and dropped her hands from her head. "We're looking for drugs," she said. "Did you see any?"

Vivian frowned. "Drugs?"

"Boxes of marijuana. Bales, I mean. Big ones."

"Um, no, I can't say as I did." She directed her frown at Janelle. "Marijuana?"

"What she means," Janelle said, her voice tight, "is that we're on the lookout for anything out of the ordinary. We don't want to be in any danger out here."

Rosie rocked her chin up and down. "We don't want to get in any crossfire with the people who want the drugs."

"Ohhh, now I understand," Vivian said. She smiled reassuringly at Rosie. "You don't have to worry about that out here. The tribe patrols this road almost every day. Plus, the Humane H$_2$0 people drive down here a couple times a week to refill the water tanks. It might feel like it's all empty and deserted out here in the desert, but it's not."

"What about the dead guy this morning?" Rosie said.

Vivian's smile disappeared. "The desert can be a dangerous place," she admitted, "but mostly for migrants." She addressed Janelle. "Just make sure you head back to the city before dark."

"Will do. Are the petroglyphs easy to find?"

"Just climb up on the rock bench at the base of the peak. They're all over the place. You'll be blown away, I promise." She raised her hand in farewell and accelerated past them, continuing up the road.

Janelle turned to Rosie. "'Dead guy'? 'Drugs'?"

Rosie shrugged. "I was testing her."

"You were doing *what*?"

"I was giving her a test. She's way out here in the middle of nowhere, and she was just at the place where we're headed."

"You don't trust her?"

"Do you?"

"Well, when you put it that way." Janelle glanced at the receding truck in the rearview mirror. "I guess we shouldn't trust anybody out here, should we?"

"Not after what happened to Francisco." Rosie aimed her

thumb over her shoulder. "She didn't have any big bales of pot in the back of her truck, at least."

"That's a plus, I guess." Janelle sat still as Vivian's truck disappeared around a bend behind them. *Francisco. Carlos.* Why had she ever agreed with their plan to cross the border and travel so far north through the desert?

"Are we going to just sit here?" Rosie asked.

Janelle jerked. "No."

She rolled up her window, clicked the air-conditioning up a notch, and continued down the road. A few minutes later, Rosie pointed at a waist-high pile of rocks—the cairn Vivian had mentioned—almost entirely hidden behind a stand of bunchgrass growing at the side of the road.

Just past the cairn, a rutted dirt track led toward Baboquivari Peak. Janelle turned onto the track, which climbed a gradual slope. Mesquite branches pressed close on either side of the car. The trees gave way after a few hundred yards to a barren hillside studded with boulders. The peak loomed above, an imposing thumb of dark rock absorbing the rays of the afternoon sun. A raised shelf of stone wrapped around the base of the mountain.

A fluttering movement on the shelf caught Janelle's eye. She stabbed the brakes, coming to a quick stop, and sat forward, staring through the windshield. The fluttering continued. She transferred her foot to the gas and drove slowly forward, her eyes locked on the movement, poised to turn around if necessary.

The car bounced through ruts and over loose rocks as they approached the peak.

At the foot of the mountain, the fluttering came into focus as someone waving their hands above their head, as if in need of help.

Janelle sucked a sharp breath. Could it be Carlos?

12

Chuck stared wide-eyed at the pistol extended over the top of the cliff. A man's bulky upper body leaned over the edge of the dihedral, attached to the arm and hand holding the gun.

Lance.

Chuck breathed a sigh of relief.

The law enforcement ranger aimed his big pistol down at Chuck and Carmelita. He blinked his eyes. "Look what I found," he announced, returning the handgun to its holster at his waist.

"It's just the two of us," Carmelita said, standing next to Chuck at the bottom of the cleft.

"What the heck are you two doing down there?"

"We found a sun—"

"—spiral," Chuck said, cutting in before she could finish. He pointed at the rays emanating from the end of the spiral on the cliff wall. "Whoever carved this finished it off with a sun at the end of it."

"Nice," Lance said, though he did not sound overly impressed. "Spirals are one of the most common petroglyphic symbols in the Sonoran Desert. It's cool that you spotted the one down there, though." He glanced up at the blazing sun. "You can see why he added the sun at the end of the line."

"She," said Carmelita.

"What's that?"

"It could've been a she."

Lance grinned down at her. "I suppose you're right. I always think of rock artists as male. But there's no way to know for sure, is there?" He looked at Chuck. "Everybody says you're good at finding things, but I didn't necessarily believe it—until now, anyway. Far as I know, this spiral has never been reported before."

"Carmelita's the one who spotted it," Chuck said.

"Sweet," Lance said. "The Carmelita Spiral. Got a nice ring to it, don't you think?"

Color bloomed in Carmelita's cheeks. "Maybe it should be called the Saguaro Spiral, since it's in the national park."

"Actually, there are several spirals in the park. Besides, I like Carmelita a lot better."

She held Lance's gaze, her eyes bright.

"Why the gun?" Chuck asked the ranger.

Lance squatted at the top of the cleft. "Ron sent me back up the ridge to do a little reconnaissance. I heard the two of you scrabbling around down here from the trail. I couldn't tell who you were or what you were up to, so I snuck on down and—" he spread his hands "—voila."

"We were doing some recon, too," Chuck said.

"For what?"

"For exactly what we found—petroglyphs. The rocks in the wash are off limits for now, so we decided to have a look at the line of cliffs."

"That's when I spotted the spiral," Carmelita added.

Lance's eyes went to the spiraling line with the sun at its end. "Nice-looking glyph," he noted. "High quality. Perfect circularity, every loop is even. People are really gonna be impressed by it."

Carmelita's eyes went to the wedge chipped through the edge of the dihedral opposite the spiral, and from there to the bones at the back of the cleft. She opened her mouth to speak.

"We'll climb on up," Chuck said to Lance before she could say anything. "You can take a closer look some other time. First things first, though: the investigation."

Chuck belayed Carmelita, and she belayed him, as they took

turns climbing to the top of the cleft. Lance stepped back, giving Chuck room to free the rope from the shoulder straps of his daypack and the straps of his pack from around the trunk of the mesquite tree.

"It's a zoo at the rocks right now," the ranger reported. "The Border Patrol officers left, but a couple of sheriff's deputies took their place, along with the woman from the medical examiner's office. Ron got the okay from the ISB agent to get moving on the investigation. They've got crime-scene tape stretched all over the place, and one of the deputies is taking a million pictures."

Chuck gathered the rescue cord in tight loops. "Is Ron still in charge of the investigation?"

"He is until ISB arrives on scene, anyway. He's not happy about what happened, of course, but migrants are part of the landscape around here these days, dead ones included. It was only a matter of time before one of them ended up getting murdered." Lance massaged the butt of his gun with his fingers. "Besides, I'm all set against anybody who does their killing with a measly piece of wire." He looked at Carmelita. "I was more than happy to be your bodyguard when we went up the trail to call 911 this morning."

"Carm can take care of herself," Chuck said, his jaw tight. He turned to his stepdaughter. "We need to get back to camp. We should head for the trail."

"I guess this is goodbye, then," Lance said. "For now, at least." He tipped his cap, his eyes lingering on Carmelita for what Chuck judged to be a second too long.

The ranger turned and angled up the slope toward the high point at the north end of the ridge. Carmelita looked after him until he disappeared among the cactuses, then turned and headed up the slope toward the trail in the opposite direction.

Chuck climbed the slope behind her, attempting to curb his anger at Lance. Carmelita no longer was the little girl she'd been when Chuck had become her stepfather six years ago. She was a young woman now, and a beautiful one at that, taking after her mother. According to the many parenting books he'd read, the last thing he should do was become defensive about her entry into womanhood. Rather, his role was to demonstrate, through the way he treated Janelle and other women, the kind of behavior Carmelita should expect—should, in fact, demand—from the countless men who were bound to express their attraction to her in the years ahead.

Still, she was only sixteen. Who did Lance think he was, flirting with her?

Or was the ranger paying respect to Carmelita by treating her as an adult, flirtatiousness and all?

Chuck shook his head, flummoxed. If only Janelle were here. She'd know what to do.

Not until he and Carmelita neared the top of the ridge did he realize he had yet to return Janelle's phone call. He looked up the slope. They were only thirty feet from the trail. He would call as soon as they got there.

The sound of footsteps reached him, those of someone approaching along the spine of the ridge from the direction of the maintenance yard.

"Carm!" he hissed.

She looked back. He put a finger to his lips and pressed his palm downward, motioning her to the ground. She crouched behind the trunk of a saguaro and he squatted behind a barrel cactus below her.

The footfalls grew louder. He poked his head around the cactus. Era Maldonado, the botanist for the city of Tucson, strode past them on the trail in her pink shirt and purple pants. Her footsteps receded as she headed back to the scene of the murder.

"Why did we hide from her?" Carmelita whispered to Chuck when Era was out of earshot.

"It seemed like the right thing to do."

"Because…?"

"Francisco is dead. Carlos is missing."

"But she's a *botanist*."

They returned to the top of the ridge.

"Why didn't we tell Lance about the sun dagger?" Carmelita asked, keeping her voice low and glancing in the direction Era had disappeared.

"He was going to see the spiral from the top of the cliff no matter what," Chuck replied softly, "but he couldn't see the wedge hacked through the rock, or the bones, either. The spiral is nice, like he said, but the dagger is a much bigger deal. It's a *huge* deal. And the femur—if that's what it is—makes it an even *huger* deal. I'd rather keep all that to ourselves until we can get back for a closer look on our own."

"Just the two of us?"

"You, in particular. You're the one who spotted the spiral in the first place. You deserve your own longer look at it, and at everything else, too, if we get the chance, before the whole world descends on it."

"I'd like that." She looked up the trail. "But what do we do now? Are we really going back to camp, like you told Lance?"

"No." Chuck kept his voice low, looking after Era. "I want to follow her. It's like you said: she's a botanist. Why is she returning to the scene of a murder in the park when she was expressly told not to? Why, for that matter, did Ron choose her for the research team in the first place? We're studying rock carvings, not plants."

"Plus, maybe we'll find Carlos."

"That would be the best of all."

Carmelita set off along the path. Chuck followed her. They came to the rocky outcrop at the ridge's high point and poked their heads over the top of the formation, peering into the arroyo.

Two hundred feet below, a uniformed deputy sheriff ducked under a length of yellow crime-scene tape draping the petroglyph rocks and disappeared beneath the palo verde trees where Francisco's body lay. The other deputy stood in the middle of the open channel, hunched over a bulky SLR camera, toggling through pictures on the camera's rear screen. Ron stood next to the deputy, looking at the pictures along with her.

The wheeled stretcher belonging to the rescue team rested in the channel, but the rescuers were not in sight, no doubt waiting in the shade for the signal to load the stretcher with Francisco's body and roll it up the trail.

Ron jabbed his finger toward the trees and addressed the deputy holding the camera. Only the superintendent's gruff tone was discernible from the top of the ridge, leading Chuck to suspect that, more than likely, Ron was telling the deputy Francisco's body would be decomposing by now in the midday heat and should be placed in a body bag and carted away. The deputy lifted her shoulders in a noncommittal shrug, her head still bowed over the camera. Ron spun away, his body tensed, and stomped out of the channel and beneath the trees.

Before Chuck drew back from the outcrop with Carmelita, Lance's voice came from partway down the slope. The ranger was screened by shrubs and cactuses, but his words were clear.

"Well, surprise, surprise," he said, a hard edge to his voice.

"Martina sent me back for one more round," came Era Maldonado's response. Like Lance, the botanist was hidden by the vegetation below. "She wouldn't take no for an answer."

"That *woman*." Lance's tone was cold and cutting, in stark contrast to the warm jocularity he'd displayed to Chuck and Carmelita a few minutes ago.

"She's just ready to make the announcement with me, that's all. But the murder has thrown a wrench into everything," Era replied. "I'm glad I ran into you. I wasn't looking forward to explaining myself to Ron. You can smooth things over with him for me."

Lance guffawed harshly. "Oh, no. I won't be spending any of the precious brownie points I've built up with *el superintendente* on your behalf."

"That's not very chivalrous of you."

"You know very well that I'm not a very chivalrous person."

"I also know that you fake it very well."

"With the right people, sure," Lance said, his voice fading away as he and Era descended the trail into the arroyo.

13

The person waving from the rock shelf at the base of Babo-quivari Peak was not Carlos. Rather, a slender woman in shorts and a black skintight top waved frantically at Janelle and Rosie from the stone ledge.

Janelle's shoulders slumped as she drove up the last of the rocky track to the foot of the mountain. She'd known the odds of finding Carlos this far south of the national park weren't good. Still, the initial sight of a person at the base of the peak had sent her hopes soaring.

The woman waved her pale white hands above her head, brunette hair bouncing around her shoulders in time with her rocking arms, until Janelle pulled to a stop on a bare patch of dirt gouged into the slope beneath the mountain's towering west face. She and Rosie climbed out and stood in front of the car. The woman clambered off the stone bench, the lugged soles of her hiking boots gripping the pocked surface of the lava rock, and hurried toward the parking area at the end of the track.

"Am I glad to see you!" she exclaimed, stopping before them. "I thought I was going to die out here. I ran out of water more than an hour ago!"

The woman was in her late thirties, petite and fit. Her shorts and top hugged her hips and torso, and she wore a fire-engine-red daypack that appeared brand new. She did not look to be in physical distress, her high energy level and animated speech indicating she wasn't suffering in the slightest from dehydration.

"We've got a jug of water in our car," Janelle offered. "We can fill you up."

"Thank you, thank you, thank you!" the woman gushed, taking one of Janelle's hands in both of hers. "You have no idea, absolutely no idea."

Rosie screwed up her mouth. "What are you so freaked out about?"

The woman released Janelle's hand and pointed at the sun high in the clear blue sky. "They didn't tell me how hot it would be. They said I should just walk around the mountain, like, no problem. 'Go ahead and take your little pilgrimage,' they said." She pressed her fist to her belly. "It's for my ka, you see—my core, my vital human force." The woman opened her hand, spreading her fingers across her stomach. "One must breathe from within to experience that which is without," she intoned.

Rosie put her balled hand to her belly, imitating the woman. But rather than spread her fingers, she shoved her fist into her solar plexus and released a loud burp. "Yay!" she cheered. She confided to the woman, "That doesn't always work."

The woman's lips formed a thin line. "I don't imagine it would."

"I'm the only one on my whole improv team who can do it. It comes from my core, too."

The woman's lips loosened, lifting into a small smile. "I'm sure it does." She furrowed her brow. "They have improv for children?"

"I'm *not* a child," Rosie groused.

Janelle tutted her. "You're sure acting like one, though."

"What do you mean?" Rosie demanded. "Everybody burps. It's just air." She turned to the woman. "Everybody farts, too, but I can't do that on command. I keep trying, but it never works."

"Rosie!" Janelle admonished.

"Your belch is more than enough for me," said the woman.

"How about if we get you that water?" Janelle suggested.

"Actually, sister, I need more than that," the woman replied. "I need a ride back around to the other side of the mountain."

"You need *what*?" Janelle suppressed the urge to add that she wasn't the woman's sister.

"I started on the far side and climbed over the ridge and on around to this side, like they told me to. But there's no way I can make it back." Her tone was matter-of-fact, as if expecting a lifesaving ride out here in the desert, in the middle of nowhere, was no big deal.

Janelle pressed her lips together. If she and Rosie hadn't shown up at the peak, what would the woman have done?

"There's a paved road all the way to the trailhead on the other side of the mountain," the woman said. She held out her hand. "Chartreuse Lamonica. Of the Newport Beach Lamonicas." She paused. Janelle and Rosie said nothing. She added, "Orange County? South of LA?"

"You're a long way from home," Janelle noted. "And a long way from help."

"They told me I'd be just fine out here."

"Who's 'they,' exactly?"

"The people at the institute—Raquel, Marcella, Jonathan. They said I should drive out here and have a look around. All the way around, they said."

"Institute?"

"The Tucson Institute for Advanced Consciousness. It's about controlling your thought processes to find healing, acceptance, and understanding in your life. You can read all about it on their website. I'm halfway through their Life Track."

Janelle blinked. "Life Track?"

Chartreuse returned her fist to her belly and again spread her fingers. "My ka, remember?"

After dealing with Chartreuse for all of two minutes, Janelle wondered if the people at the consciousness institute in Tucson had sent her out here in hopes she might not return. "I suppose we can take you back to your car. But first, let's get you some water."

"Before that," said Chartreuse, "you have to experience what I've just experienced. You simply *have* to." She aimed her thumb over her shoulder at the peak.

"The petroglyphs?"

Chartreuse nodded. "They're everywhere around the bottom of the mountain. Want to see?"

"You bet," Rosie said.

"No more burping, though," Chartreuse warned, wagging a finger at her. "This is a sacred place."

"Got it," Rosie said, covering her mouth with her hand. "I promise I won't fart either."

They climbed onto the rock shelf at the foot of the peak. The shelf extended fifty feet to the nearly vertical face of the mountain, which rose high above them. At the back of the shelf, dozens of petroglyphs lined the rock wall at chest height. The etchings were light beige, standing out against the dark outer layer of basalt into which they were carved.

Janelle turned her back to the etchings and surveyed the flat expanse stretching away from the raised shelf at the base of the peak. Francisco and Carlos had passed by here on their way north, paralleling the graded dirt road through the reservation from water station to water station. The mesquite canopy glimmered in the afternoon sunlight, an undulating carpet of green extending as far as Janelle could see.

She scanned the scrubland, pausing where breaks in the trees revealed small patches of open ground.

Nothing moved in the openings.

No doubt Carlos was still far to the north, closer to the national park. She sighed and turned to the wall. Chartreuse led her and Rosie along the line of petroglyphs. The carvings included creatures such as lizards, snakes, tortoises, and bighorn sheep intermixed with stick-figured people, their arms spread wide, and odd humanlike etchings that Janelle had heard Chuck refer to as anthropomorphs—triangular beings, half-human and half-robot, with square heads featuring arrays of horns and feathers. Some of the anthropomorphs clutched bows and arrows, illustrating the hunting past of the ancient peoples of the Sonoran Desert.

Along with the animals and humans, all manner of geometric etchings adorned the base of the mountain. Triangles and squares and squiggles accompanied ovals with interiors filled with zigzagging lines, making them look like decorated Easter eggs.

"Here's one you definitely should check out," Chartreuse said, halting before a geometric etching, roughly three feet tall, consisting of a small trapezoid tapering downward to meet a much larger trapezoid. "It's so simple, so striking. With its handful of strong lines, it conveys all the power and confidence I'm seeking in my life."

Rosie stared at the carving. "It looks like a square bottle with a cork in it. Or a rocket ship. Or a vacuum cleaner from the future."

"Those are all pretty good," said Chartreuse. "As for me, I see a cloud being, ethereal and one with the sky, yet solid and of the earth."

"If you say so."

"I can say whatever I want, just like you. According to my guidebook, no one knows for sure the meanings of the Baboquivari petroglyphs, or if they have any meanings at all."

Janelle nodded. "My husband is studying the petroglyphs in Saguaro National Park to try to figure that out."

"My guidebook says Native Americans today ascribe basic meanings to their ancestors' petroglyphs, but even they admit it's all open to interpretation," Chartreuse said. "Part of the problem, as I understand it, is that the age of a petroglyph is almost impossible to determine. Pictographs are paintings on rock walls, so their pigments can be carbon-dated. But there's no test that can determine the age of a rock carving. The petroglyphs found here on Baboquivari Peak are believed to range in age from when humans first came to this area ten thousand years ago until just a few hundred years ago. The starkness of the outlines on the rocks doesn't necessarily reveal anything about their age, either. A really old petroglyph might be light-colored because it's in a spot that's well protected from the sun and weather, while a more recent petroglyph might be faded and dark because the sun shines on it every day or rain hits it every time there's a thunderstorm."

Rosie pointed at a human stick figure with an appendage extending downward between its legs. "I know the meaning of *that*."

"Phalluses are quite *big* in the petroglyph world," Chartreuse said. She glanced sidelong at Rosie. "Pun intended." She looked back at the stick figure. "My book says no one really knows what the many phallus-bearing figures mean, beyond the logical idea of fertility."

"And sex," Rosie said, giggling.

"One and the same, sister, one and the same," Chartreuse responded. She blew air through her lips, making them vibrate like a deflating balloon. "I thought I would get away from all the men in my life by coming to the institute." She studied the phallus-bearing human etched on the wall. "But they're everywhere, aren't they? Maybe that's one of the lessons I'm supposed to take from coming here today."

Stepping back, Janelle swept her eyes across the dozens of petroglyphs on the wall, her worries about Carlos's whereabouts receding for a brief moment in the face of the astounding variety of etchings—animals, plants, humans, and geometric figures, all jumbled together. The quality of the petroglyphs was astonishing as well—sharply cut angles, smoothly incised curves, deeper and shallower divots denoting areas of light and shadow.

Maybe any meanings the carvings contained were beside the point. Instead, maybe the best thing a viewer could do with petroglyphs today, centuries after their creation, was simply to marvel at their artistry, which was truly magnificent.

She clicked a few pictures of the petroglyphs. Before she tucked her phone away, she checked it yet again for any texts or missed calls from Chuck. Nothing. She exhaled, convincing herself Chuck and Carmelita were okay and still out of service range. She examined the etchings once more. Between a pair of empty triangles was a perfect circle twelve inches across, its interior filled with parallel lines of several dots each, from the top two-thirds of the way down to the bottom, where the lowest line of interior dots ended partway across.

"That's odd," she said, leading Rosie and Chartreuse to the circular petroglyph.

"It's not finished," Rosie said. "They must've gotten distracted."

"That's the way of the world, isn't it?" Chartreuse noted. "Everybody tries to put you off your game. You're the only one who can keep yourself centered enough to complete the tasks you set for yourself." She turned to Janelle. "I'm about ready for some of that water you so kindly offered me."

Janelle snapped a quick picture of the dotted circle and led the way back to the car.

She filled Chartreuse's water bottle and drove away from Baboquivari Peak in the mini-SUV with Chartreuse in the passenger seat and Rosie in back, the car bouncing down the rough, descending track leading to the graded dirt road.

Chartreuse took swallows from her filled water bottle whenever the track smoothed. "Ahhh," she said after polishing off half the bottle. She screwed the lid back on and wiped her mouth with the back of her hand. "Much better."

They came to the junction of the track and graded road. Before Janelle turned onto the road, Rosie cried out, "Stop! Stop the car!"

Janelle braked to a halt. *Carlos?*

Leaping out, Rosie ran to the cairn marking the junction of the track and road. Janelle hopped out with Chartreuse and they hurried over to Rosie, who stood with her hand to her forehead, staring into the scrub. "Check it out!" She pointed into the shade under the mesquite trees.

Chartreuse gasped. "I can't believe it." She extended her arm to Rosie and Janelle, displaying a thick bracelet dangling from her wrist. The bracelet was made up of square gray stones strung on a silver wire. "I got this before I came to Arizona." She looked into the trees. "But I never could have imagined…" Her voice died away.

As Janelle's eyes adjusted to the shadows beneath the branches of the mesquite trees, she saw that a number of large gray stones lay on the ground fifty feet from the road.

"They're square," Rosie said.

Chartreuse wiggled her wrist, rattling the stones on her bracelet. "Just like my feedback loop."

Rosie set off into the trees, ducking beneath low branches. Janelle and Chartreuse followed. They stopped before the square stones, which were roughly ten inches on each side, slate gray, with rounded edges, eight blocks in all.

"Your feedback loop?" Janelle asked, looking from the large stones on the ground to the small stones on Chartreuse's bracelet.

"It's their shape." Chartreuse jiggled her bracelet. "I've been wearing this for weeks now, trying to break the curse that is my life. It's based on some ancient sacrament or other. The idea is to press the edges of each stone with your fingers, one by one around the loop, and recognize that life comes with hard edges— that everything isn't so nice and perfect all the time."

"Sounds a lot like rosary beads."

"It's just the opposite, actually. Rosary beads are smooth and round. They're about letting go and letting God or whoever take control of whatever happens to your life. A feedback loop is all about taking control of your own life. It's about finding your ka, your life force, at the center of your being. The pain of your fingertips pressing against the edges of the stones symbolizes the pain of real life. Then, when you stop pressing on the stones, the pain goes away, just like in real life, too. Or I think that's what's supposed to happen." She tipped her head back, gazed up through the tree branches at the sky, and recited, "We must release life's torments if we are to experience the beauty of all that life has to offer." She looked at Janelle and Rosie. "That's the idea, at any rate. But it hasn't worked so well for me, which is how I ended up at the institute."

Janelle snapped a picture of the stones lined on the ground. "What's the connection between your bracelet and these, do you suppose?"

Chartreuse held out her wrist. "I'm not sure. All I know is, except for their size, the stones are identical to one another."

"I thought the big ones were drugs," said Rosie. "That's why I said to stop."

Janelle looked deeper into the scrub. The mesquite trees marched away from the road, the sun's rays filtering through their thin leaves and speckling the pebbly ground with light. Nothing moved beneath the trees. No sign of Carlos, or of anyone else, for that matter.

"What I *am* sure of," Chartreuse said, "is that these stones were waiting here just for me, the same way I was sure, when I was getting thirsty at the bottom of the mountain, that you would arrive to give me water." She looked at the bracelet on her wrist. "Finally, my feedback loop seems to be working."

"You don't think the stones are just some sort of odd coincidence?" Janelle asked.

"No, I do not."

"Neither do I," said Rosie. She pressed her fist into her stomach and burped, loud and low. She grinned at Chartreuse. "That's not a coincidence, either. That's on demand, sister."

*

They returned to the car and drove north on the dirt road. Janelle settled back in the driver's seat, steering with one hand, as they climbed the mile-wide alluvial fan and descended into the trees on the other side.

They were still several miles from the highway when a cloud of dust rose above the trees ahead, signaling the approach of a vehicle. She slowed in anticipation of the oncoming car, which appeared around a curve in the track.

The vehicle was a black oversized SUV, large enough to seat nine adults in three rows of seats. Its exterior was coated with dust, its windows deeply tinted. It drew nearer, the dim outlines of a male driver and passenger becoming visible through the windshield. The men had narrow shoulders and thin necks. Both wore mirrored sunglasses that hid their eyes.

Janelle pulled to a stop at the side of the road to allow the bigger vehicle to pass, as she'd done when Vivian's truck had appeared. But the black car, as wide and blocky as a tank, halted in the middle of the road thirty feet away. The driver and passenger sat unmoving, their faces impassive.

"Why don't they pull around us?" Chartreuse wondered. "What are they staring at?"

The men's inscrutable looks rattled Janelle. She rolled down her window and waved the men forward, urging them to pass.

The driver raised his right hand, which gripped something. Janelle leaned forward, squinting. It was a gun.

The man aimed the pistol through the windshield at them.

Janelle pressed the gas pedal to the floor, speeding toward the men, her rear tires spitting dirt.

The driver lowered the gun and yanked his wheel, pulling to the side of the road just as the mini-SUV, Janelle's foot pinned to the gas, shot by with inches to spare between the two cars' side mirrors. Mesquite branches scraped the side of her car and its tires clawed at the hump of graded dirt lining the side of the road. Once they were past the black car, Janelle spun the wheel, cutting back into the middle of the road and racing toward the highway.

"They had a gun!" Rosie exclaimed from the backseat. "What if they shot at us?"

"I wasn't about to let us be sitting ducks for them," Janelle said grimly, staring ahead as they sped north.

Chartreuse peered back at the black car. "Men and their guns," she muttered.

"They wouldn't get out of the way," said Rosie.

"That was all about their insecurity, nothing more," Chartreuse said. "They were trying to prove themselves to us, and to themselves. They just wanted to show us who's boss."

"*Mamá* is the boss of our family," said Rosie. "That's what Dad says."

"Matriarchal societies always function best. Those men back there just proved it."

"I take it you're not married," Janelle said to Chartreuse.

"I tried it—a couple of times. It didn't work for me."

Janelle nodded. No surprise there.

Rosie said, "Kinda like how walking around the mountain didn't work for you, either."

"That had nothing to do with men," said Chartreuse. "That had to do with my own obstreperousness."

"Obstreper-what?"

"My desire to look out for myself—me, myself, I—which is exactly what I've come to the institute to learn how to do."

"I'm the same. I don't let anybody tell me what to do, do I, *Mamá*?"

"No, you don't," Janelle agreed.

"Just like you."

Janelle managed a smile, but her thoughts were on the men

who had stared stone-faced through the windshield of the black car—and on the gun in the hand of the driver, aimed straight at them.

The road behind remained empty until they reached the highway. A white, full-size pickup truck like the one Vivian had been driving was parked at the junction. Janelle angled toward the truck to wave at Vivian. But the driver and sole person in the truck turned out to be Joel Henry, Vivian's fellow Tohono O'odham governmental employee.

Janelle exchanged waves with Joel and pulled onto the highway headed toward Tucson. The road was packed with cars and trucks traveling in both directions. Beyond Kitt Peak, she turned south off the highway on a paved road that, according to Chartreuse, extended to the small border town of Sasabe, passing the east side of Baboquivari Peak along the way.

The road to Sasabe was empty of cars. Janelle drove down it for several miles, past Kitt Peak, until Chartreuse pointed ahead through the windshield. "Not much farther. There's a dead-end road cutting over to the base of Baboquivari."

As it had on the other side, the stone mountain rose above the trees, dark brown in the sun, the sky deep cerulean blue above it.

"There's the turnoff," said Chartreuse.

A quarter mile ahead, a narrow band of pavement cut away from the Sasabe road toward Baboquivari Peak at a forty-five-degree angle.

A vehicle appeared in the rearview mirror, topping a low rise.

Janelle's mouth went dry.

It was the big black car from the other side of the peak, coming up fast from behind.

14

Chuck led Carmelita off the rock outcrop and into the arroyo. He crept down the trail, placing his steps with care to descend the ridge as stealthily as possible, the need for quiet making it impossible to return Janelle's call just yet.

Carmelita spoke softly as they rounded the first switchback in the path. "What did Era mean about Martina sending her back, and about not taking no for an answer?"

"I'm not sure," Chuck replied. "But I'd like to find out."

"I could text Lance and ask him."

"You could do *what*?"

"I could send him a text. He gave me his number."

Chuck spun to her. "He gave you his *number*?"

She stopped, facing him, in the middle of the path. "He said we should exchange phone numbers when we went up the trail together to call 911."

Chuck worked to keep his voice low. "Did you give him yours?"

"Sure. I mean, he gave me his. He said it was just in case."

"In case of what?"

"In case of...in case we got separated, I guess."

"You *guess*?" Chuck struggled to remain calm. "You heard him just now, with Era, didn't you?"

"So?"

"His tone, what he said about himself—you had to have picked up on it."

"He was just talking, that's all."

Chuck fought the urge to roll his eyes at Carmelita. The fact that she was so intelligent made it easy to forget she was still a teenager. He changed tacks. "I didn't know Lance before today, but he seems like a good enough guy—by which I mean he doesn't necessarily seem evil."

Carmelita eyed Chuck, waiting for him to continue.

"But—"

"I *knew* it," she said, pouncing.

"*But*," he forged on. He swiped his hand across his mouth. "You have to understand, Carm, that with guys, when it comes to girls, there's often a 'but.' With older guys, especially."

She narrowed her eyes at him. "Like with you and *Mamá*?"

He clamped his mouth shut. Carmelita was, in fact, correct. "Well, yes, like that," he admitted. "Your uncle Clarence looked out for your *mamá* like a hawk. He didn't introduce me to her until he'd worked with me for a long time and knew me really well."

"Like, you might've been a serial rapist or something?"

"Yes, exactly like that."

"You can't possibly believe Lance is…could be…I mean, he's a national park ranger."

"He's at least ten years older than you are and he asked you for your phone number. That's all I need to know."

"You're *fifteen* years older than *Mamá*."

"But when we met," Chuck countered, "she was fifteen years older than you are now."

Carmelita glowered at him.

Chuck turned his palms up to her. "I'm just looking out for you as best I can. I mean, I can see how handsome Lance is."

"Oh, you can, can you?"

"Everybody can. But the way he was talking with Era put me on notice."

"Maybe it's all the pressure he's under. Did you ever think of that? He's dealing with a murder, in case you're forgetting."

"I'm not forgetting."

She crossed her arms over her chest.

"I'm *not*," Chuck insisted. "It's just…"

She tapped her foot. "I'm waiting."

He scrunched his face in defeat. "Why don't we get moving?" he said, giving up. "We'll have plenty of time to talk about this later."

"Fine," she snapped. She stepped around him and strode down the path in the lead.

He sighed heavily as he followed, his eyes on the rocky ground in front of him. He was just trying to look out for Carmelita, but somehow he'd botched the job.

At the halfway point on the slope, where the band of cliffs wound around the ridge and died away into the hillside, Ron's voice came up to them from the bottom of the arroyo. "All set?"

Chuck froze, as did Carmelita in front of him.

"Yes, sir," responded a male voice Chuck did not recognize. "He's all strapped in. We're good to go."

"Okay with you if they head out, deputy?" Ron asked.

"Sure," came a woman's voice. "I've got all the pics I need."

The crunch of boots on gravel and the rasp of a tire rolling across the loose rocks of the channel came from below—clearly, the sounds of the rescue team propelling the wheeled stretcher across the wash as they carted Francisco's body to the trail and on up the ridge.

Chuck scanned the surrounding slope. If he and Carmelita hid while the team passed, they could creep on down the trail and listen, unnoticed, to Era and Lance and the others in the drainage.

He caught Carmelita's eye and pointed at the spot, fifty feet past the nearest switchback in the trail, where the cliff band disappeared into the hillside. "There!" he whispered.

She nodded and left the trail at the switchback, side-hilling past a saguaro to the point where the narrow shelf atop the cliff dove into the slope. Chuck followed, digging his boots into the sandy hillside for purchase.

"Here they come!" she whispered when he reached her, pointing back at the trail.

He crouched and looked back through the brush with her. Sunlight winked on the metal frame of the stretcher as it rolled up the trail, propelled by one rescue team member pulling from the front and another pushing from the back. Nylon webbing crisscrossed the top of the litter, cinched over a human form encased in a shiny black plastic bag.

Chuck squeezed his hands together. Inside the bag was the body of Francisco, his neck slashed.

The rescuers pivoted the stretcher on its single wheel around the switchback and continued in the opposite direction, away from Chuck and Carmelita. The other rescuers followed, trudging around the bend and on up the path beneath the weight of their massive packs.

"What now?" Carmelita whispered as the rescue team departed.

Chuck knotted his fingers, reconsidering his intention to descend to the bottom of the arroyo with Carmelita. "If someone else comes up the trail while we're near the end of it, I'm afraid we won't have time to hide."

He rose and turned away from the trail. The sun beat down on the cliff band, casting a sliver of shade along the foot of the rock wall. The cliff followed the curve in the ridge in the direction of the sun dagger. At its foot, fifty yards ahead, a flash of gray appeared in the narrow slice of shadow, rounding the bulge of the ridge and passing from sight.

Chuck leaned out from the shelf atop the cliff, staring. There was just enough room at the base of the rock face for a determined person to shove their way through the foliage growing close against the wall. But if the movement he'd spotted had been a person, that person was now out of sight around the ridge, headed toward the sun dagger.

"What is it?" Carmelita asked. "What do you see?"

"Movement," Chuck replied, pointing at the foot of the cliff. "But it's gone now."

"Could it have been Carlos?"

"Maybe. I'm not sure."

"But it's possible?"

"Yes."

"Then, let's go."

Before he could say anything more, Carmelita scurried ahead of him along the rock shelf. He followed as fast as he dared, but she easily outpaced him, disappearing around the curving side of the ridge. He rounded the bulge and found her waiting for him with a finger to her lips. He crept to her.

"I saw it when I came around the corner," she whispered in his ear, her voice vibrating. She pointed at the foot of the cliff. "Down there. But it disappeared before I could tell what it was, just like you."

"Where did you see it?" Chuck asked, his voice low.

She pointed at a dark flange of rock protruding from the base of the cliff. "It went around that outcrop."

A slice showed in the rock flange at head height. "Do you see what it is?"

Carmelita stared. "Oh, my God. It's the wedge in the rock. It's the sun dagger."

Above the rock flange, at the top of the cliff, a dark V marked the spot where the dihedral cut into the rock wall.

"But why…?" Carmelita asked.

"There's only one way to find out," said Chuck.

He led the way to the top of the dihedral and poked his head over the edge of the cleft. Everything was as before. The dozen loops of the spiral petroglyph wrapped around and around themselves on the rock wall, just above the empty dirt platform at the base of the cliff. Nothing moved in the recess below.

"Carlos," Chuck called down softly. "Carlos, are you there?"

"Could he be hiding from us in back?" Carmelita whispered.

"I can't imagine why he'd do that."

"He saw his brother get killed."

"True." Chuck pursed his lips. "If he won't come to us…"

He re-rigged the rope, descended to the bottom of the cliff on Carmelita's belay, and peered into the shadowy cleft as he untied the cord from around his waist. Before descending the cliff, he'd pulled a headlamp from his daypack and centered it on his forehead. Now, he clicked it on.

The beam lit the stack of bones at the back of the cleft. Otherwise, the shadowy recess in the cliff was empty.

"He's not here," Chuck said, looking up at Carmelita.

"I saw something," she insisted. "Or someone. I'm sure of it."

"I saw something or someone, too," Chuck replied. "Maybe whatever or whoever it was continued on around the cliff."

"Maybe." Carmelita put a finger to her chin. "Or maybe not. Can I have a look?"

"Sure."

She down-climbed the dihedral on Chuck's belay, joining him on the dirt platform. She untied the rope from around her waist and lifted her hand, palm out, toward the back of the cleft.

"Feel that?" she asked.

He raised his palm. "Afraid not."

"Follow me." She dropped to her hands and knees and crawled into the recess.

He crawled after her, directing the beam of his headlamp past her into the deepening shadows. She reached the pile of bones and leaned sideways, making room for him to draw even with her.

He tilted his head, aiming his headlamp at the stack. "It's way more intricate than I—"

A gray blur rushed from the dark depths of the cleft.

Chuck cried out and hurled himself backward as a furry ball rocketed toward him. He pressed against one side of the cleft while Carmelita shrank against the opposite wall. As quickly as the gray ball—a furry creature a foot high and a few inches wide—appeared from the back of the recess, it leapt over the cylinder of bones and shot between Chuck and Carmelita and out of the cleft, disappearing around the corner of the dihedral.

Chuck stared after the creature. "Gray fox," he said, breathing hard.

"Sweet," said Carmelita. She pointed at the few inches of space between her and Chuck. "It was right there."

"We must have flushed it this way when we were on top of the cliff."

Carmelita righted herself on her hands and knees next to the stack of bones. She again held up her hand with her palm facing the back of the cleft. "Now can you feel it?"

Chuck held out his hand. A faint breath of cool air sighed past his fingers, coming from the depths of the crevice. "Its den must be back there."

"I bet it took off when we were here earlier, and it was coming back when we saw it."

"Foxes are nocturnal, like almost everything else in the desert. The last thing it wants to do is get caught running around in the daylight."

"And now we've scared it away for a second time today."

"It about gave me a heart attack."

"I'm sure it about had a heart attack, too, the poor thing."

Chuck looked at the stack of bones. The fox had not disturbed them during its hasty escape. "I'm glad it didn't knock them over."

The stack consisted of more than a hundred small bones woven together to create a perfectly round cylinder rising several inches from the dirt-and-pebble floor of the cleft. The bones ranged in length from four to six inches and were less than half an inch thick. They were beige colored, unbleached by the rays of the sun, which did not reach the back of the crevice.

"It's obviously human-made," he said. "Exceptionally well made, in fact. Someone really put some effort into this thing."

Resting atop the cylinder of bones was the single large bone he'd spied earlier. He squinted at it in the beam of his headlamp. The bone was more than a foot long, an inch thick in the middle and thicker at its jointed ends. It was beige, like the interwoven bones beneath it, and a round, boney mass stuck out at a forty-five-degree angle from one of its joints.

He aimed his light at the ball-like protuberance at the end of the bone. "That's the head of the femur. It's definitely the thigh bone of someone who walks upright."

"Who *walked* upright."

"Correct." He directed his light at the dozens of interwoven bones beneath the femur. "The others look like they're from desert creatures—birds and rabbits and rodents." He glanced at her. "Maybe even a gray fox or two."

"But what does it mean?"

"I'd say it almost certainly has some sort of a spiritual connection with the sun dagger."

"Spiritual?"

"Hohokam sun watchers are believed to have held vigils at sun dagger sites, praying and making offerings on the solstices and equinoxes."

"So the bones are some sort of a shrine?"

"That's my best guess."

"Why is there a human leg bone on top?"

Chuck spooled out a breath. "Do you remember, before Lance showed up, that we were talking about how there's never been any indication the Hohokam people ever practiced human sacrifice in the past here in the Sonoran Desert?"

She nodded.

"Well, the leg bone might be a clue that maybe they did practice it at some point. Hohokam traders might have witnessed sacrifice ceremonies on their journeys south and brought the idea back with them. In Mayan culture, sacrifices were performed in return for the promise of good fortune from the gods. To the Hohokam, the idea of sacrificing others for the promise of good harvests might have been particularly alluring, given the challenging environment they lived in." Chuck's eyes went to the femur atop the cylinder of bones.

"Is it old enough?"

"I can't really offer an age estimate. The desert air serves as such a quick preservative that it could be anywhere from a few weeks to centuries old. Carbon dating would tell us for sure, but all human remains are hands off, of course, and collecting anything else here would have to be part of an official site survey and dig approved by the National Park Service."

He leaned forward, bringing his eyes close to the bone. "Check this out." He pointed at a series of straight lines gouged into the femur at its narrower end. "It was worked."

"Worked?"

"Butchered. The marks are evidence of fleshing and dismemberment."

"Eww."

"That's what would have happened if this bone was part of a sacrifice ritual. Mayan priests used special knives to perform their sacrifices, first removing the heart, then cutting up the rest of the body. As I said, though, no indication of human sacrifice has ever been found in the Sonoran Desert—" he dipped his head at the femur "—until, maybe, now. Which makes all of this particularly astounding, thanks to you."

Carmelita's face grew red. "I just saw the spiral, that's all."

"You spotted it because you were looking for it. That's the key to every archaeological advance that's ever been made—keeping your eyes peeled and your mind open to new ideas."

She looked at the rear of the cleft, which dissolved into inky blackness. The breath of cool air eased past them. "Speaking of which, is it worth seeing if anything else might be back there?"

"You mean, like, Carlos?"

"I'm sure it was just the fox, but as long as we're here…"

"I couldn't agree more."

He crawled past the bones and deeper into the cleft, leading the way with his headlamp. The facing walls of the dihedral narrowed to the width of his shoulders and closed down from above, forming a tunnel. He twisted sideways to fit through a particularly constricted spot in the passage. The walls fell back after a dozen feet, opening to a pitch-black chamber. He climbed to his feet and swept his light around the cavern. Fox feces the size and shape of small sausages littered the floor of the cavern. The feces were riddled with undigested rabbit hair and berry seeds, and lay amid rounded spheres of feces the size of tennis balls.

The cave was thirty feet long and twenty feet wide, its ceiling a dozen feet above his head. The air inside the chamber was comfortably cool and smelled powerfully astringent, making his nose twitch.

Carmelita crawled into the chamber and rose beside him. She turned on her phone light and shone it across the room, adding her light to that of Chuck's headlamp. Chuck stared at the far end of the chamber, now doubly illuminated. His mouth fell open.

A voice sounded from outside the cave.

15

The hulking black car loomed in Janelle's rearview mirror, approaching fast from behind on the road to Sasabe.

She gulped, staring.

Rosie twisted in her seat, following Janelle's gaze.

"Ohhh," she moaned, looking backward. "Is that them?"

Chartreuse looked back, too. "What the…?"

Janelle tightened her hands on the steering wheel. She had a decision to make and only seconds to make it. She spoke fast. "Should we pull a U-turn and try to get back to the highway?"

"No," Chartreuse said immediately. "The trees are too close. They'll be able to cut us off."

Janelle pressed her foot on the gas, racing down the road. "Should we keep heading south?"

The tiny engine in the mini-SUV whined, the tachometer redlining. Even so, the black car continued to gain on them.

"We'll never be able to stay ahead of them all the way to Sasabe," Chartreuse said.

Janelle bit down hard on the inside of her cheek. Chartreuse was right. The turnoff to the peak was a few hundred feet ahead, only seconds away. Surely others would be at the trailhead at the base of the mountain…wouldn't they?

Rosie faced forward. "Turn, *Mamá*!" she cried.

Janelle set her jaw, her hands fixed on the wheel. The vehicle roared up from behind, filling the rearview mirror.

A hundred feet to the turnoff.

Janelle stomped on the gas, pressing the pedal to the floor. The engine screamed.

Fifty feet.

She spun the wheel at the last possible second, careening onto the side road to Baboquivari Peak. Chartreuse gripped the dashboard as the mini-SUV wobbled through the turn, its tires screeching, and shot down the road.

"Ride 'em, cowboy!" Rosie cried from the backseat.

The rugged east face of the peak filled the sky ahead.

In the rearview mirror, the black car blew past the junction, continuing south on the Sasabe road. "Whew," Janelle said.

"Was that the car from before?" Rosie asked, looking back.

"I'm sure of it."

"I'm glad they went the other way."

"You and me both."

Janelle slowed as they passed from sunshine into shadow, the afternoon sun now hidden behind the towering peak.

Chartreuse let go of the dash. "Thank you for bringing me back to my car—" she aimed a thumb over her shoulder "—despite those jerks behind us."

The road ended at a square of pavement large enough to accommodate a handful of parked vehicles at the base of the peak. A single sedan sat in the lot.

"That's my rental," said Chartreuse.

Janelle pulled to a stop next to the sedan.

Chartreuse tucked her water bottle in her daypack and climbed out. She looked back the way they'd come and cursed.

Janelle peered back. The black car, having turned around on the Sasabe road, was headed up the dead-end road toward them. The car was less than a quarter mile away, ascending the open slope to the parking lot at a menacingly slow pace.

Janelle stabbed at her phone screen with her finger, calling Chuck. He had to be back in service by now. She held her breath as she waited. But the call did not go through. She stared at the screen, her eyes wide. No bars appeared in its upper corner—there was no phone service at the trailhead parking lot, shielded as it was by the looming peak.

"Get out," she directed Rosie. "*Now*."

She and Rosie left the car and hurried with Chartreuse across the parking lot to the start of the trail around the mountain.

Chartreuse shoved her arms through the straps of her daypack and swung it onto her back as they left the pavement. "What are you thinking?" she asked Janelle tersely.

"I want to put as much distance between us and them as we can. If they don't want anything from us, they'll leave."

"Oh, they want something from us all right. Remember, they've got a gun."

"Then we'll just have to stay out of their range." Janelle craned her neck, looking up at the craggy face of the peak. "Up there somewhere."

The path led from the parking lot across a patch of gravel and disappeared behind a boulder the size of a house.

On the uphill side of the huge rock, Janelle stepped off the path. "You came this way already," she said to Chartreuse. "You lead."

The trail climbed the long ridgeline linking Kitt Peak and Baboquivari Peak.

"It follows the edge of the mountain and goes up and over the ridge," Chartreuse said.

She hurried up the path, which climbed steeply through rocks and brush, winding upward along the base of Baboquivari.

They climbed high enough to see over the house-sized boulder behind them. Janelle looked back. The black car sat in the parking lot, facing the peak. The distance was too great for her to see the two men in the front seat, but she sensed them staring threateningly at Rosie, Chartreuse, and her.

The front doors of the car swung open and the two men stepped out. They wore dark T-shirts and jeans, and they were slim and short, the roof of the vehicle taller than their heads.

The driver leaned against the front grill of the car and put his phone to his ear. He held the phone out before him, tapped at its face, and returned it to his ear. He gave up after a few more seconds, shoving the phone into his pocket, and bent his head, conferring with the man beside him.

"Come on, *Mamá*!" Rosie called from where she waited up the trail with Chartreuse.

Janelle hustled to them.

Rosie pointed back past her. "Look," she said, her voice shaking.

Janelle whipped around. The two men were walking across the parking lot to the start of the trail. The lead man clutched a pistol in his right hand. "We have to keep moving," Janelle said.

They scurried upward past yucca plants and mesquite trees to a point where the path canted sharply up toward the top of the ridge.

"It climbs from here to the skyline," Chartreuse said.

Janelle glanced back at the two men. They were past the big boulder now, walking steadily up the trail, the man with the gun still in the lead.

"We're faster than them," Rosie declared. "Way faster."

"Staying ahead of them won't be enough," Janelle said. "We had phone service on the other side of the mountain. If we lead them over the ridge and back into service range, they'll just call for somebody to cut us off on the other side."

"We're cornered," Chartreuse moaned.

Janelle examined the way ahead. She pointed at a rock ledge that sloped up the side of the mountain from the edge of the trail. "Not quite."

She led Rosie and Chartreuse to the shelf and hurried up it, climbing steeply above the path. In a few minutes, they were a hundred feet above the hiking trail, which ascended less steeply in the same direction below.

Janelle glanced up and ahead as they climbed. "Almost there," she said.

"Almost where?" Chartreuse asked between panting breaths.

Janelle pointed to where the ledge leveled off and widened, serving as a gathering place for rocks fallen from higher on the peak. "There." She turned to Rosie. "What do you see up ahead?"

"A bunch of rocks."

"Well, I see something else."

16

"Helloooo!" Era's voice echoed down the tunnel.

"Era?" Chuck said, bewildered, turning to the opening leading into the cavern. "Is that you?"

"Who else?"

Light shone through the low passageway as she crawled into the cave. She stood, joining Chuck and Carmelita in the chamber, her phone in her hand with its light turned on.

Chuck swept the beam of his headlamp across her face. Her painted blue eyelids sparkled in the light. She held a hand in front of her face, blocking the glare.

He aimed the light downward. "Sorry."

She squeezed her nose with her fingers. "My God. What on earth is that smell?"

"First," said Chuck, "how did you…?"

She released her nose. "Do you honestly think Climber-Carm's the only Latina rock climber in the world?"

"You down-climbed the cliff?"

"Sure," she said. "The holds were jugs, totally solid."

"That's so bomber," Carmelita complimented her.

"But what are you doing here?" Chuck asked.

"The answer is, Lance," Era replied. "He couldn't come back here on account of Ron, so he sent me instead."

"He didn't waste any time."

"He said he could tell there was more to the spiral than just the spiral." She flashed her phone light at Carmelita. "Something about the way your dad kept cutting you off when you were trying to talk. And, *shazam*, was he ever right! That's not just any old spiral out there, it's a sun dagger." She swung her light to Chuck. "But you didn't tell him that."

"We weren't entirely sure."

"Oh, yes, you were."

Chuck grunted. "Okay, yes, we were," he admitted. "I imagine you saw the bones, too."

"You don't need to sound so sad about it. We're all on the same side, you know."

"What side is that?"

"The winning side—provided the smell doesn't kill us before we declare victory." She coughed. "It *stinks* in here. What is it?"

"Sloth dung," Chuck said.

He directed his headlamp at the end of the cavern. Arrayed on the ground at the back of the chamber, tan-colored in the light, were what his brain at first had categorized as tree branches. But branches from trees would not be identically curved like the items on the cavern floor, each roughly an inch around and two feet long. Moreover, the items lay side by side, perfectly equidistant from one another, as if set in place by an invisible hand.

Between him and the back of the cavern, tiny particles floated in the still air. The particles, raised from the floor of the chamber, danced in the beam of his headlamp.

"What did you just say?" Era asked.

"We're smelling the poop of sloths. Shasta ground sloths, to be exact."

Carmelita aimed her phone light at the end of the cavern. "Is that what that is?"

"Yep," Chuck said.

Era sneezed, the light of her phone bouncing off the walls. Chuck fought the urge to sneeze along with her as the particles assaulted his nostrils. The floor of the cave was covered with the tennis-ball-sized spheres of dried dung he'd spied along with the fox scat.

"Are you honestly saying that those curved sticks are the bones of a dead sloth?" Era asked. "And that we're standing in its poop?"

Chuck nodded. "It explains everything—the sun dagger, the stack of bones at the cave entrance."

"Including the big one?" Era asked. "I have to say, it looked suspiciously human to me."

"It's almost certainly a human leg bone. A femur."

"That's what I thought. But what's it doing here?"

"The sun dagger and cylinder of bones appear to be part of a shrine." Chuck aimed his headlamp at the rear of the cavern. "I think it was built in homage to sloths—specifically, to the one in here."

"A *sloth* shrine?"

"That's my best guess, at this point anyway. Shasta ground sloths roamed this region for millions of years, until humans showed up here ten thousand years ago. The sloths were smaller than the famous giant ground sloths of South America, but they were still plenty big—about the size of black bears. Findings of fossilized Shasta ground sloths are pretty common in the Sonoran Desert, usually in caves like this one, where they tended to hang out."

"I happen to know all that," Era said. "And I know they pooped a lot, too. Have you heard what happened in Rampart Cave, in the Grand Canyon?"

"You mean, the fire they couldn't put out?"

"That's the one." In the dimly lit chamber, Era faced Carmelita. "Years ago, visitors to a cavern called Rampart Cave in a remote section of Grand Canyon National Park accidentally set fire to the dried sloth dung that had built up in the cave over thousands of years. Nobody could put the fire out, not park workers or a forest-service wildfire crew or a special team of caver-firefighters. It burned for more than a year, incinerating the irreplaceable remains of ancient birds and animals in the process."

"So," Carmelita said, looking from Era to Chuck, "you're both saying that there were lots of sloths around here, and that they weren't potty-trained."

The beam of Chuck's headlamp lanced up and down as he nodded. "Which explains why their remains have been found all across the Southwest—in almost every large cave in Arizona, in the La Brea Tar Pits in Los Angeles, even a frozen sloth, perfectly preserved, complete with hair, skin, and muscles, in a super-cold lava-tube cave in New Mexico."

"California, New Mexico, Arizona—they really got around."

"Yes, but slowly. Like jungle sloths today, they didn't move fast, which played a role in their extinction when early humans started hunting them."

Carmelita wiggled her phone light at the curved items lying side by side at the back of the cavern. "So those are the ribs of a Shasta ground sloth?"

"I can't think of anything else they could be." Chuck aimed his headlamp at two larger bones poking from a mound of dung in front of the ribs. "And those, I bet, are its legs."

Era cleared her throat. "I still don't see how the presence of a sloth in here explains the presence of a human femur outside."

"Shasta ground sloths were the biggest creatures in the area when humans showed up. Then the sloths disappeared. It makes sense that humans would have revered them after they were gone. I'm convinced the placement of the sun dagger outside is related to the sloth bones in here, and the pile of animal bones and the femur are related somehow, too."

"What makes you so sure?"

"I'll show you when we get back outside." He turned away from the sloth bones. "Much as I'd like to see the sloth up close, we don't want to risk damaging anything. We'll report it to Ron and he'll take things from here."

Era crawled into the tunnel, exiting the cavern. Chuck took hold of Carmelita's arm, halting her before she could follow, and whispered in her ear, "No need to show her the butcher marks if she doesn't notice them herself."

"Fine," Carmelita whispered back. "But why?"

"Lance sent her here," he said softly.

"You don't trust him, do you?" she said, a bite to her voice.

"It's more that I don't like the fact that he didn't trust you."

Chuck followed Carmelita back to where Era waited at the entrance to the tunnel. The three of them studied the stack of bones topped by the femur. The filtered light at the rear of the recess muted the butcher marks on the human leg bone, rendering the gouges all but invisible to the naked eye.

"We won't touch anything here, either, of course," Chuck said. "But we can look all we want. The sun dagger and interwoven animal bones indicate the significance the Hohokam people placed on this site. The human bone on top of the pile of bones seals it, in my mind."

Era frowned. "Because?"

He looked out from the crevice at the scrubland stretching away to the west. "Humans always have struggled to survive in the Sonoran Desert, whereas Shasta ground sloths thrived here," he explained. "They munched cactuses like they were eating popcorn. As a botanist, you probably know they're credited with distributing Joshua tree cactus seeds far and wide in their dung, resulting in the spread of Joshua trees all across southern California."

"But they died out almost immediately after humans arrived," Era said, "which doesn't seem to be a feat worth worshiping."

"That was ten thousand years ago, though. The height of Hohokam society was only a thousand years ago, nine thousand years after sloths went extinct. By then, only the fossilized remains of sloths were left in cave after cave after cave, demonstrating their dominant presence back in their day. It makes sense that the Hohokam might have shown appreciation for sloths by creating shrines to them at the sites of their remains."

"Complete with human bones?"

"Why not? Shrines and rituals incorporating human body parts have been key features of human belief systems forever. Think of the heart-extraction ritual of the ancient Mayans, the Temple of the Buddha's Tooth in Sri Lanka, the bones of saints worshiped in Catholic cathedrals."

"It still seems like quite a leap, connecting the dagger and bones and femur to sloth worship."

"It *is* a leap. It's just a theory, one of many I'm sure will be considered. But that's how archaeology works. This is just the beginning. Next will come an archaeological survey and dig that will add a whole lot more context to what we've seen so far."

They crawled out of the cleft and rose, facing the lands of the Tohono O'odham people.

Chuck took a moment to search the scrubland spread before him. He treated the terrain as if he was on his annual fall elk hunt in the Colorado mountains, mentally dividing the expanse into quadrants and sweeping each quadrant with his eyes, his brain on alert for any movement that might be Carlos backtracking along the route he and Francisco had taken from the border.

"To your point about ritualism and human remains," said Era, also looking out at the desert, "Edward Abbey's remains are out there somewhere. They're everywhere out there, in fact."

"He wrote *The Monkey Wrench Gang*, didn't he?" Carmelita asked. "With the crazy environmental warrior guy, Hayduke?"

"That's him," Era confirmed. "Abbey, I mean. He lived in Tucson. He told his friends that when he died, he wanted to be left out in the desert for the birds and animals to eat. He didn't want his body buried six feet underground or burned to ashes. He wanted it to provide sustenance to desert critters. His friends did what he asked, and ever since, his fans have been trying to find the place where his body was left so they can build a shrine to him there."

"From the Mayans straight through to today," Chuck noted,

gazing out at the desert, "the attraction of death never ends." He turned to Era. "Speaking of which, what made you go back to the petroglyph rocks this afternoon after Ron told everyone to stay away?"

"He may be in charge of Lance and Martina, but he's not in charge of me," Era said.

Chuck looked away. Not exactly a straight answer.

Era glanced from the spiral to the bones. "Now that I've seen all this, I'm really itching to get back to the rocks again—with you."

"Why's that?"

"You showed me yours." She raised her eyebrows. "I can't wait to show you mine in return."

"Count me intrigued," said Chuck. Not to mention, returning to the drainage—with Era set to take the heat from Ron, or at least share it—would enable Carmelita and Chuck to keep an eye out for Carlos at the water station, and perhaps find a way to search for him in the vicinity.

Chuck offered to belay Era while she climbed back up the cleft, but she turned to Carmelita instead. "How about you, ClimberCarm? Would you like to belay me?"

"Sure," Carmelita said.

Era grinned. Flecks of bright pink lipstick speckled her front teeth. She knotted Chuck's rescue cord around her waist while Carmelita looped the thin rope behind her back and sat on the flat patch of ground at the bottom of the crevice. The rope ran from Era's waist to the top of the cliff, through the straps of Chuck's daypack secured to the mesquite trunk, and back down to Carmelita on the dirt platform.

"Ready?" Era asked.

"Belay is on," Carmelita confirmed.

Era gave the cord a tug. Carmelita closed her fingers around the rope, securing it in place.

"Just making sure," said Era.

Turning to the cleft, she began to climb. She ascended the dihedral with fluidity and grace, moving upward from hold to hold with no wasted energy, her feet and hands acting in perfect synchronicity with one another—until, all at once, just before she reached the top of the cliff, her hands and feet left the facing rock walls of the cleft and she fell, plummeting down the crevice, straight toward Chuck and Carmelita below.

17

"I see projectiles," Janelle said, eyeing the rocks strewn on the wide portion of the ledge on the east face of Baboquivari Peak.

"What's a projectile?" Rosie asked.

"Ammunition."

"Ooo, I like it."

"So do I," said Chartreuse, standing with Rosie and Janelle at the point where the rock shelf plateaued.

Janelle peered over the lip of the shelf. The two men strode up the trail, more than a hundred feet below. The man in the lead, armed with the gun, glanced up. At the sight of Janelle looking down at him, he stopped and raised his pistol, aiming it up at her.

She jumped back, her heart galloping, and waved Rosie and Chartreuse away from the edge of the ledge. "Grab some ammo," she directed, her voice low, pointing at the dozens of stones that, over time, had tumbled from higher on the peak and landed on the flat shelf.

They scurried about the ledge, gathering the rocks into piles while remaining out of sight of the men below. Janelle again poked her head over the shelf, sighting in on the men. They had resumed their trek up the trail and were now directly below. Ducking back, she pointed over the edge, targeting them for Rosie and Chartreuse.

Rosie grabbed a softball-sized rock from one of the piles and threw it out and over the shelf in the direction Janelle had indicated. Janelle held her breath as the rock plunged downward, disappearing from sight. The hard *chock* of the rock striking the side of the mountain echoed through the air, followed by two more *chocks* and a hollered curse in Spanish.

"Ha!" Rosie exclaimed.

Using both hands, she lifted a rock the size of a bowling ball, swung it backward between her legs, and heaved it forward, underhanded, off the ledge. Janelle poked her head over the edge of the shelf and watched as the rock tumbled down the mountain. The men stared up, mouths agape, as the rock bounded toward them. They leapt to the side at the last second, avoiding the plunging rock, which shot past them and on down the mountainside.

Janelle teamed with Rosie and Chartreuse in tossing rock after rock off the ledge, raining projectiles down on the men. The rocks pinballed off boulders and ribs of stone on the mountainside, their trajectories changing with each strike. There was no refuge for the men on the open trail below. They cursed and jumped back and forth, dodging the plummeting stones.

Janelle beckoned Rosie to help her with a stone the size of a microwave oven resting near the lip of the shelf. They sat behind the big rock, shoved it off the ledge with their feet, and crawled forward to watch. The rock gained momentum each time it struck the mountainside and launched into the air. By the time it reached the trail, it was a whirling dervish careening wildly downward. The men lay flat on the path as it whizzed past them, inches above their heads.

The boulder crashed on down the slope and the men climbed to their feet. The lead man pointed his gun up the mountain and squeezed off a shot. The bullet ricocheted harmlessly off the rock wall well above the ledge, and the sharp crack of the gunshot reverberated off the face of the peak.

The shooter lowered his gun and shoved the man next to him, propelling him down the trail. The men strode back toward the parking lot.

"We did it!" Rosie cheered.

Chartreuse brushed her hands on her shorts, leaving dusty streaks. "I have to say, I've never done anything remotely like that."

"They shot at us," Janelle said, looking after the men, her heart pumping hard. "They followed us all the way around the mountain, they climbed up here after us, and they shot at us. What could they possibly want?"

"*Drogas,*" Rosie said. She turned to Chartreuse. "My uncle Clarence says drugs are the biggest problem of all out here in the desert. He says that's why my cousin Francisco was killed."

"Killed?"

Rosie nodded solemnly. "Just this morning."

Chartreuse turned to Janelle. "Who? *What?* This morning?"

"That's why we came here," Janelle said. "We're looking for his brother, Carlos. He's somewhere in the desert, missing."

Chartreuse blanched, the skin over her cheekbones turning white. "It never occurred to me to ask what the two of you were doing out here."

Janelle looked down from the shelf at the retreating men, her hands on her hips, her heart rate gradually slowing. "We didn't know about those two before we picked you up."

"Plus, you needed our help," Rosie reminded Chartreuse.

"That's right," she admitted. She glared at the departing men. "All males are the same. They're power-hungry beasts wanting to lord it over us women."

"All of them?" Rosie asked.

"All the ones I know, anyway."

"Not me," Janelle said. "Not by a long shot."

"You're lucky, then."

"Maybe so. Or maybe you've just been unlucky."

"Raquel, my lead therapist at the institute, says it's up to me to make my own luck."

"You just did," said Janelle.

"*We* just did," said Rosie.

The two men returned to the parking lot, climbed into their car, and drove away, the receding taillights glowing red in the shade of the mountain.

"I'm glad they didn't stick a knife in our tires before they left," Chartreuse said. "I figured for sure they would strand us out here. I mean, they shot at us."

"Maybe they're confused," said Rosie. "They can't decide for sure if they're bad guys or not."

In the distance, the black car crossed from shade into sunlight and turned onto the Sasabe road, heading back toward the highway and Tucson.

"Time for us to get out of here," said Janelle.

Chartreuse pointed at the rock wall rising at the back of the ledge. "Not just yet."

18

Chuck backed against the wall of the cleft to avoid Era as she plunged toward him and Carmelita from the top of the cliff.

The rescue cord ran around Carmelita's back, up to the mesquite-tree anchor point above the dihedral, and back down to Era. The rope stretched tight, then tighter, slowing Era's fall, as Carmelita gripped it with her brake hand. Era's weight first caused the cord to tighten around Carmelita's back. Then, the last of its elasticity spent, the taut rope hoisted Carmelita off the dirt platform at the bottom of the cleft.

At the same instant Carmelita left the ground, Era's plunge halted, leaving the two of them dangling together in midair between the facing walls of the dihedral, a couple of feet off the ground.

Era grinned at Carmelita. "You caught me!"

Chuck stepped forward and helped Carmelita to the dirt platform. She relaxed her grip on the rope, allowing Era to return to the bottom of the cleft beside her.

"Sorry 'bout that," Era said to Carmelita. "I just couldn't resist the chance to fly with you."

Chuck rounded on her. "You fell *on purpose*?"

"It's okay," she said as she freed the rope from around her waist. "I was the only one at risk. ClimberCarm was all safe and sound down here on the deck."

"You yanked her right up into the air," Chuck snapped.

"Yeah, yeah, yeah, I understand, daddy-o—it came as a surprise." Era beamed at Carmelita. "Because it was meant to." She reached out and massaged Carmelita's shoulder. "You did great."

"Thanks," said Carmelita.

Era turned to Chuck. "Acting as a belay anchor is a big deal. The only way to know for sure if you've got it right is for it to happen when you're not expecting it."

Chuck huffed. "You're saying you did that just to test her?"

"And to fly with her." Era grinned. "Nothing wrong with a couple of rock women getting a little air together."

She turned to the V of the cleft and climbed back up the cliff unroped, popping out of the top of the crevice after less than a minute in her bright clothing like a spring flower emerging from the ground.

"Yoo-hoo!" she called back down. "Who's next?"

Chuck was gratified to see that Carmelita made no move to follow Era up the cliff without a belay. Simple though the climb was for Carmelita, she heeded the longstanding entreaties by Chuck and Janelle that she never risk climbing unroped, tying the cord around her waist and verifying with Chuck that she was on his belay. She flashed the cleft, climbing to the top of the cliff with a level of ease, speed, and grace that far surpassed Era's climbing abilities.

"You *levitated* up that thing," Era praised her when they stood together atop the cliff. She squeezed Carmelita's bicep. "You must eat a ton of spinach."

Chuck climbed the cliff on Carmelita's belay, his anger at Era's stunt slowly ebbing. He'd enjoyed the sport of rock climbing since he was young, and knew the level of crazy the sport sometimes attracted. He stowed the rope in his pack and the three of them headed back along the top of the cliff with Era in the lead, her steps, like Carmelita's, light and assured on the narrow shelf.

Carmelita fell back until the botanist was out of earshot and said softly to Chuck over her shoulder, "She's *whack*."

"As in nuts?" Chuck asked. "Yes, she sure is. I have no idea what she was thinking."

"I do," Carmelita said. "Or, at least, I think I do. She let her competitive juices get the best of her. She's seen my Climber-Carm profile, with the list of competitions I've won."

"She can take surprise falls on your belay all she wants, but it won't make any difference—you're a way better climber than she is. I watched both of you climb the dihedral back there. She couldn't hold a candle to you."

Carmelita waved off his compliment, but when she glanced back at him, her eyes were alight with pride. She looked ahead and changed the subject. "I can't stop thinking about the femur. Do you really think the cuts on it mean the person it belonged to was sacrificed and butchered in the name of a *sloth*?"

"I'd say the odds are pretty good," Chuck said.

"What would it take to prove the site was associated with human sacrifice?"

"First and foremost, some sort of a physical structure. Human sacrifice by the Mayans was highly ritualized. It involved huge temples at the end of long, stone-paved procession ways. The sacrifices were performed in the temples on elaborate stone altars. If Hohokam traders brought the Mayan idea of human sacrifice back to the Sonoran Desert, you'd imagine they'd have constructed the same sort of thing here in some fashion or other."

"I'd have bet they were too preoccupied with just surviving in the desert to get involved in extravagant sacrifice rituals."

"That's exactly what everyone in the archaeological community has supposed—until today."

Carmelita aimed another appreciative look over her shoulder at him before increasing her pace and catching up with Era.

Chuck stopped and scanned the scrubland quadrant by quadrant with slow sweeps of his eyes. Nothing. He looked up at the sky. If Carlos was dead and his body was out there somewhere, it likely would be attracting circling vultures by now. But nothing moved in the air, either.

He pulled his phone from his pocket. With Era out of earshot ahead, he finally could check in with Janelle. When he dialed her number, however, the call went straight to voicemail. He ended the call and held his phone before him. Maybe she was talking with Yolanda and Hector. Or with immigration authorities. He grunted. She'd see his missed call, at least, even if she wasn't able to call him back before he dropped back into the arroyo and out of service range.

He set out along the ledge. Carmelita and Era waited for him at the trail and the three of them descended the switchbacks to the bottom of the drainage together. They emerged from behind the prickly pear cactus into the channel. Lance left a group of officials on the far side of the wash that included Ron, the medical examiner, and the two sheriff's deputies.

As Lance marched over to them, Chuck swiveled his head, his quick look around revealing no sign of Carlos.

"What are you doing here?" Lance demanded, stopping in front of them.

"I'd rather talk to Ron," Chuck said curtly.

He stepped past Lance. Era sidestepped the ranger, too. When Chuck did not hear Carmelita's trailing footsteps, he turned back. She remained in place, looking at Lance. Chuck jerked his head at her. "Come on," he said gruffly.

She left the ranger, who followed her with his eyes, his beefy arms hanging out from his sides.

Chuck stopped before the officials. Era stood next to him, and Carmelita halted a step behind.

Ron stuck out his jaw. "What did I tell you about staying away from here?"

"The rescuers left with the body," said Chuck. "We saw them."

"So?"

"You said we needed to stay out of the way of the investigation."

"Which remains ongoing."

"We won't get in your way. I just want to get back to the work you hired me to do. I'm only scheduled to be in Arizona a few more days."

The medical examiner extended her hand, first to Chuck, then to Era, then, reaching between them, to Carmelita, introducing herself as Barbara Francis from the Pima County Office of the Medical Examiner. Her pale blue eyes were set close on either side of her downturned nose, and her shoulders were slightly stooped.

"Ron brought me to the park," Chuck explained to her, "to survey the petroglyphs on the rocks here in the wash."

"Let's be clear," Ron responded. "I brought you in to survey *all* the petroglyphs in the park. It was you who wanted to start with the ones here."

"For good reason," Chuck said to Barbara. "The etchings on the rocks in this drainage represent the largest collection of rock carvings in the park. It makes sense to begin with them."

Turning to Ron, Barbara lifted and dropped her rounded shoulders. "The body's gone, and the rocks aren't in the way of anything I need to do. I don't have any problem sharing space with them if you don't." She tilted her head up the line of boulders. "Besides, we're already doing just that."

Chuck turned. Martina sat before the first of the petroglyph rocks, at the upstream end of the string of boulders, facing the etched face of the stone.

"Her, but not us?" Chuck said to Ron.

"She went straight over there from the trail. She didn't even pay me the courtesy of asking."

Barbara chuckled. "And you didn't have the guts to kick her out."

"I just want to get out of here myself, ASAP."

"That goes for me, too." The medical examiner addressed the sheriff's deputies. "Shall we?"

The officials headed back beneath the trees. Martina waved Chuck and Era over from her seat on the sandy ground in front of the refrigerator-sized stone. They walked up the line of rocks to her.

"Are you doing your own survey of some sort?" Chuck asked.

"We decided to head out here and get back to work," she replied.

"We?"

"Era and I. We're a team."

Era nodded. "That's how we think of ourselves."

Chuck looked from one to the other, his eyebrows raised.

"We've been coming out here together for a while now," Martina explained. "Quite a while, in fact."

"Today was going to be our big day," Era said. "This morning, I mean."

"To be honest," Chuck said to Era, "I've been wondering how you, in particular, ended up on the research team."

"I'm not exactly the first person to come to mind when you think of petroglyphs, am I?"

"Ron put the team together for me," Chuck said. "Everyone else makes sense." He looked down at Martina in her worn hiking clothes and dirt-flecked boots. "You, with the park, of course. Harper from the university. Vivian and Joel from the tribe." He turned to Era. "But you're a botanist."

"Ron knew of my interest in Sonoran rock art," she explained. "I've been studying the petroglyphs in the desert around Tucson, gathering ideas for the decisions I make."

"Let me get this straight. The rock art around Tucson, which is from hundreds or even thousands of years ago, determines the kinds of plants you put in the city's median strips today?"

"*Helps* determine. But yes, that's essentially correct. A decades-long drought hit the Southwest back in the 1200s, forcing the Hohokam to change the types of crops they planted, and to make significant improvements to their irrigation systems. By looking at the record they left behind on the rocks, I can get a sense of the decisions they made—which changes were most effective, and which didn't work at all."

While Era spoke, Martina watched Ron and the others gathered around the bloodstained patch of ground where Francisco's body had lain.

"The Hohokam people were great agriculturalists," Era went on. "They had to be to grow crops in such a harsh climate, even before the drought. And they were master astronomers, too. Talk about smart. Can you imagine what it took to track the movement and cycles of the sun and moon and stars through the sky over months and years and even decades? Yet that's exactly what they did, with no computers, no written records, nothing." She tapped Martina on the shoulder, drawing her attention. "Speaking of which, wait till you see what I just saw up on the ridge."

"Do tell."

Era leaned down and said in Martina's ear, "They found a sun dagger. It's up in the cliffs."

"A *sun dagger*?" Martina exclaimed, her voice low. She looked at Chuck. "You're sure?"

He nodded. "My daughter spotted it. Carmelita."

"It comes complete with a shrine of bones," Era said. "Including a human femur. And it's all out in front of a cavern containing the remains of a Shasta ground sloth."

Martina's jaw dropped. "What are we doing down here? We should head right back up there."

"None of it is going anywhere," Era said. "I told Chuck we'd show him what we found in return."

Martina arched her brow. "Oh, you did, did you?"

"We were going to show everybody else today."

"Yes, we were. But…"

Era turned to Chuck. "It's been just the two of us until now."

"Plus Lance," Martina reminded her.

"Oh, yeah. I was trying to forget."

"Whatever *it* is," Chuck said, "must be pretty special."

"It most certainly is," said Era.

Martina nodded in agreement, glancing at Ron and the others, who continued to show no interest in what she, Era, and Chuck were up to. She patted the ground beside her and said to Chuck, "We figured Ron would let us stay if we didn't make a fuss. I came straight over here and hunkered down in front of the rock." She looked at Era. "But you weren't here."

"I got here before you did, actually," Era said. "But Lance sent me back up the ridge to the dagger site—and am I ever glad he did."

Chuck dropped to the ground and glanced sideways at Martina and Era. The two were similar in certain ways, but markedly different in others. Martina, with her Italian heritage, and Era, as a Latina woman, were alike in their walnut eyes and dark hair and complexion. But they were separated in age by some twenty years, Era in her late twenties, Martina well into her forties. Their clothing and makeup styles contrasted—Era's colorful attire and decorated lips, cheeks, and eyes versus Martina's worn and stained clothing and makeup-free face. And their personalities differed: Era's impetuousness versus Martina's earnestness.

What had Martina meant when she'd referred to herself and Era as a team? And why, really, had she and Era returned to the petroglyph rocks this afternoon? Ron's order that the research team stay away from the murder scene had been explicit, yet here the two women were.

Chuck, at least, had an ulterior motive for returning to the site—he was searching for Carlos.

Were Era and Martina harboring an ulterior motive as well?

19

"You can do the honors," Martina said to Era once she and Chuck were seated in front of the rock.

Chuck turned to Era, next to him. "I'm betting whatever you found must have something to do with botany."

"Yes and no," she allowed.

"More yes than no, I'd say," Martina said. "When it comes to Era, everything has to do with plants, one way or another. That's just how she operates."

Era smiled. "True enough."

She turned to the carved rock. Chuck faced the boulder, too, focusing on the petroglyphs etched into the surface of the stone.

As with the seven other large boulders lined along the edge of the channel, a variety of subject matter was inscribed on the rock's face—human stick figures, anthropomorphic figures, geometric shapes, and household items including pots, urns, and jars, some squat and round, others tall and slender.

All manner of reptiles, birds, mammals, and plants were represented on the boulder as well. Among the reptiles were round tortoises with crosshatched shells and blocky feet, and thin lizards juxtaposed with fat horned toads. Flying ravens adorned the rock, as did desert bighorn rams with thick horns curling from their skulls, ewes with short, blunt horns, and tiny lambs cantering among their elders.

Chuck recognized etchings depicting the primary crops grown by the Hohokam people—beans, corn, squash, even tobacco plants with their distinctive sprays of flowers on top. Other plants were depicted, including saguaro cactuses, palo verde trees, and yucca plants with needled leaves and upthrust stalks.

"Quite a collection," Chuck noted of the jumble of carvings etched into the weathered face of the basaltic rock before him. "But I bet you only see the plants."

"You know me too well already," Era said. "Which gives me the opportunity to point out that, in addition to their astronomic capabilities, the Hohokam were master agriculturalists. From the very beginning of their culture, they made good use of the little rain that fell from the sky. They were forced to hone their agricultural skills even more when the drought really took hold in the 1200s, building check dams and lining their irrigation canals with clay. Their culture reached its zenith during those years, as if dealing with the stress of the drought made them the best possible version of themselves."

"I still don't see what all of that has to do with you and the city of Tucson."

"My job is to develop the city's botanical plan as it relates to changing conditions on the ground. We've faced decreasing rainfall and increasing temperatures here for the last twenty years. We know by now that these conditions are not going to end anytime soon. Given the realities of climate change, we've pretty well accepted that the recent dryness is the new normal for the Sonoran Desert."

Era looked past the rock at the hundreds of saguaros protruding from the green layer of vegetation that covered the ridge.

"The effects are most apparent in the saguaro cactus. It's the climax plant of the Sonoran Desert, which means that as the saguaro goes, so go all the other cactuses around here. In the 1930s, local ranchers brought in a species of bunchgrass from Saudi Arabia that grows well in hot, dry climates. It's called buffelgrass. Now, a century later, buffelgrass is overwhelming the entire region. It outcompetes cactuses for water, turning what was a diverse ecosystem featuring dozens of cactus species into an invasive grassland monoculture. A recent study here in Saguaro National Park found that, of ten thousand saguaro cactuses surveyed, only a few were less than a decade old. Saguaros only grow where conditions for them are perfect. If you change things just a little bit—introduce buffelgrass or raise the air temperature or decrease the amount of rainfall—it's lights out for them."

Chuck considered the stately saguaros standing straight and tall on the opposite hillside. "Sounds grim."

"It is. But people are starting to do what they can about it. Volunteers are pulling buffelgrass in the park, working to eradicate it from within the park boundaries."

"And you're doing what you can, too," said Chuck, "by, of all things, studying petroglyphs."

"The Hohokam didn't leave a written record of the improvements they made during the drought in the 1200s. Not on paper, anyway. The Mayans, south of here, left all sorts of agricultural records on sheets of bark paper called codices. But that's the tropics. I need desert information. Petroglyphs are the only form of historical record left by the Hohokam people, so that's what I've been looking at as I develop my botanical recommendations for the city. That's how I got to know Martina, and through her, Ron, who put me on the research team."

"And here you are," Chuck said.

Era glanced at Martina. "And here *we* are."

"Despite the murder this morning."

"Because of the murder, I guess you could say," Era said. "The murdered *migrant*, that is. Climate change is forcing more and more people around the world to abandon their homes. If we don't sort things out, forced human migration will destroy the planet lots faster than any invasive species like buffelgrass."

"You sound like you're a social anthropologist instead of a botanist."

"The human and natural worlds are completely intertwined. They always have been and they always will be. I consider myself a botanist with a sociological bent, while Martina calls herself a naturalist with a sociological bent. We complement each other very nicely, I'd say."

Chuck looked back and forth between them. "You're friends?"

"*Compadres*, we call ourselves," said Era. "We've been comparing notes for the last year or so."

"On petroglyphs?"

"Yes. And I think you'll find what we've spotted out here to be very interesting, indeed."

Chuck stared at the etchings on the rock in front of him. "There's a lot to look at."

"It's almost overwhelming," Era agreed. She repeated, with emphasis, "*Almost.*"

"It took us a long time to see it ourselves," Martina said. "Era's the one who saw it first."

"But you were here with me at the time," Era reminded her.

"To see *it*?" Chuck asked.

Both women nodded.

"Ready for me to show you?" Era asked him.

"No. Not yet." He leaned back and studied the face of the stone, allowing his eyes to drift from petroglyph to petroglyph. "I have this rock listed in my notes as Rock 1, because it's the farthest upstream," he noted, giving voice to his musing. "I'm still puzzled over why there's a line of eight stones carved with petroglyphs here. The boulders obviously were positioned along the edge of the wash, like some sort of Stonehenge in the desert. This is the only petroglyph site I know of in the entire Southwest where the rocks were actually moved and set in place. To me, that's one of the most interesting aspects of this site, if not *the* most interesting aspect. The boulders are big enough that moving them would have required a levering system of some sort. It would have been quite an operation. But why?"

"We've discussed the same thing over and over ourselves," said Era.

"How many times have you been out here?"

"At least a dozen." She glanced at Martina. "Wouldn't you say?"

Martina nodded.

"All, in your case, for botanical purposes?" Chuck asked Era.

"For me, that's how it started. I wanted to look at the plants depicted on the rocks here by the wash. I thought there might be meaning behind the fact that the rocks are set along a drainage, even though the drainage is usually dry. From there, I was taken in by the sheer beauty of the petroglyphs. We've been out here at dawn, dusk, midday, on sunny days and cloudy days, when it's been burning hot and freezing cold."

"We? Always the two of you?"

"We came out with Vivian a couple of times, too, early on," said Era.

"We did, didn't we?" Martina said. "I'd forgotten that. We came out here with Harper at the beginning, too, as I recall."

"Martina's the one who first hooked me on petroglyphs," Era said. "We've visited sites all around Tucson together—Honey Bee Canyon, Picture Rocks, Sutherland Wash. We've driven out to Baboquivari Peak a bunch of times, too. The Baboquivari petroglyphs are the most extensive in the area, but the boulders here, all lined up and all by themselves, have really captured my imagination. I've even come out here a few times on my own, just to sit and watch as the light changes on them."

"I have, too," Martina said. "All my visits are what convinced me to propose putting the water station out here. After visiting the rocks over and over again, I saw how many migrants were walking up the wash and on through the park to get to Tucson. The bodies of two migrants were found here in the arroyo just last year. Both had died of dehydration. I'm glad Ron allowed the station to be placed inside the park boundary, no matter what Harper thinks. Nobody else has died anywhere near here since then—until today, that is. And today's death wasn't due to the elements."

Chuck exhaled. Francisco. "When did you first start coming out here?" he asked Martina.

"Right after I got here from Minnesota. Like I told your wife this morning, the petroglyphs are a big part of what drew me to Arizona. I admit I've turned into a rock art freak since I moved to the Southwest. I just can't seem to get enough. It's been great sharing this with Era. She's as crazy about rock art as I am." She leaned forward and said to Era, "Aren't you?"

"Crazy is as crazy does," Era agreed.

"How many visits did it take until you noticed whatever it is you noticed?" Chuck asked.

"Months," said Era. "Eight visits, at least. Maybe ten."

Martina nodded. "And that was after I'd been out here several times before that on my own."

"But you think I'll spot it today, right away?"

"Ron says you're the master," said Martina.

"That sounds like a challenge."

Chuck studied Rock 1 once more, taking in the adult bighorns and their cavorting lambs, the wriggling lizards and soaring ravens. He moved on to the geometric shapes—the squares and triangles and curvilinear lines. Then to the human forms—the stick figures with their oversized hands and widespread fingers, the blocky anthropomorphs with their earrings and necklaces.

"Is what I'm looking for apparent now, in the midday light?"

"It's apparent in any light—dawn, dusk, whenever," said Era. "Once you see it, that is."

He stilled his mind. A minute passed. Another. Finally, he grunted. "I'll take a hint, if you've got one."

Era looked at Martina, who nodded her okay.

"The hint is this," Era said. "It's not just this stone."

"Ah-ha." Chuck slid backward on the ground away from Rock 1. "You didn't tell me that before."

"You told us not to."

"I did, didn't I?"

He focused on the next rock down the drainage, the one he'd labeled as Rock 2 in his notes, and quieted his mind once more. He moved from rock to rock on down the line in similar fashion. The petroglyphs on each of the stone faces were similar in their variety—reptiles next to humans beside geometric shapes separated by squiggly lines—dozens of petroglyphs etched on each stone, none seeming to have any particular relation to one another.

Then, he saw it.

PART THREE

"Spirals are the high verb of rock art. They are the trappings of motion…when the spiral is a migration symbol…its center represents a place the people are preordained to reach."

—Craig Childs, *Tracing Time*

20

"Whoa!" Rosie exclaimed, eyeing the vertical rock wall at the back of the ledge on Baboquivari Peak.

Janelle stared at the wall along with Rosie and Chartreuse, her eyes growing large. A simple yet magnificent petroglyph panel adorned the rock face at the rear of the stone shelf. The panel featured more than a dozen life-size human stick figures holding hands and standing in line, each with one leg raised, as if moving in unison. The figures appeared three-dimensional in the shade, one tick away from assuming true human form and stepping from the wall onto the ledge.

"It looks like they're having a dance party," Rosie said.

"Maybe it's a rain dance," said Chartreuse.

"Or a rock dance. The rocks we threw at those guys were lying right in front of the dancers."

Turning from the panel, Janelle peered at the shadow of Baboquivari Peak stretching across the desert as the afternoon sun descended in the west. "It's getting late. Time to get out of here."

"Before those guys come back," Rosie agreed.

Chartreuse paled and turned to Janelle. "Do you think they might do that?"

"No, I don't," said Janelle. "I got the sense they didn't really want to come up the mountain after us in the first place. They couldn't check in by phone to ask whoever's in charge what they should do."

"But when they reach cell service, their bosses might tell them to turn around."

"I don't think that'll happen. They'll have to assume we'll be calling 911 as soon as we get back into service range ourselves."

"That's exactly what I'm planning to do."

"Good," said Janelle. "Thanks."

"As for right now, I'm with you," said Chartreuse. "I want to get as far away from this place as I can—as fast as I can."

Janelle took a couple of pictures of the dancing figures. As she pivoted to head back down the sloped ledge to the trail, a small petroglyph at the end of the line of dancers caught her eye. The etching was a circle with lines of dots inside it, its size the same as the circle petroglyph on the other side of the mountain. Unlike the circle partially filled with dots on the west side of the peak, however, the circle here on the east side was entirely filled with dots in a series of straight lines. As she had on the far side of the mountain, Janelle snapped a picture of the circle-and-dot etching.

She stepped to the edge of the rock shelf and stared out across the landscape. While the primary migrant route was on the west side of Baboquivari, the raised ledge offered an expansive view of scrubland stretching away from the east side of the peak. She pushed back her sunhat and scanned the scrub, looking for signs of movement in the unlikely event Carlos was making his way south through this part of the desert. Once again, however, she saw nothing.

She pulled down her hat and descended the slanted shelf with Rosie and Chartreuse.

"Let's stick together back to the highway," she suggested to Chartreuse when they reached the trailhead parking lot.

"And hope those men really are gone for good," Chartreuse replied.

Rosie held up her phone. "We should trade numbers."

They tapped at their phones and exchanged nods.

Janelle tossed her hat in back and drove away from Baboquivari Peak with Rosie beside her in the front seat. She kept an eye out for any sign of the black car, ready to make a run for the safety of the crowded highway if she spotted it. But the vehicle did not reappear. She turned toward Tucson on the highway, trailed by Chartreuse in her sedan.

"Call Chuck, would you?" she asked Rosie, handing over her phone as she accelerated up the highway. "I'm sure we're back in service by now."

"Sure." Rosie checked the phone. "There's a missed call from him."

"Good!" Janelle exclaimed, relieved.

Rosie dialed and put the phone to her ear, but she shook her head after several seconds. "It's going to voicemail."

Janelle held out her hand for the phone, but Rosie spoke into it instead. "Hi, Dad. It's me, on *Mamá*'s phone. We're coming back. Some guys tried to get us, but we're okay. We rolled the biggest rock ever down on them. They shot at us and then they ran away." She ended the call.

Janelle raised an eyebrow. "'They shot at us'? That'll definitely get him to call back."

She crossed the last of the scrubland of the Tohono O'odham Reservation and started up the rise west of Tucson, tucked in with the heavy traffic streaming toward the city.

"How far is it to the turnoff to the park?" she asked Rosie, thinking of the unanswered call.

Rosie hunched over the phone, studying the map on its screen. "We're almost to the turnoff." She pointed ahead through the windshield. "Right over the hill, I think."

"Try calling Clarence, please."

"*Por supuesto.*" She dialed and cried out after a moment, the phone to her ear, "Hi, Uncle Clarence, it's me, Rosie!" She launched into breathless narration, repeating what she'd said in her message to Chuck. After a pause, she extended the phone to Janelle. "He wants to talk to you."

Stiffening, Janelle put the phone to her ear. "*Hola*, Clarence."

"Somebody *shot* at you?"

"It wasn't as bad as it sounds. They didn't know what they were doing."

Clarence made a strangling noise. "What world are you living in, *hermana*?"

"Calm down. *Mamá* and *Papá* are listening, aren't they?"

"Well, yeah."

"They're worried enough as it is."

"Just promise me you're okay."

"We're fine, I promise. What about you?"

Clarence described what for them had been an unproductive drive on the dirt road north of the highway, and on several of the road's branches. "The only thing we have to report is that we saw Joel, the Tohono O'odham guy, out there."

"In a white pickup?"

"*Sí.*"

"We saw him, too, at the junction with the highway. What was he up to?"

"I'm not sure. I recognized him as we passed, but he didn't stop. I'm sure he didn't recognize us. There's no reason he should have."

"We saw Vivian on the road south of the highway. She was taking pictures of petroglyphs for Chuck. I guess Joel must've been checking on the water stations."

"*Probablemente*," Clarence said. "We're thinking it's about time to call it quits."

"Agreed. Rosie and I will meet you at the hotel after we swing by the trailer."

"You're going back to the park?"

"Just to the camper. What have you heard from Chuck and Carm?"

"Nothing. You?"

She pictured her parents listening to Clarence's half of the conversation. What good would be gained by their learning how long it had been since she'd talked with Chuck and Carmelita? "We're heading to the park to meet them," she said. "The highway's busy, so I'm getting off the phone now. I'll fill you in as soon as we catch up with them."

She handed the phone to Rosie, who ended the call.

"Why didn't you tell them we haven't talked to Dad and Carm yet?" Rosie asked.

"I decided half the truth was better than the whole truth right now for your grand-*papá* and grand-*mamá*."

"Are you worried about them?"

"Grand-*papá* and Grand-*mamá*?"

"No. Carm and Dad."

Janelle straightened her arms, pressing her upper body back in the driver's seat.

"No," she said, keeping her eyes on the road. "I'm sure they're fine."

They turned onto the road to the park. Chartreuse passed behind them on the highway, continuing toward Tucson.

In the passenger seat, Rosie worked her phone, her thumbs flying.

"Who are you texting with?" Janelle asked.

"Chartreuse."

"But she's driving."

Rosie rolled her eyes. "She's got voice-to-text."

"Has she called 911?"

"I'll ask her."

Rosie tapped at her phone and bent over it, waiting. She looked up at Janelle. "She says she's too stressed out, and she'll do it later."

Janelle nodded and glanced out the window at the desert flowing past the moving car. With Carlos still missing, she was okay with Chartreuse's decision, at least for the time being.

Rosie returned to her phone, texting steadily until they pulled up to the camper. On the far side of the maintenance yard, the private vehicles belonging to the rescuers were gone. In their place was a silver SUV.

Janelle climbed out with Rosie. The drapes were drawn on the camper, just as she'd left them. There was no sign of Chuck and Carmelita.

Rosie tucked her phone in her pocket. "Chartreuse says she's almost back to her institute place. She's going to take a nap and then do some yoga. I told her I'd get hold of her if we needed her for anything."

"What would we need her for?"

Rosie toggled her head from side to side. "You never know." She scanned the far side of the maintenance yard and turned to look at the ridge rising behind the camper. "Are we going to go after them?"

Janelle nodded. "I think that's a good idea."

Rosie looked back across the yard. "The same as the others."

Janelle frowned. "What others?"

"The professor lady who got us into Antonio's room at the hospital, for one."

"Harper?"

"Uh-huh. The super-tall lady with the big *A* on her shirt." Rosie pointed. "I saw her leave in that gray car this morning. But now she's back. So's the other one, with the flower clothes."

"Era?"

"Erasmus. Yeah. See?" Rosie pointed at a small sedan, nearly hidden behind the medical examiner van. "And the one with the dirty clothes, too." She pointed at a forest-green SUV parked next to the sedan.

"Martina," Janelle said.

"That sounds right."

"How can you remember all that?"

"For practice. I studied the people getting into their cars this morning. That's an improv thing. It's okay to joke about people's cars. Like, you can say a short person is driving a big truck to make up for being short."

"To *compensate*, you mean?"

"I guess. Carm would know for sure."

"So," Janelle noted, "Harper and Era and Martina have come back—the professor, the botanist, and the naturalist."

"Maybe they're in cahoots together."

"About what?"

"I don't know."

"That's a good word though—cahoots. Almost as good as compensate."

"That's why I said it. They're compensating by being in cahoots together."

Janelle smiled.

Her phone buzzed in her pocket.

21

Chuck sat up straight, taking in the faces of all eight petroglyph stones at once. The etched stones, lined one after another down the wash, appeared in his field of vision as a single, continuous panel of petroglyphs.

And *that* was the secret—all the petroglyphs, on all eight rocks, viewed as one.

"It's a snake," he said wonderingly.

Era beamed. "We have a winner!"

Though the petroglyphs on all the stones were a hodgepodge of human, creature, plant, and geometric etchings, Chuck now saw that the shapes of the overall arrays of petroglyphs on the rock faces differed from one another. The etchings on Rocks 2 through 7 extended all the way across the faces of the boulders from side to side, but the carvings did not fully cover the boulders from top to bottom. Instead, the top and bottom borders of the arrays of petroglyphs curved upward and downward and were set higher and lower on the dark faces of each of the rocks, with the upper and lower borders aligned from one boulder face to the next. The result was that the arrays of petroglyphs on the center six boulders, seen together, presented to the eye the sinuous shape of a snake's body slithering along the faces of the stones.

At the downstream end of the line of boulders, the array of petroglyphs on Rock 8 formed the distinctive, triangle-shaped head of a western diamondback rattlesnake, the venomous Sonoran Desert reptile. A curvilinear line, extending from the snake's snout to the downstream side of the boulder, represented the snake's tongue, which reached to the far edge of the boulder in a curving S.

Chuck returned his attention to Rock 1. There, right in front of him, was the snake's tail, its rattles formed by two rows of pottery urns etched into the face of the rock. Six urns completed each row, set close against one another, with the two rows sitting directly above and below one another. The overall visual effect was that of a dozen rattles at the end of the western diamondback's tail.

Chuck looked downstream from the snake's tail on Rock 1, following with his eyes the curved tops and bottoms of the petroglyph arrays on Rocks 2 through 7, to the triangular head of the rattler on Rock 8. He passed his hand across his eyes in amazement. "Does anyone else know about this?"

"Like, out in the big wide world? Not that we know of," Era said.

"Within our little world, though," said Martina, with a hard look at Era, "Lance."

Chuck cocked his head. "Lance knows?"

Era nodded guiltily. "He spotted me heading out here a few weeks ago. I told him what we'd found."

"Which didn't make me too happy," said Martina.

"I told you I was sorry," Era replied.

"So," Chuck urged, "*Lance*."

"He's been pushing for us to announce it ever since," said Era. "I think he's going to try to take credit for it when we do."

"I can believe that," Chuck said.

"He and I had a thing, just for a little while," Era confessed. "I mean, who wouldn't?" She widened her eyes at Chuck. "It was pretty fun, I have to admit. He kept trying to play the tough guy, but I was holding the reins on him the whole time." She glanced at Rock 1. "We were going to do the big reveal to you and the rest of the research team today. It's time. Martina and I have recorded it with still photos, video, even drawings. We've looked online for anything comparable anywhere else on earth and we haven't come up with a single thing."

"I don't imagine you will." He turned to Martina. "The only thing I've heard of that's even remotely like this is the old Ojibwe route of yours in Voyageurs."

"You know about that?"

"Ron told me that's what brought you to Saguaro."

"The two aren't identical, but I get what you're saying," Martina said. "The markings on the rocks in Voyageurs lead right through the middle of the park, from portage point to portage point. They're heavily weathered, barely visible. It took me years to convince anyone of their significance. When I finally did, though, everybody jumped on it, like, overnight. I should've waited longer to tell people. I was working on a paper, but I never even got it published. The academics swooped in with their research permits and their teams of grad students, and it was all over for me."

"So you headed south."

"As far away from Voyageurs as I could get. I swore if I ever had the same kind of chance, I wouldn't let it happen to me again."

"But I've been getting antsy," Era said to Chuck. "Especially since Lance weaseled his way in on it." She glanced at Martina. "Well, since I told him." She looked back at Chuck. "We've got our paper written, we're all set to go. I mean, we've known about Sassy for going on six months now."

"Sassy?"

"That's what we named her. It seemed like she deserved it. She's been hanging out right here, in plain sight, all these years."

"Thanks for helping me see her," Chuck said.

"We've known for a while now you were coming," Martina said. "We were all ready to go this morning." She looked at Era. "I didn't tell you this yet, but I hinted about it to Harper when I saw her at the hospital today. I hardly told her anything, but she got pretty fired up all the same."

"This is definitely going to change the way people see and study rock art," Chuck said. He eyed the snake. "From now on, everyone will be looking for interlinked petroglyphs like this. There's going to be a mad rush to all the petroglyph panels on the planet—and I'll be one of the ones doing the rushing."

"Add in the sun dagger and the bones and the cavern," said Era, "and this place is going to explode."

Chuck twisted, looking for Carmelita. She'd be as excited about the snake as he was. He would show Sassy to her first, after which they would come up with some excuse or other that would enable them to search the area for Carlos.

Beneath the trees, the medical examiner and deputies conversed with Ron. But Lance was nowhere to be seen. Neither was Carmelita.

Chuck scrambled to his feet and scanned the vegetation on both sides of the channel.

Nothing.

He cursed beneath his breath.

"What is it?" Era asked, climbing to her feet. "What's wrong?"

"Carmelita's gone."

"Lance is, too," she noted, looking around. "Which is not a surprise."

"What makes you say that?"

"Lance is good at whatever he puts his mind to. And the main thing he puts his mind to is women. And girls, it would appear."

Chuck shivered. "You're speaking from your own experience?"

She nodded. "But I wouldn't be too worried if I was you. They'll be back before long. I mean, he knows you're here." She looked up the arroyo. "There they are now, in fact."

Carmelita and Lance rounded the upstream bend in the drainage and strode down the open channel together. Chuck met them in the middle of the wash.

"Where were you?" he demanded of Carmelita, his tone sharper than he'd intended.

She took a step back from him. "You were busy. Lance asked me to help him."

"Don't worry," Lance said, standing next to Carmelita. "I kept my eye on her the whole time."

Chuck glowered at the ranger.

Carmelita scowled at Chuck in return. "All we did was hike to the end of the drainage," she said.

"It'd be good to find the murder weapon," Lance explained. "I figured another look, with another set of eyes, wouldn't hurt."

"Lance says it was a wire of some kind, almost like it was professional."

The ranger nodded. "It was a sanctioned killing, that much is clear. The killer knew the victim, which is how they were able to get close and take him by surprise."

"It'll be up to the ISB agent to make that determination," Chuck said.

"The more help from the rest of us, though, the better. That's what I told Carmelita." Lance jutted his big chin at her approvingly and said to Chuck, "She's one smart cookie. But I'm sure you already know that."

"I do." He took Carmelita by the elbow. "I've got something I want to show you."

She tugged her arm, attempting to free it from his grasp, but when he held firm, she allowed him to lead her to Era and Martina at Rock 1, while Lance walked over to the other officials beneath the trees.

Chuck gazed down the line of etched stones. Now that he knew what to look for, the outline of the snake was obvious.

Carmelita crossed her arms, facing the petroglyphs carved into the first rock in the line. "What is it?"

"I'll let Era and Martina show you." Chuck turned to them. "If you'd like."

"Of course." Era stepped behind Carmelita and turned her at the waist to face the string of boulders marching down the wash. "What do you see?"

Carmelita lowered her arms to her sides. "Petroglyphs. Lots of them."

"Keep looking." She hissed in Carmelita's ear, the tip of her tongue vibrating. "Sssssnake," she said.

"Oh, my God!" Carmelita exclaimed, covering her mouth and staring downstream. "I see it!"

"We call her Sassy," said Martina.

Era pivoted Carmelita to again face Rock 1. "She's a rattle-snake. See?"

"I see her rattles, clear as anything," Carmelita marveled.

"It took Martina and me months to spot her, but we didn't have any help." Era dropped her hands from Carmelita's waist. "Once you see her, though, you can't unsee her ever again."

Chuck scanned the line of rocks from the snake's tail on Rock 1, at the upstream end of the line of boulders, to its triangular head and curved tongue on Rock 8, at the downstream end. Beyond the final petroglyph stone, the dry gravel wash rounded the north end of the ridge in a gentle bend before spreading out at the mouth of the arroyo and disappearing on the flat scrubland of the Tohono O'odham Reservation. Across the wash and on around the west side of the ridge were the sun dagger and cylinder of bones—including the butchered human femur lying atop the smaller bones.

Chuck looked up at the ridge.

Rosie. Janelle.

How far back up the trail would he need to go to call them again and make sure they were safe?

175

22

Janelle answered her buzzing phone, which displayed a picture of Chuck's tanned face, his eyes, framed by deep crow's feet, looking at her from the screen.

She put the phone to her ear. "Finally."

"Same back at you," Chuck said between heavy breaths. "It's good to hear your voice."

Tears welled in her eyes, taking her by surprise. "Yours, too."

"I just listened to Rosie's message," Chuck said. "I can't believe it. Are you okay?"

She described the events on Baboquivari Peak. "They took a potshot at us," she concluded, "like Rosie said. But it was clearly just a warning shot. They left after that."

"But—" he began.

"We're fine," she cut in. "We're at the camper."

"Yeah!" Rosie hollered into the phone from Janelle's side. "We're here, but you and Carm aren't." She nudged Janelle with her elbow. "Ask him about the others."

"Rosie wants to know about the people from the research team," Janelle said. "Their cars are here."

"Era and Martina came back to the rocks," said Chuck. "Turns out they've been studying the petroglyphs for months." Wind whistled through his phone. "Carm and I are ahead of them, on our way back."

"What about Harper?"

"The professor? We haven't seen her."

"She must be out there somewhere."

"We'll keep an eye out for her." A sustained gust of wind

howled in Chuck's phone. "Here come Era and Martina now. We'll see you when we get back."

Janelle lowered her phone. "They're on their way back here," she told Rosie.

"Can we go meet them?"

"I don't see why not."

Halfway to the top of the ridge, Rosie pointed up the slope. "Somebody's coming!"

The afternoon sun lit a hiker descending the trail toward them.

"It's Harper," Janelle said, recognizing the professor's thin physique.

"Hello there!" Harper called down to them. "What are the two of you doing here?"

"We're meeting Chuck," Janelle called back.

They met on the trail.

"I had no choice but to return here this afternoon," Harper said without prompting. "It was the correct course of action." In her formal manner of speech, her explanation sounded rehearsed.

"You *had* to come?"

"There was a great deal of discussion among those of us gathered at the hospital about what happened here in the park last night. We know a murder occurred. Someone perished."

My cousin, Janelle wanted to say.

Harper tilted her head at Rosie. "Actually, you had a great deal to do with my coming back out here."

Rosie put a hand to her chest. "Me?"

"I appreciated how forthright you were at the hospital. You wanted to see the boy, Antonio, and you weren't afraid to say so." Harper turned to Janelle. "Your daughter made me think in a more forthright manner about the situation here in the park.

Was I missing something? Was the murder related, somehow, to the work of the research team on the petroglyphs?"

Janelle looked away. The answer to both the professor's questions was yes. She looked back at Harper and changed the subject. "Chuck said he didn't see you out at the petroglyph rocks."

"I hiked to the high point of the ridge. The view from there is utterly commanding. Antonio's cry at the water station has been echoing in my head all day. 'Carlos,' he said. And '*corre*.' He was telling someone named Carlos to run."

Janelle kept her mouth shut and willed Rosie to do the same.

"I'm convinced," Harper continued, "that someone else was there with Antonio and the murder victim. But who? His name is Carlos, that much we know. But when I asked Antonio about it, he became frightened and wouldn't respond."

"So you came back here instead," said Janelle.

"I consider it my responsibility. I'm a college professor. I've worked with young people like Antonio my entire career. I keep picturing his friend Carlos—another young person, no doubt—out here somewhere on his own. Perhaps Carlos is gone from this area, perhaps he made it to Tucson. But if he's still in the desert and there's something I can do to help him, I want to do it. *That's* why I came back out here this afternoon. And that's why I might well come back out here again tomorrow. And the next day. And the day after that. I can't just stand by after what happened this morning. It was terrible, horrible. Beyond horrible. Someone died. Another person nearly died. And a third person, I believe, is still out here somewhere. Someone named Carlos." She glanced behind her at the crest of the ridge. "I looked in all directions for him, but I did not see him. I saw no movement in the desert whatsoever. But I promise you I will keep looking. It is my duty, and I will not rest until I'm satisfied Carlos no longer is in the position of needing my help."

"If he even exists," said Janelle.

"Oh, he exists, I'm sure of it."

"Yep," Rosie agreed.

Harper squinted down her long nose at Rosie. "What makes you say that?"

Rosie shifted her feet in the trail. "Because you said so."

Harper turned to Janelle, her brow furrowed.

"She's just being considerate by agreeing with you," Janelle said.

The professor let out a sharp huff and stepped to one side. "The two of you may pass," she said curtly.

Janelle and Rosie reached the top of the ridge. Far below, Harper climbed into her car and drove out of the maintenance yard, returning to the city.

"She almost caught me," said Rosie.

"No, you were fine," Janelle assured her. "You were just being nice. She was awfully adamant about looking for Carlos, though."

"Why didn't we tell her about him?"

"We didn't need to. She's searching for him without our having to say anything."

Rosie pushed her dark curls out of her eyes and looked across the desert to the west. The slanted rays of the afternoon sun struck a pair of saguaro cactuses standing sentinel-like at the edge of the trail on either side of her, turning the thorns ringing the cactus trunks into glowing halos of light.

"Harper's right," Janelle said, scanning the desert along with Rosie. "Carlos is out there somewhere. We just have to find him."

Nothing moved in the scrubland until Chuck and Carmelita appeared on the trail, accompanied on their return from the petroglyph rocks by Era and Martina.

Janelle took hold of Rosie's sleeve and whispered in her ear, "Don't say anything about the men and gun until the two women leave, please."

"Why not?"

"I'll tell you later."

Rosie nodded and galloped up the trail to meet the group. She and Carmelita descended the ridge together, chattering with one another as they followed Era and Martina, while Janelle fell back with Chuck and told him about meeting Harper on the ridge.

The sun was dropping in the sky by the time they reached the camper, the softening light adding an orange tint to the green cactuses and brown rocks on the slopes surrounding the maintenance yard.

Era and Martina drove out of the yard. Carmelita turned to Rosie and Janelle, describing to them the sun dagger, bones, and sloth remains in the cleft of the cliff.

"That sounds totally cool," Rosie said when Carmelita finished. "But somebody shot at us." Facing Janelle and crossing her arms, she asked, "How come I had to wait to tell them until after the women left?"

"For the same reason you weren't sure if we should trust Vivian earlier, out at Baboquivari Peak." Janelle turned to Chuck. "Everywhere we've gone today, your researchers have been there ahead of us. Vivian was at the peak before us. Then, not five minutes after we drove past the men in the black car the first time—"

"The ones who shot at us," Rosie broke in.

"Right," Janelle confirmed. "After we got past them, we saw Joel parked next to the highway. Then, when we came back here to the park, the rest of your research team was already here."

"What are you suggesting?" Chuck asked.

"I'm just stating facts. Five of them, to be exact. Vivian and Joel out by the peak, and Harper, Era, and Martina here in the park. All of them have been circling around like vultures the whole day."

"Vultures? I'm not sure what you're trying to say. Vivian was just doing what I asked her to do, taking pictures of the Baboquivari petroglyphs for me. Joel is in charge of the water stations for the tribe, so it makes sense he'd be out there, too. As for the other three, they weren't exactly hiding. Era and Martina came back to commune with the petroglyphs. They're really into them, as it turns out. And you said Harper came back to look for Carlos. That's a good thing, we can use all the help we can get."

"It's just…" Janelle faltered. "It's just Francisco. And Carlos. And the two men who shot at us." Tears rose, burning, in her eyes. "I keep thinking about my parents, and Aunt Consuela and Uncle Miguel." A tear ran down her cheek. She wiped it away roughly with the back of her hand. "What are we going to tell them? And when?"

"The truth. We'll tell them the truth, and soon. But the more we compare notes beforehand, the better we'll be able to do that. I want to hear everything about the two men who followed you. *Everything*."

Janelle told him about rescuing Chartreuse and driving past the men on the dirt road, the high-speed approach of the black car from behind on the paved road to Sasabe, and pummeling the two men with rocks from the ledge on the east face of Baboquivari Peak.

"I can't imagine you got any pictures of them," Chuck said when she finished.

"No. Just of the petroglyphs."

She offered him her phone and he swiped quickly through the snapshots.

"Vivian showed us her camera," Rosie said. "It was huge, with a big, long lens. She said she took tons of pictures for you. I checked, but she didn't have any marijuana bales in the back of her truck."

He looked up from Janelle's phone. "Marijuana bales?"

"I was just making sure," Rosie said.

"How much do you know about her?" Janelle asked Chuck.

"Not a lot," he admitted. "I told Ron I needed digitized pics of the Baboquivari petroglyphs. I thought he might have access to some. Instead, he suggested I ask Vivian to take them for me. He said she knew every inch of the reservation, and that she was good with a camera, too. I gave her a call and she said she'd be happy to do it."

"When did you call her?"

"A couple of weeks ago, maybe?"

"Why would she have waited until now, today, to take the pictures?"

"I was asking her for a favor. I didn't really give her a deadline."

He returned to the pictures, halting at the shot of the square stones lined on the ground at the junction of the graded dirt road and the spur track on the west side of Baboquivari Peak.

"What are these?" he asked, holding up the phone.

"I saw them when I was looking for drugs," Rosie said. "I told *Mamá* to stop."

"Any idea what they are?" Janelle asked him.

He stared at the phone. "They look familiar, I'll say that much."

"The woman we picked up at the bottom of the mountain said the same thing."

"Chartreuse," Rosie added.

"She has a bracelet with little square stones that look just like the big ones," Janelle said.

Rosie pulled out her phone. "I could ask her. We've been texting a whole bunch."

"You have, have you?"

Rosie nodded. "She says I'm a calming influence on her. With my texts, I mean."

"I'm glad she thinks so."

"Should I check with her? Maybe she's figured it out by now."

"Sure," Chuck said.

He studied the picture while Rosie tapped at her phone, waited, and looked up. "Nope, not yet," she reported.

"Me neither," he said.

Janelle stood at his shoulder looking on as he worked through the pictures of the dancing-figure petroglyph panel at the back of the ledge on the east side of the peak. He stopped at the final picture, that of the dot-filled circle next to the panel of dancers.

"Huh," he said, his brow knitted.

"'Huh,' what?" Janelle asked.

"See the dots?" He enlarged the picture with his thumb and forefinger, zooming in on a handful of the dots in the circle. Some were perfectly round, while others were jagged at the edges. "They're different." He turned the screen and pointed at one of the smoothly circular dots. "This one is an example of indirect percussion, made with a hammerstone and chisel. The chisel would have been a piece of bone or deer antler—something that could be sharpened so that when it was struck by a hammerstone, it would produce the perfectly round dot you see here." He pointed at one of the jagged dots. "This one was made with direct percussion. That is, by striking the cliff face directly with a pointed stone. Direct percussion is the quick-and-dirty approach to dotting a stone wall."

"What do the different dots mean?" Carmelita asked.

"There's no way to know for sure, but the fact that they're different could indicate that they were not all made at the same time."

He zoomed the picture out until the entire dot-filled circle again appeared on the screen.

He studied the circle a moment longer. "There was another picture of a circle with dots in it, wasn't there?"

"Yes." Janelle took the phone and swiped backward, stopping at the photo of the dot-filled circle on the west side of Baboquivari Peak. "We talked about how odd this one looked, since it was only partially filled with dots," she said, handing the phone back to Chuck.

He frowned at the photo. "I think I've got it," he said finally. He turned the phone to them. "How many dots are there?"

Janelle leaned forward with Carmelita and Rosie, silently counting. There were two dots in the top line inside the circle, three dots in the second line, five in the third, and six in the fourth line, at the widest point, halfway down the circle. In the line below the halfway point, where logic said there should have been five dots to match the five in the line directly above the halfway point, there were only four dots. Below that line, there were no more dots. The remainder of the circle was empty.

"Twenty," Carmelita and Rosie said at the same time.

Janelle nodded.

"Right," Chuck said. He swiped through the pictures on the phone and again turned it to them. "How many in this one?"

The picture on the screen was that of the dot-filled circle next to the dancers on the east side of the peak. Janelle again counted silently along with Carmelita and Rosie.

Several lines of dots filled the circle from top to bottom, first a row of two dots, then a row of three, then a row of five just above the halfway point of the circle. That row was followed by a repeated row of five dots just below the halfway point, then a row of three that matched the row higher in the circle, then, finally, a row of two at the bottom of the circle, filling the circle and matching the two dots in the top line of the circle above.

"Twenty again!" Rosie crowed, looking up from the picture on the phone.

"Right again," Chuck said.

"I don't get it," said Janelle.

"There's no reason you should." He glanced at the dot-filled circle. "This is exactly the sort of thing I had in mind when I asked Vivian for photos of the petroglyphs on Baboquivari Peak. This circle and the partially filled one on the other side may be related to a new theory circulating in the Southwest archaeological community that has to do with the Mayan numbering system."

"It was vigesimal, wasn't it?" Carmelita asked.

"You mean," said Rosie, "somebody's a virgin?"

Carmelita groaned. "Not virginal. Vigesimal." She looked at Chuck. "Right?"

"Yep," he said.

"So," said Rosie, "no virgins?"

"No," Chuck said. "Carmelita is referring to the fact that the numbering system used by the Mayans was vigesimal, or base-twenty. Their numbers increased in multiples of twenty in the same way our numbers increase in multiples of ten. They embraced the number twenty for pretty much everything else they did, too. Their *pitz* ball teams were made up of twenty players, each of their major religious temples was surrounded by twenty minor temples, exactly twenty steps led from the stone-paved walkways up to the sacrifice altars in their main temples, and on and on. The new theory here in the Southwest is that Mayan cultural mores in general, and the Mayan religious belief system in particular, may have played a bigger role in Hohokam society than previously thought. It's even possible, I suppose, that some Mayan beliefs could persist all the way through to the Tohono O'odham people of today through their Hohokam ancestors."

He pointed at the picture on the phone.

"The twenty impression points in this circle and in the one on the other side of the peak could be evidence bolstering the new theory." He looked at Carmelita. "I'm guessing you've read about the celestial calendars the Mayans used to predict important spiritual events far into the future." He addressed all three of them. "The calendar predictions continue all the way to today, our present day, and even farther ahead in time. The important thing to know about the Mayan calendars is that they were vigesimal, too, just like the Mayan numbering system. There were twenty days in a Mayan month and 260 days in a Mayan year."

He wiggled the phone.

"One circle like this, with twenty dots, might be just a coincidence. But *two* with exactly twenty dots? Still possibly a coincidence, of course, especially since one of them is only partially filled. But the different edges of the dots indicate they were added over time, as if the circles were being filled in based on some sort of a calendar, like each time a religious event was held—maybe even the one depicted by the dancers on the wall."

He turned the phone back to himself.

"Could the twenty dots be tied to the vigesimal Mayan calendars and numbering system?" he wondered aloud. "There's no way to know for sure at this point, but the fact that there are exactly twenty dots in both circles is intriguing nonetheless."

Janelle envisioned the wide section of the stone shelf on the face of Baboquivari Peak. The ledge easily was expansive enough to accommodate a dance ceremony like the one depicted in the wall panel. "How could Mayan beliefs reach all the way through to today's Tohono O'odham people?"

"Through spiritual and religious similarities," Chuck said. "The name of the Tohono O'odham creator is I'itoi, similar to the name of the Mayan god of creation, Itzamna. Both the Mayan and Tohono O'odham creators are said to have led their respective peoples onto the earth's surface from the underworld. And, after leading their peoples to the surface, both creators are believed to have gone on to reside in high places. I'itoi is believed to live in a cave near the summit of Baboquivari Peak, while Itzamna supposedly lived in the clouds in the sky. Itzamna also was the Mayan god of rain, and we know how important rain is to the Tohono O'odham people."

"That still seems like quite a stretch," Janelle said.

"It is. But after what we saw in the cliff today, added to the two circles you spotted, maybe it's not so much of a stretch after all."

He swiped back through the pictures to the photo of the square gray stones beneath the mesquite trees.

"What do you see?" Janelle asked.

He shook his head. "They still seem familiar, but I just can't quite put my finger on it." He looked up at her from the phone. "Plus…"

She knew exactly what he was thinking. "…they're heavy."

23

"Okay," Chuck said when everyone was settled, "let's see what we can figure out."

He, Janelle, the girls, and Clarence and Liza were gathered with Hector and Yolanda in their Tucson hotel room.

Through the window, the evening sun was an orange ball hanging just above the freeway, which was filled with rush-hour traffic. The setting sun silhouetted palm trees lining the interstate. The tall, spindly trees were imported queen palms. If Era had her way, Chuck imagined, the trees someday would be replaced with fan palms, the only species of palm tree native to the Sonoran Desert.

He squinted at the sun dropping behind the line of trees. Given all that had happened in the last twelve hours, it was nearly impossible to imagine that he'd enjoyed the sunrise on the ridge with Janelle and the girls just this morning, when they'd breathed in the scent of the moist desert.

He broke his gaze from the window and looked around the room from where he leaned against the dresser next to Janelle. "Based on what the boy, Antonio, had to say at the hospital, we're assuming Carlos is alive, but we still have no idea where he is."

"Maybe *you* don't know where he is," said Carmelita, "but I do." She sat at the head of the bed, propped against a pillow, her stockinged feet tucked beneath her. "He's here in the city some-where. He'll get hold of us or his mom and dad soon enough."

"What makes you say that?"

"Where else could he be at this point? We searched for him all day. We'd have found him, or he'd have found us, if he was anywhere in the area."

Liza twisted to look at Carmelita from where she sat on the edge of the bed beside Clarence. "I'm sorry, Carm, but I disagree."

Chuck waited for Carmelita to direct a glare at Liza. Instead, Carmelita nodded, waiting for Liza to continue.

"If it was me," said Liza, turning to the room, "and I'd just seen my brother get killed, I'd be completely freaked out. I mean, Carlos is only seventeen, he's just a kid. This whole thing probably started out as an adventure for him and Francisco. But things went bad fast. First, they were conscripted as mules at the border. Then, in the park, Francisco was murdered right in front of Carlos's eyes. At this point, he's got every right to be curled up in a ball somewhere in the desert, just wishing everything would go away."

"Meaning what?" asked Chuck.

"Meaning we have to keep looking for him. I'm sure he'll pull himself together. He just needs time. I bet he'll come back to the water station tomorrow morning. He'll follow the original plan, just a day late. Once he regains his bearings, that's what he'll stick with." Liza turned again to address Carmelita. "That's what I think, anyway."

Carmelita stuck out her lower lip. "Hmm. I think you could be right."

"I just feel so awful for him," Janelle said. She moaned softly. "For what I did to him, and to Francisco."

"No!" Yolanda said sharply from her seat on the sofa between Hector and Rosie. "You mustn't think that way, *m'hija*. These were big boys. These were young men. They were in danger in Juárez, deadly danger. They were willing to take the risks to come here, and you were willing to take the risks to help them."

"I would've helped, too, if I'd known," said Rosie, looking up from thumbing her phone.

"You can help now," said Chuck. "You can tell us about the men who came after you."

"Okay." She dropped her phone in her lap and launched into a vivid description of the moment she, Janelle, and Chartreuse had come upon the men in their car on Baboquivari Peak's west side—what she referred to as the "first side" of the mountain—after she spotted the gray stones beside the road. She described the driver aiming his gun at them, and, later, the men roaring up behind them on the "second side" of the mountain. She recounted the men pursuing them up the trail, described throwing rocks down at them, and ended with a description of the errant gunshot by the lead man, complete with a tongue-popping sound effect, and the men's retreat back down the trail to their car.

Chuck nodded when she finished. Her description matched what Janelle had said at the camper. "The more I hear about those two guys, the more questions I have about them." He turned to Janelle, beside him. "Why would they have threatened you with their gun right off the bat? Why did they chase you all the way around the mountain? And why would they come up the trail after you? I can't think of a logical reason for any of that."

"Unless they had something to do with Francisco and Carlos," said Clarence.

Chuck inclined his head, glad Clarence had put the idea out to everyone. "Which brings us to the stones—the big square gray ones—by the side of the road." He looked around the room. "We know from Antonio that he, Francisco, and Carlos left something behind that was too heavy to carry. We know they left whatever it was at the big rock mountain."

"I bet it was the square rocks I found," said Rosie. Her phone lit in her lap. She looked at it and held it up to everyone. "Wait for it."

Chuck held his breath. A knock sounded on the hotel room door.

"There she is!" Rosie cried. She leapt up from the sofa and pulled open the door.

A thin woman in her thirties stood in the doorway. The loose blouse and bellbottomed slacks she wore were nearly as colorful as the hiking outfit Era had worn in the park backcountry. The woman's face was tanned and Botox-smooth, and her nose ended in a sculpted point. Her hair was pulled behind her head, stretching the skin of her forehead above her plucked eyebrows.

"Chartreuse!" Rosie cried.

The woman smiled and held out her hand to Rosie, making the stones on her bracelet clack together.

"I invited her," Rosie announced, drawing the woman into the room. "Everyone, this is Chartreuse. Chartreuse, this is everyone."

Chartreuse offered a circling wave of her hand. "Hi, everyone."

"You asked her to come?" Janelle said to Rosie.

"Sure." Rosie lifted her shoulders to her ears. "We're in Tucson. She's in Tucson." She relaxed her shoulders. "We traded numbers, remember? Besides, she's smart. We need to find Carlos, and she can help."

"Uh, welcome, Chartreuse," Janelle said, tugging the unused office chair from beneath the desktop and rolling it across the room. "Have a seat. How are you feeling? You look good."

Chartreuse sat down in the chair, which immediately tilted far backward. She tipped upright, her eyes round with surprise. "That was close." She patted her thighs and said to Janelle, "I'm feeling much better, thank you. They provided exceptional care for me at the institute this afternoon—a guava smoothie and ginger scone followed by a full-body massage."

"Plus yoga," Rosie said. "That's what you texted me."

"Yes, that too," Chartreuse replied. She said to Janelle, "I confess I have not called the authorities yet. I haven't mustered the energy. I gather you haven't yet, either."

Janelle studied her hands. "No, we haven't."

"Your cousin is still missing?"

Janelle nodded, looking up.

"And you think the men might have something to do with him?"

Janelle nodded again.

Chartreuse returned Janelle's nod. "That's what I've gathered from Rosie's texts. That's why I've come, in fact. At her invitation, that is."

"I see you're still wearing your bracelet," Janelle said.

Chartreuse shook the piece of jewelry encircling her wrist. "I promised myself I wouldn't take it off until I was ready to go home." She sighed. "But they tell me I've still got a ways to go, and it's *heavy*."

At her last word, Janelle glanced at Chuck.

"Can I have a look?" he asked Chartreuse.

She held out her arm. He crossed the room and bent, eyeing the bracelet up close. The small stones indeed matched the large ones pictured on Janelle's phone. "May I ask where you got this?" he asked, straightening.

"Chrysalis," Chartreuse said.

"Chrysalis?"

"Of course. It's right on the shore. I live three blocks away. It's the best."

"The best what?"

"Aromatics shop. That's how they started, anyway. Scents, tinctures, suspensions—you name it, they can mix it for you. They added jewelry after a while, but only a carefully curated selection." She proffered her wrist. "Like this. It came with a pamphlet describing how to use it."

"You don't know where it's from, other than the store?"

She flicked her fingers. "Bali, probably, for all I know. Someplace like that, anyway, where they know how to live simply and deliberately, and it's up to the rest of us to stumble along behind and figure out how they do it as best we can."

Rosie, on the couch, put her fist to her stomach and opened her hand, spreading her fingers across her stomach. "Your ka, remember?"

"Right you are." Chartreuse leaned back in the chair, only a few inches this time. She placed her fist on her stomach and spread her fingers, imitating Rosie. "My ka," she purred. "I'm certain that's what saved us from those evil men today. It's what my two weeks at the institute have taught me."

"I'm not so sure about that," Janelle said.

Chartreuse's mouth turned downward.

"But if it did," Janelle hurried on, "I'm all for it."

Chartreuse nodded, her face softening. "Rosie tells me you're still searching."

"'Tells' you?"

"We've been texting." She looked at Rosie. "Haven't we, sister?"

"Yes, we have, sister," Rosie replied. She turned to the room. "Chartreuse has some ideas for us. Good ones."

24

Chuck blinked, looking from Rosie to Chartreuse. "Ideas?"

"My inner being has produced some outward manifestations," Chartreuse said, "and Rosie has welcomed me here to share them with you."

"Your inner what has done what?"

"Let's just say that where I come from, people stab each other in the back all the time, so for me, the idea of someone being strangled isn't all that much of a leap."

Yolanda and Hector's faces grew ashen. They pressed together on the sofa, clinging to each other's hands.

"Sorry," Chartreuse said to them. She turned to Chuck and Janelle. "It's just, I thought, based on what Rosie was texting me, I might be of some assistance."

"In what way," Chuck began, "could you possibly imagine—"

But Janelle squeezed his arm. "Chuck."

He clamped his mouth shut and waved his hand in surrender. "Okay, fine." He eyed Chartreuse. "What have you got for us?"

She sat forward in the chair, making it squeak. "Rosie tells me—texts me—that you're going in circles. It just so happens I know a thing or two about that. And what I know is, when you're going in circles, the answer always, always, always lies at the center of the circle—the 'inner.'"

She paused. Everyone looked at her with blank expressions. She spoke directly to Hector and Yolanda. "My ka understands the pain the two of you are experiencing. This was to be a joyous occasion, the uniting of your family. Instead, you've experienced a terrible tragedy. For that, I am deeply sorry. But I want you to know that from your sorrow can come, ultimately, a sense of realization—if you can find your missing nephew, and those who stole your other nephew's ka."

"His 'ka'?" Yolanda repeated, her voice soft.

"His life force, Grand-*mamá*," Rosie explained.

"But to accomplish those two objectives," Chartreuse said, "you have to enlist all the support and aid you possibly can, in the same way I've come to the institute for its multifaceted approach. The team assigned to me at the institute is working to support and aid me on my journey to becoming my best inner and outer self." She turned to Chuck. "Rosie tells me you have a support team, too."

"I guess you could consider all of us here, together, a team," he said, looking around the room.

"No," Rosie said to him. "Not all of us in here. I told her about your research team."

"That's precisely what I'm referring to," Chartreuse said with an assured nod. "Like me, those of you in this room are not from here. You don't know this place. Consider what happened to me today—I nearly died, simply because I did not know how to interact with the desert. In your case, one among you has had his life force taken from him. But you don't possess the knowledge necessary to solve the unwarranted movement of his ka from one level to the next, or to locate his brother, either."

"'Unwarranted movement'?" Chuck repeated.

Chartreuse continued as if he hadn't spoken. "You must call upon more than just the unknowing circle in this room. You must call upon your larger circle, upon the knowledge of your team. To that end, Rosie has texted me their names."

"I remembered all of them," Rosie said.

Chartreuse drew her phone from the rear pocket of her slacks and tapped its face. She looked at Chuck. "Joel."

"What are you—?" he began.

But Janelle cut him off. "Let her do this, Chuck."

He looked out the window. The sun was below the horizon now, the western sky pink and purple. It would be dark soon. There would be no more searching for Carlos until morning. "Fine," he said, biting off the word and turning to face Chartreuse. "I barely know him. I barely know any of them—just from a couple of video conference calls before I came down here."

"We know more than that," Carmelita said from the head of the bed. "We know Era is crazy. And we know how hard she and the other one, Martina, worked to find the snake."

Chartreuse inclined her head to Carmelita and repeated to Chuck, "Joel."

Chuck grunted. "He's in charge of filling the water stations for the tribe. He knows the lay of the land."

"We saw him," Clarence said from his seat on the edge of the bed next to Liza. "He was driving a white pickup out on the rez when we were out there."

"Which wouldn't necessarily be an unusual thing for him to be doing," Chuck added.

"*Verdad*," Clarence agreed.

Rosie translated for Chartreuse. "That means 'truth.'"

Chartreuse nodded and checked her phone. "Harper."

"The professor," said Chuck, going along. "Tall, skinny, smart. Talks like the academic she is. She's lived in Tucson her whole life."

"Another one who knows the lay of the land, then," Chartreuse noted. She consulted her phone. "Ira."

"Era," Chuck corrected her. "Botanist. Dresses like you."

"She's nuts," Carmelita said. She looked at Chuck. "You and I both think so."

"She's a rock climber," Chuck said.

"Like I said, she's nuts." Carmelita turned to Chartreuse. "Pretty much all rock climbers are. I don't think she'll be of much help."

"Maybe," Chartreuse allowed. She glanced at her phone. "Martina," she said to Chuck.

"The park naturalist. She's Italian American, originally from the Midwest. She was big into researching an old canoe trade route in Voyageurs National Park in Minnesota before she came here." He looked at Carmelita. "She knows her stuff, wouldn't you say?"

Carmelita shrugged. "Maybe. Except for her decision to team up with Era to study the petroglyphs."

Chuck smiled despite himself. "There is that," he admitted.

Chartreuse checked her phone once more. "Vivian."

Janelle chimed in before Chuck could respond. "We saw her before we ran into you at Baboquivari Peak. Vivian's fearless. I like her. I'm sure you would, too. She has a big smile."

Chartreuse placed her phone facedown on her thigh and covered it with her hand. "Those are all the names Rosie gave me."

"There's Ron, the park superintendent," said Clarence. "If Chuck would just level with him, he might be the most help of all."

"And Lance," Carmelita added. "He could be a big help, too." She leaned forward, speaking to Chartreuse between Clarence and Liza. "He's a ranger."

Chartreuse looked at Rosie. "The one you said was hot?"

Rosie nodded emphatically. "Like, scorching."

"That's a lot of people," Liza said.

"Which is the whole idea," said Chartreuse. "That's what I'm attempting to learn while I'm at the institute—to broaden my circle, to learn to trust." She looked past Chuck, focusing on Janelle. "You have to do the same, for your cousin."

Chuck pressed his lips together. Who did this woman think she was, showing up here and telling all of them what to do? She'd been rescued by Janelle and Rosie just a few hours ago at

Baboquivari Peak, helpless and unprepared. Yet here she was, dispensing advice like some sort of guru.

Janelle leaned her shoulder into Chuck, keeping him quiet.

"Thank you, Chartreuse," she said. "This has been very helpful. Clearly, our circle of trust wasn't big enough today. Tomorrow, we'll make it bigger. We'll enlist the members of Chuck's research team, every single one of them." She looked at her mother and father. "We will find Carlos, I promise." She looked around the room. "And we'll do everything we can to find out who killed Francisco, too."

25

Chuck woke before dawn and padded down the narrow passage to the camp trailer's tiny bathroom. He held up his phone on his return, lighting the corridor as he passed by Carmelita and Rosie's curtained bunks on his way back to the small bed he and Janelle shared behind a sliding door at the back of the camper.

They had left the hotel room soon after Chartreuse last evening, picking up takeout pizza and returning to their campsite not long after dark. Chuck had spent the night tossing and turning next to Janelle, who'd been equally restless. He was beyond exhausted by the events of the long day, entirely spent. Even so, he barely slept, waking over and over again to the memory of Francisco's slashed neck and sunken eyes. Rosie's gunshot sound effect—the pop of her tongue off the roof of her mouth—haunted him, too, reminding him of the deadly danger, to use Yolanda's words, Rosie and Janelle had faced on Baboquivari Peak.

At bedtime last night, Carmelita and Rosie had tugged their curtains the length of their bunks, enclosing themselves in their sleeping nooks. But now, in the light of Chuck's phone, Carmelita's curtain hung open a few inches. He stopped and listened for the sound of her breathing, but only Rosie's nasally breaths issued from the lower bunk.

He drew aside the upper curtain and shone his light onto Carmelita's bed.

It was empty. Carmelita was gone.

"I know damn good and well where she is," he growled to Janelle a few minutes later. "And I know who she's with, too."

They stood outside in the predawn darkness. Their quick circuit around the camper had turned up no sign of Carmelita with her phone in hand, texting or talking with one of her friends in Durango.

"She's with Lance," Chuck said. "I'm sure of it."

He raised the flashlight he'd grabbed from the camper, directing its beam across the maintenance yard. The parking area in front of the metal sheds had been deserted the night before. Now, however, the flashlight illuminated a white park-service pickup truck parked in front of the garages.

Chuck cursed. "Did you hear that pull in here?" he asked Janelle.

"No," she replied. "Do you really think she's out there with him?"

"Where else could she possibly be?"

"Surely she'd've told us."

"She's sixteen and figures she's all grown up. Besides..." Chuck stopped.

"Besides, what?"

He kicked at the ground with his foot. "I wasn't exactly on my best behavior with her yesterday. She disappeared at one point, searching the perimeter with Lance. I jumped her case pretty hard about it when she got back."

"In front of Lance?"

"Yes."

"You shouldn't have done that, Chuck."

"You're saying it's my fault she's gone?"

"I'm not saying it's anyone's fault. But I'm not ready to say she's done anything wrong yet, either."

Janelle tapped at her phone, composing a text, and pressed send.

"You think she'll text you back?" Chuck asked.

"She will if she knows what's good for her."

"When you were sixteen, would you have texted your parents back?"

She did not reply, staring at her glowing phone instead. The screen did not light up with a response. She exhaled through her nose and said, "We have to go after her."

"I'll do it," Chuck muttered. "You'll need to stay here with Rosie. One of us has to be in cell range. Just keep on texting her. She'll reply at some point. When she does, let me know."

"Where are you going to look?"

"The arroyo. The petroglyph rocks. Where else?"

"You should check the sun dagger, too. Lance sent Era out there in his place, and I'm sure he would love to see it for himself. Maybe he talked Carmelita into showing it to him."

Chuck nodded, his neck stiff. "I'll check there first, on the way to the rocks."

"Don't be too hard on her."

"I can't believe you're saying that."

"She thinks she's helping."

"Sure, but—"

"Go," Janelle broke in. "Find her, Chuck. Make sure she's okay."

From the top of the ridge, he left the trail and angled down the slope toward the dihedral, the light of his headlamp glancing off the outstretched arms of chollas and ocotillos. He reached the break in the cliff without hooking his skin with any thorns and aimed his headlamp down into the dihedral. The cleft was deserted, the etched spiral bright in the beam of his headlamp against the dark face of the rock.

"Carmelita?" he called, loud enough to carry into the cavern. "Lance?"

He waited through a count of five and again called their names. Nothing.

He climbed back up the slope and hurried along the trail, the light of his headlamp bouncing along the path's uneven surface in front of him. He climbed to the high point on the ridge and took out his phone. Its screen was blank. No texts from Janelle or Carmelita.

He returned his phone to his pocket and switched off his headlamp, the growing morning light now adequate for him to make his way without it. He hurried down the switchbacking trail to the foot of the ridge and halted, listening, behind the head-high prickly pear cactus that shielded the end of the trail from the wash.

He peered through the disk-shaped prickly pear leaves, searching for signs of movement. Again, as at the sun dagger site, nothing.

He eased into the open. The petroglyph rocks, big and blocky, stood like oversized offensive linemen on the far side of the drainage, opposite the water station.

He strode past the blue water barrel to the center of the channel, his boots crunching in the gravel. In the dusky light of early morning, the imprints of the helicopter's parallel skids were just visible in the loose rocks, nearly obliterated by the footprints of the many people who'd visited the site yesterday.

He turned a slow circle, scanning the vegetation lining the channel. Still no movement.

He walked to Rock 1 and eyed the snake curving down the line of petroglyph rocks, discernible even in the dim light. Yesterday, Lance had taken Carmelita upstream from the rocks to search. Assuming the ranger had convinced her to return with him to the arroyo before dawn this morning to continue searching before the others arrived, it made sense that he would head downstream with her next.

Chuck walked down the line of stones to Rock 8 and squinted in the gray light at the triangular head of the snake, formed by dozens of elaborate petroglyphs, tongue curling from its snout.

A tremendous amount of work had gone into creating the snake—placing the large stones in line along the edge of the drainage and carving the hundreds of petroglyphs to hide the reptile in plain sight. Why?

There had to be some explanation.

Chuck faced the direction indicated by the snake's pointing tongue. With a start, he realized that he was looking across the wash straight toward the sun dagger and cavern on the west side of the ridge. Cactuses and shrubs formed a seamless wall on the far side of the drainage, save for a single narrow slit between two bushes at the edge of the channel. The tongue of the snake pointed directly at the black slit, which was clearly visible to him only now, in the half-light of dawn, before the bright light of day rendered it virtually undetectable.

He crossed the wash and knelt to examine the slit, which turned out to be an incision between a pair of thornless creosote bushes. The opening, which led into the wall of foliage, was a few inches wide and extended two feet up from the ground. He crawled forward, pressing the branches back with his shoulders. Upon passing through the slit, he entered a tunnel-like passage hacked through the thick vegetation away from the wash.

Climbing to his feet, he found he could stand fully erect in the shoulder-wide corridor, which was lined on both sides and above by the shorn ends of cactus and shrub branches clipped by whoever had created the passage.

He squatted and looked back through the slit. The eight petroglyph rocks were framed by the narrow opening, perfectly aligned, the tongue of the rattlesnake pointing at him.

He turned his back to the opening. The tunnel extended in a straight line away from him as far as he could see, its floor, cleared of roots and rocks, as smooth as a sidewalk.

Rising, he ventured down the passageway. A hundred feet from the drainage, a shadowy block rested on the level floor of the corridor.

26

Chuck hurried to the block sitting in the middle of the tunnel. It was a square gray stone, its edges rounded, about ten inches in length, width, and height. Its size and monochromatic gray color were identical to the stones pictured on Janelle's phone and lying beside the dirt road near Baboquivari Peak.

He rose and proceeded down the passage, moving quickly in the wan light filtering through the overhead branches. A second square stone sat in the middle of the path a hundred feet from the first. The second stone was the same shape, size, and color as the initial stone. He stepped over it and hurried on. A third matching stone rested in the passage a hundred feet beyond the second stone.

The vegetation on either side of the passage and over Chuck's head thinned as the distance from the drainage increased, making the passageway feel more like a hallway and less like a tunnel. Still, the corridor through the cactuses and shrubs remained distinct as it followed the base of the ridge, its trajectory directly away from the pointing tongue of the snake and the line of petroglyph rocks.

He came upon additional square stones resting in the middle of the path every hundred feet as he sped along the passage. By the time he passed the tenth stone and spotted the eleventh another hundred feet ahead, he knew he would reach the corridor's end, and whatever awaited him there, at the twentieth stone in the path.

Twenty. That was the key—save for the confounding fact that the stone-marked passage was *not* a thousand years old. Rather, the passageway was a recent creation, as proven by the freshly cut branches lining it, and by the placement of the stones on the newly smoothed floor.

He came up short.

The stones.

The square gray stones pictured on Janelle's phone had looked vaguely familiar to him. Now, he remembered why.

Chuck had earned his anthropology degree over seven long years as a working student taking classes part-time at Fort Lewis College in Durango. One of his classes had focused on the ancient peoples of Mesoamerica—the Olmec, Aztec, Toltec, and, of course, the Mayan people.

All the ancient Mesoamerican cultures had been highly religious, given to elaborate rituals and obeisance to myriad gods. Mayan religious practices, in particular, had revolved around sacrifice, sometimes of animals, but primarily of humans. The ritualized Mayan form of human sacrifice had focused on heart extraction performed in elaborate temples. As Chuck had noted to Janelle and the girls, entry to those temples was gained from stone-paved walkways up stairways consisting of exactly twenty steps.

What Chuck hadn't recalled until now was that the Mayans had constructed their temples using stones quarried from the substratum of distinctively smooth-grained limestone, monochromatic gray in color, underlying much of the Yucatán Peninsula homeland of the Mayan people. Mayan records noted that sacrifices were performed only in temples constructed of squared Yucatán limestone blocks, on altars made of the same locally quarried blocks, and only after sacrifice victims were paraded to the temples along pathways paved with the same local stone.

Chuck hurried to the eleventh square block resting in the middle of the passage and crouched over it, studying it closely. The block was smooth-grained and monochromatic gray—the type of limestone found exclusively on the Yucatán Peninsula.

Rising, he peered up through the cactuses and shrubs at the cliff band running parallel to the corridor along the west face of the ridge. Several hundred feet ahead, the dihedral showed as a dark slash in the cliff face.

Chuck's breath caught in his throat. His instincts told him the passage leading from the petroglyph rocks along the base of the ridge should be ancient. But someone had cut the corridor through the vegetation only recently.

And what of the femur at the back of the cleft in the cliff above?

The human leg bone should be ancient as well. But, as he'd told Carmelita, here in the dry Sonoran Desert, there was no way of knowing the age of the femur without carbon dating it.

He stared down the corridor.

Someone had hewn the passage toward the sun dagger and stack of bones, and that same someone, presumably, had lined the corridor with limestone blocks from the Yucatán Peninsula.

Lance?

Chuck broke into a run.

The corridor grew brighter as he raced down it, the thinning foliage allowing more light to reach the passageway. He leapt over stone after stone in the path, keeping count as he ran. He reached the eighteenth stone, still running, and looked up to see the dark cut in the cliff band two hundred feet ahead.

The path through the foliage revealed no footprints. Had Lance convinced Carmelita to accompany him this way? If she had grown suspicious, had he forced her at gunpoint to do as he demanded?

Chuck's heart thumped in his chest. The desert was quiet save for his heavy breaths and the pounding of his boots on the corridor floor. He came to the nineteenth stone and slowed his pace, peering ahead.

The passage continued for another hundred feet to the twentieth stone. The final stone was directly below the dihedral, which was hidden from above by the arching branches of a palo verde tree. Beyond the final stone was what he'd both expected and feared: a stack of the same square gray limestone blocks as those set in the passage and left near Baboquivari Peak. The stones at the end of the passage were stacked side by side and on top of one another, forming an altar.

The end of the passage was deserted. Carmelita and Lance were not in sight.

Chuck approached the altar slowly, breathing hard. A stain spread thickly across the stack of stones. The stain was dark, nearly black, the color of dried blood. His breath left him in a rush.

He stopped before the altar. Two lines of four stones each made up its base, and four more stones were lined on top, for a total of twelve. Though the dried bloodstain indicated the make-shift altar had been put to use sometime prior to this morning, the altar was eight stones shy of the required twenty to make it an officially sanctioned Mayan ritual site.

The faint buzzing of flies reached him, coming from beyond the altar. He stepped past the stacked blocks, pushed aside a low-hanging palo verde branch, and came upon a pile of bones lying on the ground at the foot of a cholla cactus. The bones were obviously human—curved ribs, flanged pelvis, long spine, and only one femur. Resting in the sand beside the mound of bones, its empty eye sockets staring up at Chuck, was a skull.

Flies were busy stripping the last bits of muscle and fiber from the bones, which were the same ageless beige color as the fully stripped and butchered femur in the recess at the base of the cliff above.

Chuck stared at the pile of bones, his blood running cold. Where was Carmelita? Where had Lance taken her?

He envisioned the ancient trade route leading south from the Sonoran Desert to the Yucatán Peninsula—the same route trodden northward today by desperate migrants from Central

America. The route passed Baboquivari Peak, the sacred mountain of the Tohono O'odham people, and turned east to the water station in Saguaro National Park.

But it did not end there.

From the water station, the route continued up the arroyo and on to Tucson—the direction Lance had taken Carmelita yesterday morning during his purported search for the murder weapon. Had the ranger taken Carmelita upstream with him yesterday in order to assure she would be comfortable returning up the wash with him in the predawn darkness today?

Chuck spun away from the human remains and sprinted back past the altar and along the corridor, leaping over the stone blocks in the passageway one after another. The foliage thickened as he neared the end of the passage. He slowed at the last stone in the path and crept forward to the slit in the creosote bushes at the edge of the wash.

No movement showed in the channel beyond the narrow opening. He crawled through the slit, scrambled to his feet, and sprinted past the petroglyph rocks and water station and on around the curving bend in the drainage, racing upstream.

27

Janelle sat at the small dinette table in the front of the camper, gripping her phone with both hands and willing a text from Carmelita to appear on its screen. She'd texted Carmelita every five minutes since Chuck's departure half an hour ago, imploring her to respond, so far to no avail.

Unable to wait any longer, Janelle rose from the table and shook Rosie awake. The two of them pulled on hiking clothes, loaded their daypacks with water and snacks, and set out up the ridge, lighting the trail ahead with their headlamps.

"I'm sooo tired," Rosie grumbled, stumbling over rocks in the path in the predawn darkness.

"You and me both," Janelle agreed.

"Then why are we doing this?"

"We're making sure Carm's okay."

"That's what phones are for."

"She's not texting me back."

"That's her problem."

"It's a problem for all of us, unfortunately."

"I hate her."

"No, you don't."

"I'm just so tired!"

They reached the top of the ridge and turned off their headlamps as the night gave way to day. Beneath the brightening dawn sky, the lights of Tucson twinkled in the broad bowl at the foot of the Santa Catalina Mountains.

"*Caramba*," Rosie said softly, looking out over the city.

"Makes the hike up here worth it, don't you think?" Janelle asked.

Rosie shook her head, her hair bouncing around the nape of her neck. "Nope."

A vehicle appeared on the road leading to the maintenance yard from Tucson, its headlights cutting through the last of the night's shadows. The vehicle pulled into the yard and stopped next to the park-service pickup truck. The car was big and black. Two people, too distant to identify, climbed out of it.

Rosie put her hand to her mouth. "Do you think that's them?" she asked, a tremor in her voice.

"Yes, I do," said Janelle, fighting to keep her voice from shaking as well.

The two people from the black car set out on foot across the gravel yard. One turned toward the camper, the other headed for the trail up the ridge.

"Let's get a move on," Janelle said, her heart racing.

Rosie took off along the ridgetop, moving quickly now. Janelle drew deep breaths as she followed. Why were the men here? Who had sent them?

She checked her phone. Its screen remained blank.

She paused where, yesterday, Chuck had pointed down the slope at the break in the cliff marking the hiding place of the sun dagger and cavern. She saw no sign that Chuck, Carmelita, or Lance were below. She jogged along the trail, catching up with Rosie. They reached the rocky outcrop at the north end of the ridge just as the sun rose, painting the desert with golden light.

Rosie pointed at Baboquivari Peak on the western horizon, its summit lit by the rising sun. "There's our mountain. We creamed those guys, didn't we?"

"We scared them away—but not for long, unfortunately." Janelle looked back at the winding trail. It was deserted. The man who'd followed them out of the maintenance yard had yet to reach the top of the ridge. Turning, she peered from the outcrop into the drainage. The gray gravel channel, still deep in shadow at the bottom of the ridge, was devoid of movement.

She checked her phone. *Nada*.

Should she and Rosie hide behind the outcrop and remain in cell service range? Or should they descend into the arroyo ahead of the man?

Janelle shoved her phone into her pocket. Carmelita and Chuck were somewhere below. Carlos, too, perhaps. There were plenty of places for Rosie and her to hide from the man down there if necessary.

"Ready?" Rosie asked, pointing into the arroyo.

Janelle squared her shoulders. "*Absolutamente*."

Rosie clambered off the outcrop and strode down the trail, descending into the arroyo. Janelle followed, leaving the sunlight and dropping into shadow. At the bottom of the ridge, they stepped from behind the prickly pear cactus onto the gravel wash.

Rosie spun in a circle. "Nobody's here, *Mamá*."

Nothing moved in the arroyo. The water barrel sat next to the dry channel, the flag hanging limp from the pole above it. On the far side of the wash, yellow crime-scene tape ran from the centermost petroglyph rocks back beneath the palo verde trees, outlining the site of Francisco's murder.

Rosie looked up at the ridge. "That guy is coming."

Janelle drew her lower lip between her teeth. She and Rosie needed a weapon, something, anything, to protect themselves from the approaching man. Yesterday, the fallen stones on the ledge high on Baboquivari Peak had served that purpose. What about today? The plastic tape marking the murder scene hung limply from the petroglyph rocks and ran back beneath the trees.

"Come with me," she told Rosie, leading her across the channel.

Janelle pulled the tape free of the rocks, gathering several feet of it in quick loops. She grasped the loops in her hands and pulled them tight. The combined portions of tape held firm, together forming a strong length of plastic rope.

"Get all of it," she directed Rosie. "Hurry."

They hustled around the perimeter of the murder site in opposite directions, gathering the tape as they went, and met back up with loops of tape dangling from their arms.

Janelle pointed back across the drainage. "There."

She hurried to the prickly pear cactus at the end of the trail off the ridge. Dropping her armload of plastic tape in the middle of the path, she knelt and grasped the thornless base of the cactus where it emerged from the ground. The bottom of the cactus, six inches around, was as stout and unyielding as the trunk of a tree.

Working quickly, she wrapped several lengths of tape around the cactus trunk, drew the tape portions together, and strung them across the trail and into the shrubs on the other side of the path. She beckoned Rosie to kneel with her. Together, they covered the tape with handfuls of loose sand from the trail and smoothed the sand over the combined lengths of plastic with their palms.

Janelle sat back, assessing their work. In the early morning shadows, the buried tape was invisible.

She and Rosie ducked into the scrub lining the trail across from the prickly pear cactus. Working as a team, they strung Rosie's part of the crime-scene tape back and forth several times and knotted the ends, creating a ten-foot length of corded plastic rope.

The sound of a shoe striking a loose rock and sending it tumbling along the trail came from the slope above. Janelle put a finger to her lips and handed Rosie the length of plastic rope. Kneeling in the brush next to the trail, Janelle grasped the buried lengths of tape where they emerged from the sand opposite the cactus.

The approaching man breathed heavily as he descended the last stretch of the trail.

Janelle twisted the lengths of tape in her hands. She and Rosie were well hidden in the brush. They could allow the man to pass, then hike back up the trail and out of the arroyo without having been seen. But that would leave the man free to do whatever he'd come here for, with Chuck and Carmelita unaware of his arrival.

Janelle tightened her grip on the lengths of tape, the plastic edges digging into her palms. The man was one of the two men who had chased Rosie and her up the mountain yesterday. They had shot at them, trying to kill them.

She clenched her jaw. She would not let the man pass.

The man drew within thirty feet of the end of the trail, the tread of his feet carrying through the cool morning air.

"We've got him," Rosie whispered softly in Janelle's ear.

Twenty feet.

Janelle caught sight of the man through the branches. He was short and slight and wore the same dark clothes as yesterday—definitely one of the men who had pursued them. The man's hands swung free at his sides; he did not hold a gun this morning. But he had been armed yesterday. He likely was armed today as well.

Fury blazed inside Janelle. Yesterday, she'd had no choice but to flee with Rosie from the two men. But this morning, she had the upper hand.

The man drew even with the prickly pear cactus, striding down the path, his head up and his eyes forward, looking out at the channel.

Janelle yanked the gathered lengths of tape from their shallow burial place across the trail. The fabricated rope snapped out of the loose sand. She leaned back, pulling the rope taut across the path from the trunk of the cactus, directly in front of the man's shins.

The trip line hooked both of the man's feet. He toppled

forward, arms flailing, and struck the ground on his stomach with a resounding "oof."

Janelle lifted the tape, raising the man's feet into the air, and launched out of the brush. The man shoved his hands beneath his stomach. Rosie crawled from the bushes, dropped the length of corded plastic rope, and pressed the man's head into the ground, while Janelle used her bandaging skills, which she'd honed as a paramedic, to ensnare his legs, winding the lengths of tape around his ankles once, twice, a third time, and drawing the loops tight.

"Hold this," Janelle said, extending the end of the looped portions of tape to Rosie. "Keep it tight."

Rosie tugged hard on the gathered loops of tape, cinching the man's ankles against the trunk of the cactus.

The man kicked his secured legs ineffectually, still scrabbling with his hands beneath his stomach, his face turned to one side. Janelle pulled one of the man's arms free from beneath him and twisted it behind his back, shoving his wrist upward between his shoulder blades.

"Ayyy!" the man cried, his face contorted. Still, he worked his other hand beneath his torso.

Janelle yanked the man's other arm from beneath him. His hand appeared, clutching a handgun. She shoved the man's trapped arm higher on his back, his shoulder and elbow bending horrifically.

He screeched and released the gun, which fell to the ground.

Janelle drew the man's hands together behind his back and used the length of corded tape to tie his wrists and secure them to his ankles, leaving him lying on the path snugged to the prickly pear cactus.

She grabbed the pistol from the sand and knelt next to the bound man, her heart pounding. The man twisted his head to her and cursed her in Spanish.

She lowered the gun, taking deep draughts of air, not yet trusting her legs to support her if she climbed to her feet.

From upstream came a gunshot, the loud blast echoing down the arroyo.

28

Chuck charged full-tilt up the gravel channel.

Yesterday, during his brief search while Janelle and the girls had tended to Antonio, he'd ventured up the arroyo to where the drainage narrowed at its head, ending in a tight V of cactuses and shrubbery at the foot of the low hill that abutted the north end of the ridge. He had turned back from that point to meet Ron and the research team upon their arrival at the end of the trail.

Now, he slid to a stop before the wall of vegetation. No human-incised slit showed in the cactuses and shrubs, but when he crouched close to the ground, he spotted a low break in the shrubbery at the point of the V marking the head of the channel. The thorny branches of a cholla cactus grew low over the opening. Clinging to the branches were threads torn from the clothing of those who had ducked through the break in the brush.

Chuck crawled through the opening, ignoring thorns fallen on the ground that punctured the skin of his hands and poked into his knees. He rose on the other side. A faint path angled away from him up the hillside, past the trunk of a towering saguaro. He hurried around the saguaro and came to an abrupt halt.

Lance was sprawled on the ground on the far side of the cactus.

The ranger lay on his back, unmoving, face to the sky. His hands gripped his neck, which was slashed open beneath his jawline. Blood, fresh and bright red, pooled in the sand under the gaping wound.

Chuck covered his mouth with his hand, gagging.

Lance's eyes were open and unblinking, his mouth agape. His broad chest was collapsed and still beneath his Kevlar vest. He was dead.

The ranger's gun holster was empty, his large silver pistol missing.

Chuck swung his head, searching wildly, not daring to call out Carmelita's name.

The path climbed the low hill that separated the national park from the outskirts of Tucson. The slope of the hill rose gradually from the head of the drainage. They—whoever "they" were—must have taken Carmelita up the trail in that direction.

Chuck leapt over Lance's body and raced up the dim trail. Above him, cactuses and shrubs lined the rounded top of the hill, aglow in the first rays of the morning sun. He searched for signs of movement on the path ahead but saw none.

He neared the hilltop and stooped to remain in the shade, scurrying upward, the rays of the sun lancing past his ducked head. He stopped and froze in place when the sound of heavy breathing reached him from the other side of the hill.

If he continued to the top of the rise, the sun would strike him full on, blinding him and, at the same time, revealing his presence to whoever was on the other side.

He scrambled sideways along the slope for a hundred feet, crept to the top of the rounded hill, and peered back the way he'd come. The east side of the hill, drenched in morning sunlight, angled gently down to the city. The slope was sparsely covered with creosote bushes and a smattering of saguaro, prickly pear, and barrel cactuses.

Through breaks in the vegetation, Chuck spotted three figures climbing the hill's east side, toward the petroglyph rocks—and the sacrifice altar. He made out Carmelita's slender frame, a second person wearing hiking clothes, and, slumped and taking stumbling steps between those two, someone wearing jeans and a sky-blue T-shirt.

Three people, not just Lance's killer and Carmelita.

It appeared that Carmelita was helping the person in the middle from one side, while the person in hiking garb was aiding the middle person on the other side. At the same time, Chuck presumed, the person in hiking clothes was guarding Carmelita with Lance's gun.

Chuck hurried over the rise, descended until he was below the threesome, and sprinted back across the slope.

The killer had to be someone Lance had known and trusted, someone the ranger had willingly allowed to accompany him in his truck in the predawn hours. Further, the killer had to be someone Carmelita knew as well. Even with assurances from Lance, Carmelita would not have set off into the night with someone she did not know. That left only those she had met since her arrival in Arizona.

Chuck came to the faint migrant path and turned and raced up it, heading away from Tucson, the sun now at his back. The path to the top of the rise was empty. Carmelita and the other two people were now on the hill's west side.

He ducked as he neared the crest of the hill. The sounds of breathing came from over the rise. A dark, disc-shaped shadow, as big around as his fist, moved on the ground next to the path. He stooped, staring: a tarantula, parallel to the trail, heading for the top of the hill. The male spider was out in the open in the early morning on its straight-arrow autumnal march in search of a mate.

Chuck plucked the big, hairy spider from the ground and, cupping it in one hand, sprinted over the top of the hill. Rays of sun shone past him, lighting Carmelita, in a fleece top and running tights, the stumbling person, and the person in hiking clothes descending the slope together.

The three were forty feet down the slope from Chuck, their backs to him, nearing the shadow line. The killer's fingers were hooked through a pair of steel rings attached to a length of wire encircling the stumbling person's neck. Sunlight winked off Lance's silver handgun, which was tucked in the killer's waistband.

Chuck squinted at the killer, suddenly understanding why the gray blocks had been used to line the passage and build the altar, and recognizing that the ancient, north-south trade route, which long ago had connected the Mayan and Hohokam peoples, had been subverted now, a thousand years later, by a wellspring of all-consuming hatred that had resulted in the murders of Francisco yesterday and Lance today—and now threatened Carmelita's life as well.

Chuck drew a full breath. "*¡Corre!*" he cried out.

29

Chuck's use of Spanish had the effect he hoped for. Carmelita reacted instantly to his cry, releasing the stumbling person and darting off the trail and into the brush before the killer could react.

"Martina!" Chuck yelled next.

The park naturalist yanked the pistol from her waistband and aimed it sideways, in the direction of Carmelita's disappearance into the vegetation.

"Behind you!" Chuck cried.

Martina pivoted and aimed the gun up the slope at him. Blood splattered the front of her shirt in a bright red arc. She tugged on the steel rings with her left hand, turning her captive to face Chuck along with her.

Chuck pressed his hand, holding the tarantula, against his leg. The captive's face was pallid and drawn. Chuck had stared at it yesterday morning behind the petroglyph rocks. The face was that of Francisco, but clean-shaven. It was Francisco's identical twin, Carlos, who looked at Chuck from Martina's side with vacant eyes. Carlos's cheeks were sunken, his wrists secured in front of his body with a plastic zip tie.

Keeping Lance's gun trained on Chuck, Martina snugged the length of wire beneath Carlos's jaw, drawing him close to her side.

"It's over," Chuck said, raising his free hand to her. "Please, Martina. Don't."

He took a step down the hill.

"I'll do it," Martina vowed, cinching the wire tighter around Carlos's neck. At the bite of the wire into his skin, Carlos tipped his head back. Martina squinted up the slope at Chuck, the sun full in her eyes. "I swear to God, I'll do it right here."

Chuck took another step toward her, his free hand still raised. In his other hand, the tarantula pressed its legs against his closed palm, the hairs on its back brushing against his fingers. He spoke, seeking to connect with Martina and establish a line of communication with her. "How about if we talk about the sense of Mayan history we share?"

"We?"

"Yes, of course, *we*." Chuck lowered his hand and took a third step, followed by a fourth, continuing his advance. The tarantula pressed harder against his encircling hand. How long, entrapped as it was, before it would lose its sense of direction? "You and I both know how easy it is for societies to fail, how quickly progress can be replaced by dysfunction, leading to decay and collapse."

Martina eased up on the loop beneath Carlos's jaw. A trickle of blood escaped from under the wire and ran down his neck, painting a thin red stripe past his Adam's apple. Martina turned the barrel of the gun away from Chuck. Looking at Carlos, she pressed the muzzle to the trickling blood, smudging it across Carlos's skin.

While Martina's eyes were on Carlos, Chuck stepped sideways, directing his shadow, cast by the sun behind him, straight at Martina—and aligning it with the straight-arrow trajectory the tarantula had been following before he'd picked it up on the east side of the hill. He opened his hand, dropping the tarantula to the ground beside him.

"I saw it first in Minnesota," Martina snarled, turning back to Chuck and aiming the gun at him once more. "I saw it so much more clearly when I came here."

"The Mayans."

"You *do* get it," she said.

He held her gaze while, at the bottom of his vision, the

tarantula crawled ahead of him, hidden by the dark shadow of his body, following the trail in the same direction it had been headed on the other side of the rise, straight for Martina. "How much of this is about you, and how much is it about the Tohono O'odham?"

His question struck a chord—Martina's mouth curled in obvious repugnance.

"The Tohono O'odham don't understand," she growled. "They think they're helping by maintaining the water stations. But they're only making things worse. My grandparents came here the right way, the legal way." Her eyes slid sideways to Carlos and her voice filled with disgust. "But not these people. They just keep coming and coming. They're drowning us. They're destroying everything my family has worked so hard for."

"But it was you who proposed the idea of placing the water station in the park."

"Bees to honey," she said, Lance's pistol still aimed at Chuck. "No one else was making them pay. It was up to me."

"You decided you had to act," Chuck said, his tone nonjudgmental, keeping her talking.

In his peripheral vision, he tracked the tarantula's advance down the trail, careful to keep his shadow over it.

"I had no choice," Martina said.

"You decided to kill."

"No!" she declared, shaking her head hard and fast. "*Sacrifice*. You're the one who said it. The Mayans. The snake showed me the way."

"Sassy."

"I saw where her tongue was pointing. That was when I knew."

"You found the sun dagger."

She nodded. "I've only done what she called me to do, nothing more."

"You found the bones and the sloth, too, didn't you?"

Again Martina nodded.

Chuck took another step. He was fifteen feet from Martina now, the spider on the move ahead of him, nearing Martina. "You cut the tunnel through the brush."

"All the way to the foot of the cave," she confirmed. Her fingers, twisted through the steel circles at the ends of the wire, trembled. "Shasta sloths went extinct when too many humans came to the desert. We'll go extinct, too, if we let the illegals overrun us."

"*Illegals*?" Chuck snapped, his true feelings apparent in his voice for the first time.

Martina's face darkened. She raised the gun to Chuck's face, her finger tightening on the trigger.

"Why the Mayans?" Chuck asked quickly.

"That should be obvious." She glanced at Carlos, her trigger finger relaxing. "These...these *people* are flooding here from Guatemala, Honduras, El Salvador."

"Where the Mayans thrived."

"*No.* Where the Mayans *failed.*"

"The stones," Chuck said, taking another step. "They're from the Yucatán, aren't they?"

"From Tikal," Martina confirmed. "The center of Mayan trade."

"But why?"

She forced Carlos's chin upward with her left hand. "These *moochers,*" she snarled, her face hard. "I won't allow them to bring their failures to America. They don't deserve to live here, and they don't deserve to die on our land either."

"So you brought their land here to them instead?"

She dipped her chin, the low sun penetrating her beady eyes. "I had the stones quarried and shipped to the border. From there, I paid coyotes to have mules carry them to the park for me."

Chuck blinked. The level of evil required for Martina to do what she'd done was beyond imagining. "The altar isn't finished. It only has twelve stones. But there's blood on it already."

"I had to get started. The calendars."

"The Mayan calendars?"

She nodded firmly. "Both of them, the Tzolkin and the Haab, point to this month of this year as the most auspicious cycle in centuries. I'm sure you know about the observances taking place all around the world right now—the parade in Amsterdam, the drum ceremony in Kyoto, the mass puja in Rajasthan."

Chuck struggled to pull together the disparate pieces in his mind. "You…you…"

"*Sacrifice*," she said bluntly. "Two human offerings are required at the altar before the end of the cycle. A few weeks ago, one of the mules collapsed out in the desert before he reached the water station—a gift from the gods that I accepted as such. It took me all night, but I got him to the altar while he was still alive. I placed his femur on the shrine, preventing him from walking in the afterlife." Her eyes went to Carlos, beside her. "But this one and the others left the stones behind. When they admitted what they'd done, I did what I had to do in response."

The tarantula was within a yard of Martina, headed for her left foot.

"You killed Francisco," Chuck said.

"I had to, which meant I couldn't sacrifice him at my altar."

"You tried to kill the boy, Antonio, too."

"That was Javier. I told him not to use his gun. Too noisy. He used a rock instead." Martina pulled on the wire, eliciting a yelp from Carlos. "This one ran off, trying to make it to the city. Mendes chased him down and secured him. It was too late by then to do anything more. We had to hike back so I could meet the research team. I sent Javier and Mendes south to look for the stones."

"But they didn't find them," Chuck said, picturing the eight blocks lying untouched beneath the trees near Baboquivari Peak.

"They found your wife instead. They followed her."

Chuck bristled. "They shot at her, and at my daughter, too."

"They'd have done much more than that if I'd been in contact with them."

"But you weren't. So you went after Carmelita instead."

"That was all on Lance." She glanced at Carlos. "I knew I would need help getting this one to the altar alive this morning. I had to move fast to stay ahead of everyone. I told Lance I knew of a break in the case and asked if he wanted to see what I'd found. That was all it took. He was so eager to one-up Ron. I knew I could grab his gun and make him do what I needed. I'd planned to hike here from the edge of the city like I did yesterday with Javier and Mendes. But when Lance picked me up, he told me he'd invited your daughter to join us. I had to play along."

"But you *didn't* play along. You killed him."

"He kept asking questions. Finally, he figured it out. I heard it in his voice." Her eyes glinted in the sunlight. "He never saw the wire. He went down so easy, like cutting down a tree. When I had his gun in my hand, your daughter did as she was told."

Chuck took another step. "You know you won't get away with this."

"This isn't about getting away with anything. It's about making a statement." Martina looked sidelong at Carlos. "He has to die today, this morning, as required by the Tzolkin and the Haab." She motioned for Chuck to approach her with the barrel of Lance's gun. "You have a choice. You can help me get him to the altar, or you can die right here." She re-centered the gun on Chuck's chest.

He took another step down the hill, drawing within ten feet of Martina. In the middle of the trail, the tarantula reached her foot. It probed the suede leather of her hiking boot with its pedipalps, climbed onto her toe and up the laces of her shoe, and disappeared beneath her pant leg.

Chuck held Martina's gaze. A second passed. Another.

She jerked, her eyes darting to her lower leg.

The instant she looked down, he ran at her.

She lifted her foot and shook it, one hand holding Lance's gun, the other clinging to the wire around Carlos's neck. She tottered on one leg, her hands flailing, the sun full in her eyes.

The gun discharged, the blast of the shot loud in Chuck's ears. The bullet whipped past his head as he crashed into Martina and Carlos, taking both of them down in a heap.

The gun tumbled from Martina's right hand, but the fingers of her left hand remained curled through the steel rings attached to the wire. Chuck shoved his hand upward, cramming his fingers between the wire and Carlos's neck just as Martina yanked hard on the steel circles.

The tightening wire sliced into Chuck's skin. Blood spurted from his fingers and pain seared through his brain. He rolled atop Martina, pressing her to the ground, and shoved his forearm against her neck. With his free hand, he grasped the fingers of her left hand and bent them backward until they made popping noises.

Martina screamed and released the steel rings. The wire slipped through the slashed skin of Chuck's fingers. Carlos rolled away, coughing and grasping his neck with his zip-tied hands. Martina kicked and twisted beneath Chuck, pummeling him with her fists.

"Stop!" Carmelita cried out. She stood over Martina, holding Lance's gun in both hands, the barrel aimed at Martina's face.

Martina grew still. She looked up at Carmelita, her breaths coming in harsh gasps. "Do it," she begged. "Please. Do it."

For a moment, Chuck thought Carmelita would shoot the gun. But her hands began to shake and she removed her finger from the trigger.

Chuck rolled Martina to her stomach. Rising, he pressed his foot squarely on her back, shoving her facedown into the earth. He made a fist with his bleeding fingers and held his hand tight against his chest, pain veiling his eyes.

Carlos sat up, the wire hanging loose around his neck. Tears streamed down his cheeks as he looked up at Chuck and Carmelita. "*Gracias,*" he said. "Thank you, thank you."

Carmelita laid Lance's pistol on the ground and stepped away from it.

"Carm!" Janelle cried. She and Rosie charged up the trail from the drainage.

Janelle took Carmelita in her arms and looked past her at the blood dripping from Chuck's clasped fingers.

Carmelita stepped out of Janelle's embrace, removed the length of rescue cord from Chuck's daypack, and bound Martina's wrists and ankles with loop after loop.

Janelle took Chuck's injured hand in hers and assessed his wounds. "This won't take long," she said. She set to work, stanching the bleeding with dressings from her medical kit.

Rosie approached Carmelita. "We saw Lance back there," she said. Tears brimmed in her eyes. "I'm so, so sorry, Carm."

Carmelita collapsed, sobbing, in her sister's arms.

The tarantula dropped to the ground from Martina's pant leg and set out once more, resuming its straight-line journey across the desert.

EPILOGUE

Chuck relaxed in a chair on the patio of Tucson's venerable Saguaro Corners Restaurant, his bandaged hand resting on his stomach. He leaned his head back on the chair's frame and took a deep breath.

Ahhh.

The piney scent of desert moistness filled his nostrils, as it had after the brief rainstorm three days ago. Tonight, however, the pleasing scent came from the irrigated creosote bushes surrounding the historic eatery, which overlooked the Rincon Mountain District of Saguaro National Park on the east side of Tucson. Towering overhead at the edge of the terrace, the restaurant's famous neon saguaro cactus glowed lime green against the purple dusk sky.

The evening air was calm and cool, the patio filled with the lively chatter of patrons, including those seated with Chuck at the large, outdoor table in the center of the terrace: Janelle, the girls, Clarence, Liza, and—once again at Rosie's invitation—Chartreuse.

Chuck sat forward in his chair, retrieved his margarita from the table with his unbandaged hand, and took a deep swallow.

Two days had passed since Martina's arrest for the murders of Francisco, Lance, and the still-unidentified migrant. Local news outlets were filled with sensational stories of the killings, offering prurient accounts of the murders and detailing the legal proceedings now underway against Martina and her hired henchmen—Javier, hogtied by Janelle and Rosie at the foot of the ridge, and Mendes, apprehended after Era, Harper, and Chartreuse arrived as planned at the maintenance yard at dawn, ready as members of Chartreuse's suggested larger circle of trust to help with the search for Carlos. When Chartreuse recognized the big black SUV parked at the yard, she, Era, and Harper deflated the car's tires, called 911, and kept eyes on Javier as he fled on foot along the road back to Tucson until the police arrived and arrested him.

Chuck and Janelle had turned down numerous requests for interviews from reporters over the last two days. To Chuck's surprise, Chartreuse had refused requests directed her way as well—so far, at least.

The research team, minus Martina, was to return to the arroyo tomorrow to commence the delayed study of the national park petroglyphs. Chuck warmed at the thought of sharing conjecture with Era and the others about Sassy the rattlesnake curving along the line of rocks, her tongue aimed at the sun dagger and cavern on the west side of the ridge.

He returned his glass to the table, the oaky tequila and tangy lime juice tickling the back of his throat.

Migrant proponents in Tucson had expedited Carlos's asylum paperwork with the local authorities, enabling him to leave the city yesterday, bound for Albuquerque with Yolanda and Hector. Clarence and Liza were to follow in a rental car tomorrow.

Antonio had been released from the hospital just this morning, and was recuperating at the home of Harper, under her temporary custody, while he contacted his family in Central America and began the asylum-claim process.

Across the table from Chuck, Chartreuse lifted her bare arm to everyone. "I thought about smashing it to bits with a hammer," she said of the bracelet that no longer dangled from her wrist. "In the end, though, I buried it in the institute's garden. Maybe it'll bring some peace to the ones who died."

"How would it do that?" Rosie asked.

"I'm not really sure," she admitted. "It's just, smashing it didn't feel right."

"Did you figure out why it had the same rocks as the big ones I found in the desert?"

"It turns out your mother was right." Chartreuse glanced across the table at Janelle, who sat next to Chuck. "I asked Jaden, the owner of Chrysalis, to check one of the pamphlets that come with the bracelets. The stones are Yucatán limestone. They're supposed to have healing powers related to Mayan notions of emotional certitude and immortality. I told her she had to get rid of the ones in her shop, but she said she couldn't. She had too much money invested in them."

Rosie's eyes widened. "So other people are going to buy them?"

"Not on your life, sister. I made a deal to buy the whole lot of them from Jaden at her cost. I'm going to throw them into the ocean from my boat. They'll be at the bottom of the Pacific by this weekend."

"You're going home?"

Chartreuse nodded. "I'm checking out of the institute tomorrow. Raquel has declared my progress nothing short of extraordinary." She looked around the table. "Which, I must say, is thanks to all of you."

"I want to see your house," said Rosie. "I bet it's huge."

"It is," Chartreuse confirmed.

"And your boat."

"You're welcome to visit whenever you like."

"I'd like to help you throw the bracelets in the water. For Francisco. And for Lance, too."

Carmelita stiffened in her seat, her face growing pale.

Liza leaned toward her from across the table. "Lance was one of the good guys, Carm."

Carmelita blinked back tears. "I know."

"Yep, he was," Rosie said, nodding. "When I was running up the hill with Mamá, I saw you holding his gun. It was huge."

"Everything about Lance was big," Liza said. "Bigger than life."

"He saved me," Carmelita said softly, repeating what she'd said to investigators yesterday in Ron's office, with Chuck and Janelle at her side. "If it wasn't for him, it would have been me. Martina told me so. She…she said I'd been expendable and that she'd been planning to kill me. But after what she did to Lance, she needed me to help her with Carlos."

Liza lifted her glass into the air. "Here's to Lance."

Carmelita nodded to Liza as everyone echoed the toast around the table.

"What I keep trying to figure out," Clarence said to Janelle, "is why Martina got down on the ground with you when you were working on Antonio before the helicopter came. She should've been hanging back, worrying he'd recognize her if he came around."

"I've thought about that, too," said Janelle. "I think it was dark when he, Francisco, and Carlos met her at the water station, so she thought he wouldn't recognize her if he regained consciousness. She was trying to manage the situation as best she could. That would fit with all the questions she asked about him when Rosie and I came out of his room at the hospital."

"She couldn't help herself," Chartreuse said, nodding. "She wanted to control the narrative."

"But it controlled her instead," said Rosie.

"Actually," said Clarence, "Chuck and Carm are the ones who really controlled her." He aimed the neck of his beer bottle at them. "Here's to the two of you." He tipped the bottle toward Janelle and Rosie. "And to you two badasses, too. You took out Javier."

Chartreuse swung her bottle of sparkling water around the table. "Here's to every single one of you. Honestly, I've never met anyone like you in my life."

Rosie grinned at her. "We've never met anyone like you, either, sister."

Chuck pressed his shoulder against Janelle, his salt-rimmed glass raised. "Here's to the whole lot of us, then." He tilted his glass at Chartreuse. "You included."

"And to Sssssassy," Carmelita said, holding her glass high. "I can't wait to find out what secrets she leads us to."

ACKNOWLEDGMENTS

Sincere appreciation goes to my early readers—Margaret Mizushima, John Peel, Mark Stevens, Sue Graham, C. Matthew Smith, and Pat Downs—for alerting me to a number of questionable decisions I made in preliminary drafts of *Saguaro Sanction*. This book is much the better thanks to their sharp intelligence.

My talented teammates at Torrey House Press—Kirsten Johanna Allen, Anne Terashima, Michelle Wentling, Rachel Buck-Cockayne, and Kathleen Metcalf—are champions of the National Park Mystery Series in marvelous ways that have led directly to the series' ongoing success. I cannot thank them enough for their keen attention to and strong belief in every book in the series.

David Jonason's magnificent artwork graces the cover of *Saguaro Sanction*, providing a dazzling entrée to the book for which I am exceedingly grateful.

In addition to my many visits to rock art sites around the Southwest, the fictional depictions of petroglyphs in *Saguaro Sanction* are based on the fascinating, all-true descriptions of rock art by Craig Childs in *Tracing Time: Seasons of Rock Art on the Colorado Plateau*. My sincere thanks to Craig for the evocative quotes from *Tracing Time* that introduce parts one, two, and three of *Saguaro Sanction*.

FURTHER READING

Craig Childs's *Tracing Time: Seasons of Rock Art on the Colorado Plateau* captures the wonder and enchantment of petroglyphs and pictographs in prose that is illustrative, instructive, and reverential. Childs's deeply personal chronicle enables readers to comprehend why ancient rock artists devoted so much time and effort to creating their transcendent works on rock walls across the Southwest.

Published in 1986, Polly Schaafsma's *Indian Rock Art of the Southwest* continues to offer the most comprehensive survey available of Native American rock art in Arizona, New Mexico, Utah, west Texas, and northern Mexico, providing a fascinating visual introduction to the ancient records left on stone of Native American spiritualism and culture across the Southwest.

The fictitious migrant route that lies at the heart of *Saguaro Sanction* is based in part on "Death in the Desert," James Verini's heartbreaking story in *The New York Times Magazine* of migrants traveling north from the US-Mexico border through the Sonoran Desert.

For deep dives into Saguaro cactuses and the Sonoran Desert, look no further than T*he Saguaro Cactus: A Natural History* by David Yetman et al., and *A Natural History of the Sonoran Desert*, published by the Arizona-Sonora Desert Museum.

ABOUT SCOTT GRAHAM

Scott Graham is the author of twelve books, including the National Park Mystery Series from Torrey House Press, and *Extreme Kids,* winner of the National Outdoor Book Award. Graham is an avid outdoorsman who enjoys whitewater rafting, skiing, backpacking, and mountain climbing with his wife, who is an emergency physician. He lives in southwestern Colorado.

TORREY HOUSE PRESS

Voices for the Land

The economy is a wholly owned subsidiary of the environment, not the other way around.
— Senator Gaylord Nelson, founder of Earth Day

Torrey House Press publishes books at the intersection of the literary arts and environmental advocacy. THP authors explore the diversity of human experiences with the environment and engage community in conversations about landscape, literature, and the future of our ever-changing planet, inspiring action toward a more just world. We believe that lively, contemporary literature is at the cutting edge of social change. We seek to inform, expand, and reshape the dialogue on environmental justice and stewardship for the human and more-than-human world by elevating literary excellence from diverse voices.

Visit www.torreyhouse.org for reading group discussion guides, author interviews, and more.

As a 501(c)(3) nonprofit publisher, our work is made possible by generous donations from readers like you.

Torrey House Press is supported by Back of Beyond Books, The King's English Bookshop, Maria's Bookshop, the Ballantine Family Fund, the Barker Foundation, the Jeffrey S. & Helen H. Cardon Foundation, the Lawrence T. & Janet T. Dee Foundation, the George S. & Dolores Doré Eccles Foundation, the Literary Arts Emergency Fund supported by the Mellon Foundation, the Sam & Diane Stewart Family Foundation, Robert Aagard & Camille Bailey Aagard, Kif Augustine Adams & Stirling Adams, Diana Allison, Klaus Bielefeldt, Joe Breddan, Rose Chilcoat & Mark Franklin, Linc Cornell & Lois Cornell, Susan Cushman & Charlie Quimby, Laurie Hilyer, Kirtly Parker Jones, Kathleen Metcalf & Peter Metcalf, Betsy Gaines Quammen & David Quammen, Kitty Swenson, Shelby Tisdale, the National Endowment for the Arts, the National Endowment for the Humanities, the Salt Lake City Arts Council, the Utah Division of Arts & Museums, Utah Humanities, and the Zoo, Arts & Parks Program of Salt Lake County. Our thanks to individual donors, members, and the Torrey House Press board of directors for their valued support.

Join the Torrey House Press family and give today at www.torreyhouse.org/give.

DEATH VALLEY DUEL

A National Park Mystery
By Scott Graham

Coming next in the National Park Mystery Series

TORREY HOUSE PRESS

Salt Lake City • Torrey

1

"Move into the light, Carm!" fifteen-year-old Rosie Ortega demanded of her older sister, Carmelita, who leaned forward in a folding camp chair in the shadowy predawn darkness, cinching the laces of her neon purple trail-running shoes.

Carmelita flinched at Rosie's command.

Standing next to Carmelita, Chuck Bender stiffened, his throat growing tight. In his role as the girls' stepfather, he had suggested Rosie could film her sister's participation in the Whitney to Death 150, the annual 150-mile-long ultra-running race across the rugged desert wilderness of eastern California, from the base of Mount Whitney to the bottom of Death Valley. The competition, due to start in just a few minutes, was widely considered the toughest footrace on earth.

Rosie had taken up Chuck's suggestion with her usual gusto. Over the months leading up to the race, she'd captured hours of footage with her cell phone camera of seventeen-year-old Carmelita on her training runs, lifting weights, and stretching between her workouts. Rosie created rough-cut videos from the footage and uploaded them to the internet. The videos featured her distinctively raspy voice as she praised her sister's work ethic, quiet confidence, and clothing and hairstyle choices.

Because of their unbridled positivity, perhaps, or their refreshing amateurism, the videos proved popular online, aiding Carmelita in her goal of gaining enough followers on the internet to be offered sponsorship by running shoe and outdoor clothing companies. Last week, in fact, with the race just days away, marketing representatives from three different firms had called Carmelita with proposals for when she turned eighteen in the fall.

Chuck raised a hand in warning to Rosie, who squatted in front of Carmelita with her cell phone aimed at her sister. The last thing Carmelita needed right now, in the tense final minutes leading up to what would be by far the toughest physical test she'd ever faced in her young life, was Rosie's phone camera shoved in her face.

"I'm not moving," Carmelita told Rosie, short and sharp. She bent farther forward in her seat, presenting the back of her head to the upraised phone, and continued tightening her shoelaces.

By Chuck's count, this was the sixth time in a row Carmelita had loosened and retied her laces while seated in the camp chair, a show of nerves notably uncommon for her—though wholly justified this morning.

The Whitney to Death 150 followed remote mining tracks and rugged hiking trails away from Mount Whitney, at 14,505 feet the highest point in the lower forty-eight states, to Badwater Basin in the heart of Death Valley National Park, at 282 feet below sea level the lowest point in all of North America. In the decade since the race's inception, fewer than one in five runners had completed the route in the allotted forty-eight-hour time limit, the rest succumbing to the brutal nature of the competition—the unrelenting heat and lack of shade during daylight hours and the bitterly cold temperatures and challenging terrain at night.

Last fall, Carmelita had proposed the idea of competing in the race and had asked if Chuck, Rosie, and Janelle, Chuck's wife and the girls' mother, would serve as her support crew. When Janelle had questioned Chuck in private about the wisdom of Carmelita tackling such an intense challenge at such a young age, Chuck had convinced her Carmelita possessed the qualities needed to complete the race—the willingness to put in long training hours before the early April race and the mental fortitude to keep running when the going got tough, as it inevitably would. Most important, Chuck assured Janelle, if the race ultimately proved too demanding for her, Carmelita was mature enough to drop out before she harmed herself.

Carmelita's preparation for the Whitney to Death 150, as filmed and posted online by Rosie, had proceeded smoothly—a steady accumulation of miles through the winter months on snowy mountain trails around their Rocky Mountain hometown of Durango, Colorado, tapering as the date of the competition drew near. Over the last two days leading up to the race, she had been remarkably upbeat with Chuck while he and she had surveyed the race route together by car, with Janelle and Rosie remaining behind at their family campsite in Whitney Portal Campground, the starting point of the race, directly beneath the towering east face of Mount Whitney.

Carmelita's fixation on her shoelaces this morning was worrisome, however. On top of the extreme physical challenge the race presented to runners, the psychological pressure of the competition was enormous.

"But you *have* to move," Rosie whined to Carmelita, extending her phone closer to her sister. "It's too dark where you're sitting. Nobody will be able to see you."

Twenty feet beyond Carmelita, a floodlight on a portable tripod lit a circle of asphalt in the otherwise unlit trailhead parking lot adjacent to the campground. The steep road up Portal Canyon from Owens Valley ended at the parking lot, where the climber route to the summit of Mount Whitney began.

"Anyway," Rosie said, "you've already tied your shoes, like, a million times."

Carmelita did not respond. She kept working on her shoes. Reaching behind her, Chuck drummed the back of the camp chair with fidgety fingers, his thumb hooked over the chair's aluminum frame.

"Please," Carmelita said to him, bent over her shoes. "Stop that."

He jerked his hand away. "Sorry."

Rosie chortled, her phone still aimed at her sister. "Geez, Dad. You're more nervous than Carm is."

"He *should* be nervous," Janelle said. She stood on the opposite side of Carmelita from Chuck, zipping closed one of the many pockets on the custom-made running vest Carmelita would wear for the race, its compartments filled with packets of energy gel and balloon-like plastic bottles filled with glucose water. "You should be, too, Rosie. We all should be."

"Well, *I'm* not," Carmelita said. The confidence in her voice reassured Chuck. She snugged the laces tight on her left shoe, sat up straight in her seat, and slapped her bare thighs below her running shorts with the palms of her hands. Looking directly into the lens of Rosie's camera, she said, "Let's do this, shall we, peeps?"

She stood up and faced the circle of light, where Rachel and Doug, founders of the Whitney to Death 150, scurried back and forth, clipping tiny GPS trackers to the shirts of racers gathered in the parking lot. The two were well past middle age, pudgy and gray-haired. They were rumored to work for the Los Angeles Department of Water and Power, the largest employer in rural Owens Valley two hundred miles north of Los Angeles.

Ten years ago, so the story went, Doug and Rachel—known to racers to this day only by their first names—had dreamed up the race as a diversion from their tedious engineering jobs with the massive utility company, which gathered the snowmelt water flowing off the east side of California's Sierra Nevada mountain range and transported it via aqueduct to the LA metropolitan area.

Rachel and Doug had organized the initial competition ten years ago on their own, with no website, no press releases, and no official registration. The first race on the demanding route they laid out had attracted only a handful of racers via word of mouth. Given its extreme nature and high dropout rate, the race, still organized under the radar by the couple, had remained small in the decade since. Despite its continued stealthy presence on the ground, however, the Whitney to Death 150 by now was notorious on the internet, where legions of fans worldwide tracked the racers' progress throughout the competition, wagering hundreds of thousands, if not millions, of dollars on each year's outcome through shady online betting sites.

Chuck checked his watch: 4:45 a.m. In fifteen minutes, the few dozen racers gathered for this year's competition would set out amid quiet cheers from their support crews. No loud blast from a starting gun would mark the 5 a.m. start of the race. Instead, the runners would simply jog east out of the parking lot and descend Portal Creek Trail away from Mount Whitney, headed to the bottom of Owens Valley, their headlamps flickering amid the pine trees that grew thick beside the creek.

Having read every online posting he could find about the race, Chuck knew that as soon as the racers left the parking lot, Rachel and Doug would douse the floodlight, toss it in their car, and drive back down the road paralleling Portal Creek to the flat, open floor of Owens Valley. They would pass through the small town of Lone Pine and continue to the far side of the valley, where they would assemble the first of several racer aid stations at the edge of empty Owens Lake, drained a century ago so Los Angelenos could water their lawns. The two would offer snacks and drinks to the racers at the station. They would be joined there, and at all the other aid stations along the route, by members of the runners' support crews, who would provide individualized food and drink options to their particular runners.

Janelle handed the running vest to Carmelita and squeezed her bony shoulder. "You got this," she said to her.

Chuck rested his hand on Carmelita's other shoulder. Her

skin was cool beneath the thin fabric of her long-sleeved running shirt. "Damn straight you do," he said.

Rosie giggled, stepping back far enough to capture all three of them in her camera. "I'll have to bleep that out."

"Damn straight you will," Chuck told her, grinning.

A quiet laugh escaped Carmelita's lips, further reassuring Chuck. She rolled her shoulders, shaking off his and Janelle's steadying hands. "I'm ready," she said, iron in her voice.

Chuck had witnessed Carmelita's extraordinary willpower since marrying Janelle and becoming stepfather to Carmelita and Rosie seven years ago. He had introduced rock climbing to Carmelita two years after he'd joined the family, when she was twelve. Her natural abilities and strong competitive streak had enabled her to ascend to the top ranks of sport climbers as an adolescent. Her interest in competitive trail running had grown over the last two years until it rivaled her attraction to climbing, leading to her proposal to compete in the two-day, two-night footrace from Mount Whitney to Death Valley.

Wise counsel, Chuck knew, would have been for Carmelita to compete in shorter ultra races, in the fifty- to hundred-mile range, before attempting the ultimate competition in the ultra-running world. But that wasn't Carmelita's way. She had competed in top rock-climbing events at the very beginning of her competitive climbing career and had notched a string of podium finishes in the process.

"Carm did great against the best rock climbers in the country right from the start. She'll do fine against the best trail runners, too," Chuck said to Janelle. "Besides, it'll be no problem if she quits the race partway through. There's nothing wrong with a DNF."

"A DNF?" Janelle asked.

"Did Not Finish," he explained.

Though a DNF would nearly be expected of Carmelita in her

first attempt at the Whitney to Death 150—or any first attempt at an ultra-length footrace, for that matter—Chuck was confident of her chances in the competition. When he compared the times of her training runs with those posted online by other runners planning to compete in this year's race, he found that Carmelita's times were similar to theirs—including the times posted by the only other female teenage runner in the race, eighteen-year-old Margot Chatten, who had won a number of ultra races held over the preceding year near her San Francisco home.

While Carmelita had gained a few hundred new followers after each video Rosie posted online over the winter, Margot's follower numbers had skyrocketed in the wake of her ultra victories during the same time span. Her promo videos were slickly produced, complete with background music and high-tech graphics. They invariably featured Rick Chatten, her father and coach, humble-bragging about his daughter's race wins. An online search by Chuck revealed that Rick had made a fortune in high tech in the Bay Area and now was devoting himself full-time to his daughter's trail-running pursuit.

Carmelita shrugged on her vest, snugged its straps tight against her chest, and strode toward Rachel and Doug. Janelle, Rosie, and Chuck followed her across the pavement.

Just as Chuck entered the circle of light behind Janelle and the girls, a soft whooshing noise sounded behind him. Looking over his shoulder, he spied a car hurtling toward them through the darkness, its headlights off.

"Look out!" he yelled.

He grabbed Rosie by the arm and yanked her out of the vehicle's path. She stumbled and fell to her knees, her phone clattering on the pavement beside her.

The speeding car, a minivan, struck Carmelita's folding camp chair, which crumpled beneath the van's front bumper.

Chuck tugged Janelle and Carmelita back from the streaking minivan, which sped past them and into the light, dragging the crushed camp chair beneath it. As the car flashed by, Chuck recognized it as one he'd seen before.

The minivan shot toward Rachel and Doug. Rachel screeched and leapt out of the car's path. But Doug was facing away from the van. Before he turned around, the car plowed into him from behind. He bounced off the front of the vehicle and sprawled across the pavement.

The minivan skidded to a halt in the center of the light. Just before it stopped, its front bumper clipped the tripod supporting the floodlight. The tripod fell across the roof of the car and the light winked out in a shower of blue-white sparks.

"Doug!" Rachel screeched in the sudden darkness. "Oh, my God! *Doug!*"